We Three Queens

Titles by Rhys Bowen

Royal Spyness Mysteries

MASKED BALL AT BROXLEY MANOR
(enovella)

HER ROYAL SPYNESS

A ROYAL PAIN

ROYAL FLUSH

ROYAL BLOOD

NAUGHTY IN NICE

THE TWELVE CLUES OF CHRISTMAS

HEIRS AND GRACES

QUEEN OF HEARTS

MALICE AT THE PALACE

CROWNED AND DANGEROUS

ON HER MAJESTY'S FRIGHTFULLY SECRET SERVICE

FOUR FUNERALS AND MAYBE A WEDDING

LOVE AND DEATH AMONG THE CHEETAHS

THE LAST MRS. SUMMERS

GOD REST YE, ROYAL GENTLEMEN

PERIL IN PARIS

THE PROOF OF THE PUDDING

WE THREE QUEENS

Constable Evans Mysteries

EVANS ABOVE

EVAN HELP US

EVANLY CHOIRS

EVAN AND ELLE

EVAN CAN WAIT

EVANS TO BETSY

EVAN ONLY KNOWS

EVAN'S GATE

EVAN BLESSED

EVANLY BODIES

Anthologies

A ROYAL THREESOME

We Three Queens

RHYS BOWEN

BERKLEY PRIME CRIME
New York

BERKLEY PRIME CRIME
Published by Berkley
An imprint of Penguin Random House LLC
penguinrandomhouse.com

Library of Congress Cataloging-in-Publication Data

Names: Bowen, Rhys, author.
Title: We three queens / Rhys Bowen.
Description: New York: Berkley Prime Crime, 2024. |
Series: A Royal Spyness Mystery
Identifiers: LCCN 2024026447 (print) | LCCN 2024026448 (ebook) |
ISBN 9780593641361 (hardcover) | ISBN 9780593641385 (ebook)
Subjects: LCGFT: Detective and mystery fiction. | Novels.
Classification: LCC PR6052.O848 W4 2024 (print) | LCC PR6052.O848 (ebook)
| DDC 823/.914—dc23/eng/2040617
LC record available at https://lccn.loc.gov/2024026447
LC ebook record available at https://lccn.loc.gov/2024026448

Printed in the United States of America
1st Printing

This book is dedicated to the real Addison Rose, who is the daughter of Angel Trapp (who is actually a very nice mother). I hope Addie Rose enjoys her brief moment of stardom.

We Three Queens

Chapter 1

Friday, October 23, 1936
Eynsleigh Manor, Sussex, England

Dear Diary: My life is absolutely perfect. I'm married to a wonderful man and have the most adorable baby in the world. As Jane Bennet said, "How shall I bear so much happiness!" For once I'm living a quiet life as a normal housewife in my own home, taking care of my husband and our darling son. I feel absolutely content and calm.

I broke off from writing this, staring down at the page. Didn't it sound rather pathetic and boring for someone in her twenties? But then I had just given birth to a baby. And it was very nice to feel settled and happy in my own little corner of the world after what had been a rocky few years trying to survive on my own with absolutely no money. (Yes, I know I am related to the royal family and my brother is a duke who lives in a castle, but unfortunately none of that loot has been passed across to me!)

I was sitting on the sofa in the morning room enjoying the slanted autumn sunshine coming in through the tall south-facing windows. It was my favorite room in the house, with armchairs and sofas, upholstered in light brocades, set around small tables or, in the winter, around the big marble fireplace. The wallpaper was buttery yellow, enhancing the sunlight. Sounds from the grounds outside made me turn to the windows. Strands of morning mist drifted over the grass tinged white with frost. In the distance leaves lay in brown carpets beneath the woodland. What had been acres of unspoiled parkland where deer and rabbit roamed now saw signs of development. Oh, I don't mean we were turning it into a housing estate or industrial complex. My husband, Darcy, and Sir Hubert, my godfather, who actually owned Eynsleigh, had decided they should put the grounds to better use. We now had sheep grazing in the far meadow. The small kitchen garden had been expanded to grow various fruits and vegetables. We had the home farm up and running again and were raising chickens, also darling piglets. I tried not to think that they would one day be sold for bacon. Life is cruel on a farm. I spotted Jacob, one of our new farmhands, returning to the house with our dogs. Usually I enjoyed walking the dogs in the mornings but I was just getting over a nasty cold and the weather was a little too bleak to be outside much.

As I watched, Jacob broke into a run and the dogs bounded beside him, tongues lolling out. I smiled, glad that this was going so well. We had hired several young men from the surrounding area to help with the new farm chores. Three of them now lived together in the small farm cottage, which had been built with a touch of eighteen hundreds whimsy and looked like an adorable house from a fairy tale. Jacob immediately became my favorite. He had had a hard life, growing up in an orphanage, and then working in terrible conditions for a local farmer. In spite of all of this he was always cheerful and willing, loved all animals and had a natural affinity for them. Our dogs immediately took to him, which was a good sign in my opinion. Dogs are good judges of character!

"So there you are, ducks." My grandfather came into the morning room. I had persuaded him to come back to Eynsleigh when the weather turned beastly cold and damp. I didn't want him living alone so near to the London pea-souper fogs. He had needed a lot of persuading as he didn't feel comfortable in a big house like Eynsleigh, certainly not being waited on by our servants. Finally he had agreed since we had no posh guests staying. I was also glad of his company as Sir Hubert was away again and Darcy had been coming and going on various assignments. It could feel lonely in a big empty house.

I looked up. "Come and sit near the fire." I held out my hand to him. "It's bitterly cold today, isn't it? Is your bedroom warm enough?"

"Toasty as anything," he said. "Couldn't be better. And it's nice in here with the big fire. At least you've got enough trees to keep your fires going forever, haven't you?" He sank into an armchair. "This will warm up the old plates of meat."

I was about to ask what he meant when I realized he had lapsed into Cockney rhyming slang again. He meant feet. I had become used to "apples and pears" for stairs and "tit for tat" for hat. I found them quite endearing. And in case you are confused as to why someone who lives in a large property with servants should have a Cockney grandfather, I should quickly explain that although my father was Queen Victoria's grandson, he married my mother, a famous actress who came from humble roots (but chose to forget them). Therefore I had one grandfather who was a Scottish duke (whom I had never met since he died before I was born) and the other who was a Cockney retired policeman. He was my favorite person in the world apart from Darcy and James Albert, asleep in his cot upstairs.

"How's the little man this morning?" Granddad asked.

"Splendid." I beamed. "He's becoming so alert and interested in everything. And every time I look at him he gives me the biggest smile."

"He's a lovely little chap," Granddad agreed. "Are you going to bring him down when he wakes up?"

I grimaced. "I know I shouldn't. He's supposed to live in the nursery the way Darcy and I did, but I do love having him down here. And I think it's good for him to be exposed to everything that's going on."

"You do what you want, my love," Granddad said. "It's your house and your baby. Don't you feel bound by silly old traditions. Your brother only sees his kids for an hour each day, doesn't he? Are they any better for it?"

I laughed. "That's because Fig is not the motherly sort," I said. "I suspect Binky would enjoy interacting with them more often but as you know Fig rules the roost there."

I put down my diary and stood up. "Shall I ring for coffee?" I tugged on the bell rope.

"Do you expect that husband of yours back soon?" Granddad asked.

I sighed. "I have no idea. He is never allowed to tell me where he's going. It might be Paris. It might be Antarctica for all I know. But I do think he would have told me if he was going to be away long. Usually it's a quick trip these days, thank heavens. I'd hate to be worrying about him for a long spell, not knowing if he was in danger."

Granddad nodded. "He needs to think about settling down, now that he has a family, not go gallivanting all over the globe. Get a proper job. Go up to town on the eight thirty train each day and sit behind a desk."

"Oh, Granddad, he'd hate that," I said. "Darcy wasn't born to be ordinary. He was born to do things and live an exciting life. Besides he is settling down in a way. He's officially working for the government now." I didn't mention what as. . . .

I had now assumed my husband was a spy but he wasn't allowed to tell me.

Our conversation was broken off by the sound of rattling crockery from the hallway outside. The sound grew louder, accompanied by rhythmic thumping, and Queenie made an entrance, carrying a tray.

"Whatcher, missus," she said. "Chef told me to bring up the coffee on account of everyone else being busy."

Queenie put the tray down on the low table between the armchairs. She had poured the coffee into two cups and a rather large amount had slopped into the saucers. I thought it wiser to say nothing. I also kept quiet that she called me "missus," when my correct title was "my lady." Either she was too thick to learn or, I suspected, knew quite well but chose to ignore it in a passive way of showing she was as good as I was. Either way she was exasperating but I was fond of her, had owed her my life at one point, and she was turning into quite a good cook, under Pierre's tutelage.

"So what is Chef preparing for dinner tonight?" I asked.

"Another of them Froggy dishes," she said, giving a sniff of disgust. "I told him there was lamb left and it would make a perfectly good shepherd's pie, but instead he's doing some sort of fricassee with mushrooms to use up them leftovers."

"That sounds good," I said. "I hope you are taking notes and learning how to cook these dishes, Queenie. Then you'd be able to get a good job as a chef yourself one day."

A look of dismay came over her face. "'Ere, you're not giving me the boot, are you? Not after what I've done for you?"

"Of course not," I said rapidly. "I'm delighted to have you as our assistant cook, but one day you might want to spread your wings."

She gave a throaty chuckle. "I think I'm spreading enough as it is, missus. My uniform ain't half getting tight. Although I suspect it shrinks every time in the wash."

This was true. Queenie worked in a kitchen where there was a lot of good food, and she did love to eat. It showed.

"Perhaps you could start walking the dogs," I said to her. "A little more exercise would do you good."

"Me? Walk them bloody great things? No thank you," she

said, and made what she thought was a dignified exit, only marred by tripping over the edge of the rug.

I looked at Granddad and grinned.

"That girl will never learn," he said.

"I don't think she wants to." I took a sip of coffee. Queenie had already sugared it and it was much sweeter than I liked, but it wasn't worth the effort of calling her back. I knew I should demand the best from my servants, run my own household, but I didn't enjoy bossing people around. And in Queenie's case it would be a waste of time. She'd simply say, "Bob's yer uncle, missus," and then do exactly the same thing again.

We finished our coffee and I went up to the nursery to see how James was doing. He was awake, lying in his cot and trying to eat his feet. When he saw me he broke into a full body-wiggling smile and made lovely little noises. Of course this was too irresistible. I scooped him up.

"Oh, sorry I wasn't here, my lady." Maisie appeared in the doorway. "I was just bringing up his clean bedclothes from the laundry."

"Nothing to apologize about," I said. "I just thought I'd come up and see if he was awake. I think I'll bring him downstairs for a bit and let you get on with other things."

"Very good, my lady," she said.

As we went downstairs I compared her mentally to Queenie. Maisie was always willing, always cheerful and loved to take care of James Albert as well as her duties as my personal maid. Queenie was . . . well, she was Queenie. When she had been my maid she had lost my shoes, ruined my evening gown and done all manner of horrible things. But she had been brave and worked for no money when I couldn't afford to pay her. So now all was well. Maisie took care of my son and me. Queenie was happy in the kitchen.

"Well, there he is, my little man." Granddad held out his arms and I passed the baby to him. James gave a toothless grin and grabbed at Granddad's bristly face. We were just settling down when there was the sound of galloping feet on the parquet floor outside and into the room shot two large bundles of furry energy, one black and one yellow.

"I hope you've had your feet wiped," I said as our two Labrador puppies, Holly and Jolly, tried to cover me with kisses while I tried to fend them off. Sure enough Mrs. Holbrook, our housekeeper, appeared behind them, quite breathless.

"There you are, you naughty things," she said. "I'm sorry, my lady. Someone left the door open just as they arrived back from their walk." She tried to grab at their collars. "You two will be the death of me."

The dogs had now spotted the baby and if they loved anything more than me, it was him. He was now getting covered in doggy kisses. I'm sure it was most unhygienic and my sister-in-law Fig would have a fit, but James seemed to be loving it.

"It's all right, Mrs. H," I said. "Let them stay. They'll be tired after their walk."

"If you say so, my lady." She sighed. "And might we expect the master home soon?"

"I really don't know, Mrs. Holbrook. I hope so."

"Chef was wondering whether to use up leftovers if it's just the two of you."

"Whatever he cooks will be perfect, Mrs. H." I smiled at her.

She bobbed a little curtsy. "I'll tell him." And she went.

As I had predicted the dogs soon lay in front of the fire. I took James from Granddad and propped him among pillows on the sofa. Then I sat back with a sigh of contentment. Life was calm, simple and good. All I needed now was my husband home again.

Almost on cue I heard the front door slam. Voices in the foyer. The dogs were instantly alert and dashed out, barking. Then I heard a deep voice. "Down, you brutes. Down. Anyone would think I'd been away for years."

I gave a big sigh of relief. Darcy was safely home.

A few minutes later he came into the room, his cheeks still red from the cold wind.

"Well, that's a sight I've been longing to see," he exclaimed, pausing in the doorway. "My perfect family." Then he bent to kiss me before scooping up James. "I suppose I should ask why the baby is out of his nursery when it's not teatime," he said, an amused grin on his face. "What rules of polite society are we breaking here?"

"He's awake and alert," I said. "What's he going to learn alone in a nursery? I want my son to grow up to be a genius who is also at ease in society. So sit down. Do you want some coffee? Queenie only brought us cups and not a pot but I could have Mrs. Holbrook bring more."

"It's all right. It will be luncheon soon," he said. "And I did have a cup at the station, if it could loosely be described as coffee. So how are you?"

"As you can see, we're flourishing. But how are you? Where did you go, or can't you tell me?"

His face clouded. "I made a quick trip to Germany," he said. "Not my favorite place at the moment. The rhetoric is clearly becoming more warlike and antisemitic. Hitler is now virtually deified. The schoolchildren have to pledge to the führer, and everyone raises their arms in the 'Heil Hitler' salute. Quite alarming."

"Ruddy Krauts," Granddad muttered.

"We knew that was coming, didn't we?" I said. "I don't know what the rest of the world can do to stop it."

"Not much." He stretched out his hands to the fire to warm them, then looked up. "Oh, and I saw your mother."

"You did? How is she?"

"Having a grand old time. Right at the center of things," he said. "She's making a film at the request of Herr Goebbels."

"Goodness, she said they'd been asking her to do that. She must be in her element."

"She is. Except that her German is not too good and I don't think she realizes what she's saying. It's a complete propaganda film, you know. Your blond mama and adorable blond children in dirndls picking wildflowers in the meadow and living the happy German life." He had been staring into the fire, then looked up abruptly. "I don't think she realizes what danger she is in."

"She would never believe she was in danger. She said that everyone adores her. Max certainly does and he's very much in favor with the Nazis."

"That's the point. She finally has her wedding planned to Max." He reached out and took my hand. "If she marries him she'll be a German citizen, Georgie. She'll lose her British citizenship. She won't be able to get out if she wants to."

"But you know Mummy—she has everything she likes at the moment. She has a rich man who is going to marry her. And she's reviving her career as an actress. Her face will be seen on screens across Germany. She'll be in heaven."

"You don't understand these people," he said solemnly. "She might be enjoying her life right now, but there will come a time when Max might fall from favor, or she may finally develop a conscience about what is happening to the Jewish population. And then it will be too late to get out. She'll be trapped there."

"What do we do?" I asked.

"I tried to warn her," he said. "But you know your mother. She didn't listen."

Chapter 2

Monday, October 26
Eynsleigh

All is well with my world. Darcy says he'll be home for a while. We can enjoy being a family with a normal life in peace and quiet.

I should never write things like this in my diary! When will I learn? Darcy had gone up to London for the day for meetings in Whitehall. At least that is what he had said. One never quite knew. But he didn't return home in time for dinner. He had not returned when I gave James his ten o'clock feed and settled him down for the night. I lay awake for a while, listening to the wind rattling the window frames and creating all kinds of worrying scenarios in my head. Darcy had slipped across the Channel, he'd gone back to Germany, he'd been captured and would be shot as a spy. I must have finally drifted off to sleep because I was conscious of the bedclothes being moved, cold air hitting me and someone getting into bed beside me.

"I hope it's you," I muttered, "because I don't want to open my eyes."

"It might be Clark Gable," whispered a masculine voice in my ear.

"I hope not. I don't like American men and I don't like mustaches," I replied. "But if it's a handsome Frenchman . . ."

"*Mais oui, chérie*," the voice whispered, now tickling my cheek. "It is Gaston, come to visit you at midnight!"

I laughed and pushed him away. "Where were you? I was worried."

"Sorry," he said. "You can blame it on your cousin."

"Which cousin? I have quite a lot, you know. They range from hairy Scottish lads in kilts to the king."

"The latter," he said. "His Majesty King Edward."

"Golly. You had an audience with David and didn't tell me? (I used the name by which I had always known him.) "Were you reporting on international secrets? Are you getting a knighthood or something?"

He laughed then. "It wasn't an audience. It was a tête-à-tête."

"What?" Now I was fully awake.

"I got a message that HM would like to see me. Didn't say why. So I met him at the fort."

"The fort?"

"Fort Belvedere. His bolt-hole in Windsor Great Park. We started with drinks at six and I didn't get away until after eleven."

"You were drinking all that time? I'm surprised you're not

still wandering around Windsor Great Park trying to find your way home."

"We did have some food along the way, but mostly it was him talking and me listening."

"You were alone? A certain lady wasn't with him?"

"She was not, and with good reason. He has to make a big decision, Georgie, and he is quite lost."

I turned over so I was facing him. "About Mrs. Simpson?"

Darcy nodded. "He is determined to marry her."

"Oh gosh. That won't go down well, will it?"

"Absolutely not. He's already mentioned his intention to the prime minister and was told it was unthinkable. There was no circumstance under which he could marry her."

"Of course not. He's head of the Church of England, which does not permit divorce. She's twice divorced and a foreigner."

Darcy sat up, slipping an arm around my shoulders. "In many ways your cousin is quite naïve. She got him believing that he could change laws by decree to allow their marriage. Of course he can't." He paused. A great gust of wind buffeted the window and howled down the chimney, making me shiver. "He then suggested a morganatic marriage."

"What's that?" I asked.

"They could marry but she'd never be queen or an HRH and any children would not inherit the throne."

"As if there would be children at their age," I said, scornfully. "They are both over forty."

"Anyway," Darcy went on, "that is also not going to be acceptable to the prime minister. He has agreed to present it to the cabinet but he already knows the answer."

"So what is David going to do?" I asked. "The simplest thing would be to keep her as his mistress. Several of my ancestors have lived quite happily with this arrangement—think of Lily Langtry, Alice Keppel."

Darcy gave a grunted chuckle. "King Edward had more than his share of mistresses, I agree, but he also had a respectable long-suffering wife to be at his side on state occasions. You can't picture Mrs. Simpson receiving foreign heads of state or sitting on an elephant at a durbar."

"What a mess," I said. "I'm sure he won't give her up."

"He won't," Darcy said. "He made that quite clear. He'd rather give up the throne than her."

"Golly." I tried to swallow back the word too late. My attempts at curtailing my schoolgirl language were not successful in times of crisis.

"He's absolutely besotted with her," Darcy continued. "She has him completely under her spell. When we'd got through a bottle of Scotch he kept saying, 'You don't understand, Darcy, old fellow, she's the most marvelous woman in the world. I couldn't live without her.'"

"So what does he plan to do?"

"Allow the newspapers to spill the beans at the right moment, I gather. They've been remarkably obedient so far and kept the news of her from the public. But now he wants the public on his side. They adore him and he's sure that they'll want him to marry the woman he loves and thus put pressure on their local MPs. The law will be changed and he'll live happily ever after."

"That isn't likely to happen, is it?"

"I don't think so. If it were just civil law then maybe. But you can't alter the doctrine of the church and he's the official head of it."

"His poor mother," I said. I had become quite fond of Queen Mary, who had sent me on various assignments for her. She was a stickler for the rules and felt the royal family should be above reproach. She had done everything she could to get her son's attention away from "that woman," as she called her, but to no avail. His late father, King George, had been remarkably prophetic. "That boy will be the downfall of the monarchy," he had said not long before he died. I just prayed this wasn't going to turn out to be a true prophecy. We had endured one war between king and Parliament in our history and it had ended with the king losing his head. Someone should remind my cousin of this.

A thought now struck me. "Darcy, why did he particularly want you to listen to his lament? He has his own group of friends, doesn't he, and you were never close to him."

"Ah." Darcy gave a deep breath. "It wasn't exactly me he wanted. It was our house."

"What? What do you mean?"

"He knows that the moment the news breaks Mrs. Simpson will be hounded by the press. It could break before he's ready as the American papers are already full of it. He wants to spare her the unpleasantness that could ensue. He wants her safely far from the public eye. . . ."

It was gradually dawning on me exactly what he was saying.

"He wants her to come and stay here?" I heard my voice rising. Mrs. Simpson was not my favorite person. I had had plenty of interaction with her and even though she had rescued me from a French jail earlier in the year, I did not relish the prospect of sharing a house with her.

"That's the general idea. She'd arrive under cloak of darkness and stay until the whole mess is sorted out."

"Oh golly," I said. Our house ran smoothly enough for a young couple with a baby plus a Cockney grandfather but I was sure it was below the standards required for someone who might be the future queen of England. James Albert would have to stay in the nursery, for one thing. The dogs would have to stay in the servants' part of the house. And I'd have to entertain the dreaded Mrs. Simpson. And dress smartly rather than wear my country tweed trousers. What's more, she'd cost us a fortune in food and drink, and funds were tight right now.

"You didn't say yes, did you?" I heard the tremor in my voice.

"How could I not?" he said. "We have a big house suitably far from everywhere and he is your cousin. His own brothers are firmly against Mrs. Simpson, as you know. So someone has to help out the poor chap."

"I'm afraid I won't be able to be so sympathetic," I said. "I tend to agree with his mother. He needs to buckle down and do his duty to his country. He is the king, after all. He's supposed to devote his life to the service of his people."

"I remember you weren't so keen to marry a certain Romanian prince when presented with the suggestion." He gave my shoulder a squeeze.

"Prince Siegfried? Darcy, he was repulsive and had fish lips and was not interested in girls. Anyway, I'm only a very minor royal and the fate of England didn't hang upon the match." I snuggled against him as an icy draft was now finding its way in through the curtains. "Besides," I went on, "he's not being asked to give her up completely. He can install her at one of his many residences and see her when he likes."

"I agree that would be the sensible thing to do. I did recommend it, rather than creating a constitutional crisis. We'll just have to see what Parliament decides. His fate is in their hands. They may agree to the morganatic marriage and then all would be well, except she wouldn't be crowned with him. If not . . ." He broke off. There was a long moment of silence. "I have no idea what might happen."

The details of this terrifying visit were just beginning to dawn on me.

"And how do we intend to pay for this? You said yourself that we're strapped for cash at the moment, having invested all that money into setting up the farm again. Those piglets won't be big enough for bacon for a year. No lambs until next spring. At the moment we're selling a few eggs and cabbages, as far as I can see. That doesn't exactly bring in enough to pay for Mrs. Simpson's taste in alcohol and food. As it is I'm worried that we might have to let Pierre go."

"Why do you think I agreed to work for a salary, rather than taking on assignments that appealed to me?" he asked. "We just have to get through a few months until the first lambs in the spring. We'll survive, I promise you. And in the meantime, the king has asked for a favor, Georgie, and I think we should help out at this difficult moment for him. Give him time and space to make up his mind and hopefully do the right thing."

I tried to think gracious thoughts. All that came into my head was a picture of Mrs. Simpson, lounging in my favorite armchair, smoking a cigarette and telling me that my wardrobe needed sprucing up, my hair styling and my wine cellar improving. "How long would this be for?"

"Oh, not long. He'll have to make up his mind by the end of the year."

"The end of the year? Two months of being polite to Mrs. Simpson? It's all right for you. You'll be going up to London for meetings and things. I'll be stuck here with her all day and every day."

"It may not be as long as the end of the year," he said. "It depends when your cousin learns his fate and decides to act. It could be in the next week or so."

"Will he be coming down to visit her? If I know David he won't be able to keep away from her and then the cat will be out of the bag pretty quickly."

"He assured me that he would stay away until the situation becomes clear. He does not want to subject us to being besieged by the press."

"I'm glad to hear it." I gave a sigh. "So you already said yes?"

"I told him I'd have to talk to you about it, and presumably Sir Hubert since it is technically his house. If we can locate Sir Hubert on whatever mountain peak he is climbing right now."

"I believe he's in America," I said. "Last time he wrote there was talk of making a film about the Grand Canyon. But I wouldn't know how to contact him. Mrs. Simpson will have gone again by the time he comes back to England . . . one hopes."

Darcy squeezed my shoulder again. "You should have been

queen," he said. "You're prepared to do your duty to your country."

"Oh gosh no." I laughed. "If I'd been in the running for the throne I'd have had to renounce it to marry you, you bloody Catholic."

"You'd have renounced the throne for me?"

I gazed at him adoringly. "Definitely," I said.

"That makes a chap feel good," he said. "Actually that makes a chap notice that he's holding a desirable woman in his arms and it's time he did something about it."

And he did.

Chapter 3

Tuesday, October 27
Eynsleigh

Why did I ever think I could have an ordinary, quiet life? It's getting more complicated by the minute.

In the morning I wondered how I should break the news to the servants. I wasn't at all sure how they'd take it. The first person I told was Granddad. I could have predicted his reaction.

"Well, that's me out of here pretty sharpish," he said. "That woman won't want the likes of me in the house."

"Oh, Granddad, please don't go." I took his hand. "I'm sure it won't be for long. I know you feel awkward when we have guests, especially guests like her. So I'd quite understand if you joined Mrs. Holbrook in her sitting room rather than being up here with us. You do like her, don't you?"

"She's a very kind woman," he said. "Refined. Polite."

"Go on. You like her. I can tell." I gave him a cheeky grin.

"I admit I do enjoy her company," he said. "And I wouldn't mind at all spending time in her sitting room if it doesn't upset the protocols of the house. I don't know the rules about mixing masters and servants, but since I'm neither I imagine I can come and go as I please."

"Exactly. So you will stay, then? I really need you to back me up."

He gave a little sigh. "We'll see how it goes, shall we? I don't imagine it will be a piece of cake for any of us. Won't we have reporters peering out from every bush and hounding us every time we take a walk?"

"That's the whole point," I said. "She's in hiding. Nobody is to know she's here. The servants will be sworn to secrecy. And it's only until the king and Parliament have sorted out her status."

"I could tell you what her status was," Granddad said with a sniff. "Bloody annoying. That's what she is. A social climber of the worst sort and quite wrong to be the consort of a king. If I were him the sooner I sent her packing back to America the better."

"You know he's not going to do that," I said. "He adores her. You've seen him. He's like a little boy when she's around. She bosses him and he obeys."

"Perhaps she's the mother he never had," Granddad said. "His own ma wasn't very cuddly was she. And I heard his governess was horrible to David and his brothers. Sadistic. Used to pinch them to make them cry and then make it seem she was the only one who could comfort them."

"I personally don't find Mrs. Simpson warm and cuddly," I said. "But she fills a need in the king's life and I am fond of him. I do want him to be happy. But she simply can't be allowed to be queen."

"We'll just have to see," Granddad said. "Let's just hope they sort it out quickly."

"Amen to that," I agreed.

MRS. HOLBROOK WAS quite flustered when I shared the news with her. "A society lady? Coming here? And it's to be a secret?"

"Yes. Only for a short while. She needs a place of absolute peace and quiet. Nobody is to know she's here."

"Had some sort of breakdown then, has she?"

I was tempted to say "not yet" but I nodded. "We won't discuss it and you just instruct the staff to take good care of her and to behave in exemplary fashion."

"I will, my lady," she said. "We won't let you down, I promise."

I wondered what would happen when pictures of her flooded the newspapers and my servants realized whom exactly they were serving. Then they'd need to be reminded to remain silent. I thought they'd pull this off . . . except Queenie, of course. She could not be trusted to keep her mouth shut. She'd mean well but then it would come bursting out at the wrong moment. I could just picture her in the village when someone said something about Mrs. Simpson that they'd read in the papers, replying, "You don't bloody well know what you're talking about. She ain't like that at all cos she's staying with us right now."

We might have to keep her locked in the house until the lady went. Locked in the kitchen might be even better.

After I had broken this news to Mrs. Holbrook the next discussion was on where to put our visitor. Which bedroom would be suitable for an American lady who presumably was used to warm rooms and hot baths? Eynsleigh, built in the time of Queen Elizabeth, was not known for warm rooms or hot water heaters that worked well. Drafts blew down chimneys and under doors. Floors were icy cold; so were hallways. It did cross my mind that she might not stay long if it was too uncomfortable for her. There was one particularly grim bedroom that was reputedly haunted. Now, if we put her in that one . . .

Then I gave myself a stern reprimand. The king had asked Darcy for help and in spite of my cousin's faults I was really fond of him. We couldn't let him down. I'd have to grit my teeth and be nice to Mrs. Simpson. We decided on the blue bedroom at the back as it had a lovely view and was close to a bathroom. It was also away from prying eyes. And it had a working fireplace. One of the maids could light her fire every morning. And I wouldn't have Queenie bring up her morning tea.

"Don't worry about it," Darcy said when he sensed that I was getting upset. "We're doing them a favor and if they don't like it, then she can go somewhere else. We don't have to run around trying to please her."

"You know what she's like," I said. "She expects everyone to do exactly what she wants and be adored all the time."

Darcy didn't answer this, knowing it to be true. Instead he put an arm around my shoulder. "Never mind, old thing. It won't be for long. We'll survive. Then your godfather will be home and we'll have a lovely Christmas."

"Yes." I smiled at this, picturing James's eyes when he saw the lights on the Christmas tree. Lots to look forward to and just the one small inconvenience. I could handle it. We passed a pleasant morning. Later in the day when the sun came out we put James in his pram and wheeled him out to look at the chickens and pigs. Everything seemed to be flourishing.

"We'll have a good supply of bacon this time next year," Darcy said, heartlessly. Why did men have to be so thoughtless?

Having settled James back in his nursery I found Granddad in the morning room and rang for coffee.

"Had a good walk?" he asked, looking up from his newspaper.

"Lovely, thanks. It's really cold out there but bracing. James was absolutely fascinated with the chickens and pigs."

"Such a lively little chap." Granddad beamed. "Reminds me of your uncle Jimmy at the same age." A wistful look came over his face. My uncle Jimmy was killed in the Great War. I never knew him.

"Ah, coffee." I looked up as Phipps, our footman/chauffeur, came in with a tray on which there was a pot of coffee, hot milk, sugar, three cups, and a plate of biscuits. Clearly Mrs. Holbrook and not Queenie had prepared the coffee today. Everything was just so. I had just poured for Granddad and me when Mrs. Holbrook came in.

"The midday post is early today, my lady. I reckon that postman wants the afternoon off." She smiled as she handed me a letter. I took it, then froze. I recognized that crest on the envelope, and the handwriting. It was a letter from my sister-in-law Hilda, Duchess of Rannoch, better known as Fig.

Oh golly. Fig wrote only when she wanted something. It was never good news. . . . With great trepidation I opened the envelope.

My dear Georgiana,

(I could almost hear Fig's imperious tones.)

I hope that you, Darcy and your young son are all in good health. We have had beastly weather here in Scotland. Gales every day. Binky said he's never seen so many trees felled in the parkland. At least we'll have wood for the winter.

I am writing to you about our son Podge. As you know, we have his name down for Eton when he turns thirteen but now comes the matter of a prep school. He'll be seven in the new year and it's time for him to go away to school. I have been researching various school choices. (Binky is hopeless as always. He says that Podge would do just as well with a tutor at home. Of course he won't. School isn't just academic subjects. He needs to be playing rugby and toughening up before he goes into the army like the rest of the males in my family.)

I looked up from the letter. Podge's sweet little face came into my mind. A gentle sensitive child. Great imagination. He was going into the army over my dead body! But I had to admit that he'd probably be better off at school than alone in a nursery in the wilds of Scotland. I was brought up with a governess and although it wasn't in any way horrible it was lonely, and I was quite unprepared to tackle the big wide world when I was sent to finishing school. I began to wonder why Fig was sharing all this. Did she want Darcy's advice on schools . . . ? But no, she certainly wouldn't want that. Darcy, being raised a Catholic, had gone to Catholic boarding schools run by monks. The last thing that Fig would want for her son.

I read on.

We have some good recommendations from friends and family. We are especially interested in a school not far from you. Chorley Moat it's called. My brother sent his son Archibald there and says it's an outdoorsy type of place with plenty of rugger and cross-country runs. We have to make sure that Podge doesn't grow up feeble like Binky, who is absolutely hopeless at sports.

So the reason for writing this letter is to let you know that we'll be coming down next week to view the school, and maybe some others in the south of England, and would like to stay for a few days, if that's all right. I presume with a new baby you will be home and our visit wouldn't be an inconvenience. We are bringing our chauffeur and motorcar so we won't need driving anywhere. We are bringing both children (we might as well see whether there are any schools nearby suitable for Addy when she is old enough. It would be convenient to have both children in the same part of the country and of course they could then spend half terms and short holidays with you rather than traveling all the way up to Scotland. . . .).

"Bloody cheek," I muttered.

"What is it, ducks?" Granddad asked as he drained his coffee cup and put it back on the tray.

"My sister-in-law," I said.

"Oh. Her." He made a face. "Bad news?"

"The very worst. She wants to come and stay here again while they check out schools for their son and daughter. She thinks a school near us would be good because then the children could come to us for the shorter holidays."

He nodded. "That might be good for them, poor little things. It can't be much fun stuck up there with only those parents and a nanny."

"I suppose so," I said. "And I am fond of them, but foisting her children on us is damned cheek, isn't it?"

"She ain't exactly the motherly type, is she?"

"She's absolute poison," I said. "And now I have to be polite and entertain her again and . . . oh golly, Granddad. They'll be here at the same time as Mrs. Simpson."

He grinned. "That's all right. Those two women can be rude to each other."

I thought about this. "They have met," I said. "And I believe Fig was a little in awe of Mrs. Simpson, so that might work well to stop her from being too obnoxious."

Granddad gave a little sigh. "Well, at least that has made up my mind for me. Mrs. Simpson and your sister-in-law. That's too much for a bloke like me to handle. I'll be out of here in the morning."

"Oh no, Granddad. Please don't go."

He reached across and patted my hand. "I know when I'm

not wanted, ducks. Mrs. Simpson would be bad enough but your sister-in-law looks at me as if I'm something the cat brought in. Besides, my little house needs me there. What if there's a frost and a burst pipe, eh? I've things I need to take care of. But I'll be back for Christmas, if you'll have me. We'll have a grand old time, won't we?"

I looked at him with longing, knowing how much his calm presence meant to me. But I did understand. I too had suffered from Fig's critical gaze and I was the daughter of a duke.

"Don't be away too long," I said. "I'll send you a telegram as soon as all these people have left."

At that moment Darcy came in. "Oh good. Coffee," he said. He too was holding a letter. His looked rather official.

"Don't you dare tell me that your letter is summoning you somewhere far away," I said, "because I've just learned that Fig and Binky are descending on us, and I do not plan to entertain Fig and Mrs. Simpson alone."

"Quite the opposite," Darcy said. "This letter makes my position official. I am now officially employed by His Majesty's government on a salary, not being paid under the counter, so to speak."

"Oh, jolly good." I smiled at him. "But does that mean you won't be going abroad all the time? You'll be working in London?"

"I expect I may be doing my share of traveling," he said, "but I should be home more. It's only right now that I have a family." He paused, just realizing what I had said. "Wait a moment. Did you say Fig was descending on us?"

I nodded. "They are checking out schools for Podge. They

want one near us so he can come to us during half terms, rather than traveling back to Scotland."

"That makes sense," Darcy said. "Poor little chap. He'll be better off at school than stuck up there."

I tried to picture James Albert going off to school when he was only seven. That was something I did not intend to allow. I stood up. "I better alert Mrs. Holbrook that we'll need to make up more bedrooms," I said. "I don't imagine she'll be thrilled."

I crossed the room and gave the bell a good tug.

Chapter 4

Wednesday, October 28
Eynsleigh

Any day now my home is going to be invaded by two poisonous women. I just hope we all survive it.

"Do we have any idea when this lady might be arriving?" Mrs. Holbrook asked me. She looked worried. I had briefed the staff that this lady was an important person who wanted complete privacy. If any member of our staff dared to mention that she was staying with us, they would be instantly dismissed. Probably the name Mrs. Simpson would mean nothing to any of them, as it had not yet appeared in the British newspapers but it might any day now.

"I'm afraid we don't. I've heard nothing."

We were examining the bedroom we had chosen for Mrs.

Simpson and deciding where to put Binky and Fig. The children would sleep in the nursery with their nanny in the small bedroom next door. I decided to bring James's cot down to our room for the duration of the visit.

It was a toss-up which of the uninvited guests would arrive first. I hoped it would be Fig and Binky so that I could brief them about Mrs. Simpson. Actually that would work well. Fig would be subdued, if jealous, around Mrs. Simpson, as she was with any fashionable woman (not having the best dress sense herself nor the money to dress well). She certainly couldn't boss Mrs. Simpson around. She'd be quiet and deferential. She might even not wish to stay long. . . .

But of course life is not meant to run smoothly. I had just finished giving James his late-night feed and was trying to get him back to sleep. He had been unusually fretful, perhaps because he sensed my own tension. I was walking up and down, singing to him, when I saw the beams of headlights strafing our driveway. Who could possibly be arriving in the middle of the night? I put James hurriedly into his cot and went downstairs. The servants were long in bed. I opened the front door in time to see a petite dark-haired woman coming toward me, while a driver attempted to unload what looked like an awful lot of luggage from the boot.

"Thank God you're awake," she called to me, thus reaffirming she was the infamous American lady we were expecting. "I know how ridiculously early everyone goes to bed in the English countryside and I was afraid I'd have to sleep on the doorstep." She reached me and held out a hand. "How are you, Georgiana, honey. So good of you to do this." She glanced back at the motorcar, where a chauffeur was now staggering toward the front door with a mountain of suitcases.

"The fool got lost in the country lanes. We wound up going up a cart track to somebody's barnyard and had baying dogs all around us. Not the best experience for the nerves."

She walked ahead of me up the steps and into the foyer. I noticed she was wearing a full-length dark mink.

"I'm sorry but the servants have all gone to bed," I said. "I was only up because I was feeding the baby."

"Of course. You've given birth to the son and heir. Very commendable of you. And let's hope he enjoys being the heir more than a certain man does." She paused to look back at me while she removed her gloves. "He never wanted to be king, of course. Hates it. You know David. He doesn't like to boss anybody around. And he expected his father to go on living another twenty years like the old queen, not die so soon. Most inconsiderate of him."

She was looking around. I could tell she was examining the quality of everything within sight. Since Sir Hubert had good taste and had inherited this very elegant house I didn't think she could find much wrong, but she looked at me, frowning. "The place does have central heating, doesn't it?"

"I'm afraid it doesn't," I said. "And we didn't know when you were arriving so you'll find your bedroom rather cold tonight. But the maid will light your fire before you get up in the morning."

"God Almighty. I really am in the depth of the boonies here," she said. "David said he wanted me well away from the reach of the newspapers, but this really is the middle of nowhere. How you British can live with no heat I just can't understand."

Part of me wanted to apologize, to try to find her a hot-water bottle, but then I thought heck no. We were doing her a favor. She hadn't bothered to tell me when she was arriving. If she was cold tonight then too bad.

"If only you'd have let us know when you were arriving we'd have had the room nicely warm for you," I said sweetly.

"I didn't know until the last minute myself," she replied. "David wanted to say good-bye to me but he couldn't risk tipping off the press. So I had to escape through the back door. Very hush hush." She watched as the chauffeur deposited the last of many cases and boxes on my hall floor.

"I'll be off, then, madam," he said.

"Yeah. You can go," she said, waving a hand in his direction. "I hope you find your way back quicker than it took you to get here."

"I'd offer you a cup of tea but the servants are all in bed," I said.

"That's all right, miss," he said. The way he was looking at me seemed to indicate he thought I should just pop down to the kitchen and heat up the kettle.

"It's Lady Georgiana. I'm the mistress of the house."

His expression changed. "Sorry, my lady. I had no idea when you opened the door yourself. I'll be on my way, then."

And he beat a hurried retreat.

"I'll show you to your room," I said. "At least it's all made up for you. I'll help you bring up a small case but you'll have to wait until morning for the rest of your things."

"I suppose I can survive for one night." She gave a long-suffering sigh. "I wonder which bags I'll need to get through the night." She handed me a smallish suitcase then added a hatbox to it while she herself picked up a jewel case.

"I can't leave this in the front hall," she said. "I take it you do have a maid who can look after my things?"

A malicious thought shot through my head. I'd lend her Queenie. Then I remembered she had already had one encounter with Queenie last Christmas. It had not gone well. But it would be fun to see her face if Queenie were presented. . . . Be charitable, Georgie, I commanded myself. We are doing this for your cousin.

"My personal maid is also helping me with the baby at the moment," I said, "but I expect she can find some time for you. Where is your own maid?"

"I don't have one at the moment. The last girl proved unsatisfactory—she was eager to blab to reporters—and I've been living out of suitcases. I haven't felt settled enough to hire a new girl. When I know what's going to happen, then I'll hire a new maid if I have to. I expect they have maids coming out of the woodwork at Buckingham Palace."

Oh dear. She really expected she'd be moving in soon.

We had been climbing the stairs as we spoke. I pushed open her bedroom door.

"We've put you in here at the back so that no snooping reporter can spot you." I opened the door and went ahead into the room. It certainly felt frosty. I put down the cases and turned on the bedside lamp.

"There is a hot-water bottle in the top drawer and plenty of hot water in the bathroom. It's at the end of the hall."

"Oh God." She was looking around. "Still I suppose one

must suffer for love." She placed her jewelry case on the bedside table. "Sometimes I wonder why I ever agreed to marry the boy. It's all turning out to be too complicated. Still, he is having a tiara made for me, which will be nice, and Your Majesty does have a ring to it, doesn't it?" She gave a brittle laugh, which made me think that she wasn't entirely thrilled about her future.

I left her and went back to our room, where Darcy was now walking up and down with James Albert over his shoulder. The latter was still protesting loudly. Darcy gave me an exasperated look. "Thank God. Here, go back to your mother." He handed the baby to me. I did the only thing that worked well, sat on the bed and offered him a late-night snack. He sucked for a few minutes then fell blissfully asleep.

"What was all that about?" Darcy asked. "I wake up to the child screaming and no sign of you."

"That's because Mrs. Simpson chose to arrive," I said. "You'll find the front hall full of her baggage. I showed her to her room and she is not happy that we have no central heating."

"That's good," Darcy said. "Perhaps she won't want to stay long if we make it too uncomfortable."

"My thoughts exactly," I said. "Move over. My feet are freezing."

I slid into bed beside him. "Maybe central heating might be a good thing," Darcy said. "If the farm starts to make a profit we could suggest it to Sir Hubert."

"Who knows when he'll turn up again," I said. "He was in America but he's probably gone on to Alaska or North Russia by now." I snuggled up against Darcy. "I'm glad you're home," I said. "Don't you dare go abroad and leave me with Mrs. Simpson and Fig."

He chuckled, wrapping me in his arms. "That might be grounds for divorce," he agreed. "But I do have to go up to town in the morning."

"Coward," I said.

"No, honestly. I have meetings, I'm afraid. I'm sure you'll handle her just brilliantly."

"Hmmpf" was all I could think of saying.

Chapter 5

Thursday, October 29
Eynsleigh

We are surviving Mrs. Simpson so far. Now all we need is Fig to make life even more difficult.

Mrs. Simpson did not stir until late the next morning so I presumed her bed was warm enough, as Sally the housemaid had been instructed to light her fire at an early hour. I was in a quandary whether to keep the breakfast items warm in their chafing dishes in the dining room, in case she showed up for breakfast, then decided against it. When she did stir she tugged on her bell and requested black coffee and toast brought up to her room. At least she was going to be easy to please in the mornings.

She finally appeared around eleven thirty looking, I thought privately, rather the worse for wear. Granddad had departed immediately after breakfast, anxious to get away before he had to face "that woman."

"You will come back soon," I said, giving him a big hug. "I'll miss you."

"You've got plenty of company for the moment," he said. "Not that I envy you. But you're doing your duty for king and country."

I'd kissed his bristly cheek, relishing the smell of lavender water that I had always found so comforting. And then he was gone, driven to the station by Phipps. I was reading the morning papers when Mrs. Simpson finally appeared. No mention of her in the news yet. I had decided to keep James confined to his crib upstairs today. I didn't think Mrs. S would be too fond of babies.

"Did you sleep all right?" I asked politely.

"I had an awful night," she said. "All those ungodly noises."

"Noises?"

"You know, shrieks and hoots and moaning wind. Like a horror film."

For a moment I thought she was referring to James's crying, although he had gone to sleep pretty quickly, but then I realized. "We have a screech owl in the north tower," I said.

She rolled her eyes dramatically. "God, I hate the country. Give me London or New York any day. And when I'd finally dozed off, then that dratted girl came in to light the fire, and then a constant procession of servants bringing my luggage in. I've hardly slept a wink."

"I'm sorry. I thought you'd like your room to be warm when you wanted to get up," I said. "You must let my housekeeper know what time you'd like to be woken with coffee in future."

"Certainly not before nine," she said. "Frankly there's little point in getting up at all here. Nobody to talk to. David says I'm not allowed to make phone calls, except to him. I can't even get my hair done. It's like a prison. I might as well be stuck on Alcatraz or Devil's Island."

"At least we promise not to beat you or feed you bread and water," I said dryly. I wanted to remind her that this was my home she was criticizing and that I wasn't exactly thrilled about having her here. But my good breeding prevented it . . . for the moment at least. I would see how far she could push me before I told her what I was thinking.

"Now that you're up, would you like anything more to eat?" I said. "I'm afraid you're too late for breakfast, but we'll be having coffee any minute and luncheon is at one o'clock."

"Nothing to eat," she said. "I'm on a diet. I want to look good in my wedding dress. Oh, and just a salad for lunch, with maybe some smoked salmon and a little clear soup."

"I'm not sure about a salad at this time of year," I said. "We eat what we grow. But I do have an excellent French chef and he can prepare you almost anything. I'll ring for him, shall I?"

Pierre came into the morning room and suggested steak tartare and wilted spinach salad to go with her consommé. She seemed quite pleased with this. "I must say your chef is remarkably civilized for an outpost like this," she said. "Where on earth did you find him?"

"Paris," I said. "Where else."

It felt like a small victory.

"So where is your dear mama these days?" she asked. "Still with what's-his-name in Germany?"

"She is," I said. "They are finally going to get married."

"Such a sensible country, Germany," she said. "Now that Herr Hitler is in charge everything runs so smoothly there. David is quite impressed. And the German ambassador here in London is utterly charming. He sends me red roses." And she gave a little smirk, making me wonder if she was perhaps too friendly to the German ambassador, or that the gentleman was deliberately courting her in the hope of gleaning a few state secrets.

WE GOT THROUGH the rest of the day. Mrs. Simpson hardly said a word over lunch, took a long rest in the afternoon and then spent hours on our phone talking to the king. "At least they seem to have a good chef," I heard her say. "But apart from that it's unbearably dreary."

She brightened up a bit over dinner because Darcy had come home and every woman finds Darcy attractive.

"Don't you find it incredibly boring down here after London?" she asked him. "But then of course you do travel a lot."

"Actually I'm enjoying being a family man and a farmer," Darcy replied. "Has Georgie shown you around the estate yet? We've got piglets and sheep and chickens."

I saw her shudder.

Pierre outdid himself at dinner and cooked an amazing bouillabaisse and a tarte tatin. Mrs. Simpson clearly forgot about her diet and had seconds of both. She seemed in quite a cheerful mood after Darcy had plied her with wine and then a brandy.

"At least your room will be warm tonight," I said.

"You're not thinking of going to bed yet?" she asked, horrified.

"We live a country life here," I said. "And I have a baby who gets me up at all hours to be fed."

"You don't let the nanny do that?"

I had to smile. "We don't actually have a nanny yet and besides, I'm breastfeeding."

Now she did look stunned. "Yourself?"

"Nobody else would volunteer to do it," Darcy said with a chuckle.

"But my dear girl, how totally primitive. They make good bottles these days, and you could have servants give the child his nighttime feeds."

"But I enjoy feeding him," I said. "I know my mother never nursed me but I like that special contact with my son."

"But your figure, honey. It will spoil your figure."

"I think her figure will be fine." Darcy gave me such a warm smile that I blushed.

As we went up to bed we heard her talking to the king again on our telephone. "You might have warned me how primitive it would be," she was saying. "I feel as if I'm back in colonial times." There was a long pause and then she said, "Yes, of course I love you."

I wondered who was going to pay the telephone bill.

THE NEXT MORNING we were just finishing breakfast when we heard the scrunch of tires on the gravel.

"Is that the delivery van picking up the produce?" Darcy asked. "They're early."

I got up and looked out of the window. "Much worse," I said as I watched a chauffeur emerge from the driver's seat, and then go around to open a door for Fig. "It's my beloved sister-in-law."

"Well, at least she can entertain Mrs. Simpson," Darcy said. "Maybe they'll bore each other to tears or annoy each other so much that they'll both leave."

"With our luck they'll become bosom friends and decide to stay over Christmas," I said. I gave a big sigh. "Golly, Darcy, what have we done to deserve this? What gods have we offended?"

"You shouldn't have said how contented you were with your life." He ran a caressing hand over my shoulder.

"True." I brushed away toast crumbs from the corners of my mouth with my napkin, smoothed down my skirt and went to face the music.

Phipps had opened the front door by the time I reached the foyer. I heard him say, "If you'll wait here, Your Grace, I'll announce you to the mistress."

"Oh, for heaven's sake," Fig said. "We're family. We don't need to be announced. Which room are they in?"

I stepped forward to intervene. "Hello, Fig. Hello, Binky. Lovely to see you. Welcome to Eynsleigh."

"What-ho, old bean." Binky gave me a big bear hug. "You're looking very pretty. Clearly motherhood agrees with you."

Fig merely gave me a nod. "Beastly journey down. Sleet and snow all the way through Yorkshire and then Podge was carsick. We spent the night at the London house and nearly froze to death because it didn't seem worth getting the boiler going." She shot Binky a look of venom. "Actually Binky hadn't a clue about how to get anything going. Podge and I managed to light a fire in the drawing room."

"You didn't bring servants?"

"Well, no, of course not. Why would we need servants if we are staying with you. We talked about bringing the chauffeur but Binky said he could drive, and I'm sure I can borrow your sweet little maid to look after me."

"I'm afraid Maisie is rather busy at the moment," I said. "She is looking after our other guest and helping me with the baby."

"Other guest?" Fig's voice was sharper than ever. "You didn't warn us about another guest."

"If you remember we didn't actually have a conversation. You wrote to say you were coming. And the other guest was rather foisted on us at the last minute."

"Who is it? Do I know her?"

"You've met her before. An American lady. Mrs. Simpson."

"Her?" Fig's face flushed an angry red. "The king's . . ." She sought for a word that she could use in polite company. . . . "Special friend?" she concluded. "The one we met last Christmas at Sandringham?"

"Soon to be more than special friend, one gathers," I said.

"He doesn't want to marry her, surely?" Binky asked. "He can't marry her. Twice divorced and he's the head of the church. I mean, that simply isn't done."

"Am I interrupting a touching family reunion," said a voice from the stairs, and Mrs. Simpson glided toward us, a defiant smile on her face.

Luckily, as I had predicted, Fig was a little in awe of Mrs. Simpson. She did have that effect on people. So they were frostily polite to each other. But it was quite clear that Mrs. S found my family as horribly lacking in social graces as I was. Nobody drank the latest cocktails. Mrs. S suggested bridge after dinner and Binky trumped her ace when he was her partner. It was only at mealtimes that everyone cheered up, because the food was so delicious and we never knew what we were going to have next.

"Do you select your menus for the week, Georgiana?" Fig asked as we sat at lunch and had just eaten a rich soup. "I must say I'm impressed. I suppose you learned about foreign food when you were sent to that expensive finishing school in Switzerland. I wouldn't know what to ask for, and Binky doesn't know one French dish from another."

"That's right. Give me a big portion of haggis and mashed turnips and I'm quite content," he said.

Mrs. Simpson shuddered.

"Actually Pierre is given carte blanche with the menus most of the time," I said. "He loves to experiment with new dishes." I looked across at Fig. "You should bring down the children and let them try French food. Educate them young. That's what we plan to do."

Podge and Addy, who had come with their nanny, had been installed in the nursery, where Fig intended they should stay, unseen and unheard, but instead they had been having a lovely time with Darcy, running free on the estate. He had taken them to the farm, introduced them to the boys who lived in the farm cottage and let them help with the animals. They both had rosy cheeks and looked like normal happy children for once.

"Your ideas on child-rearing are most strange, Georgiana," Fig said. "Nursing your own baby? And letting him sleep in your bedroom? And what's more you haven't hired a proper nanny yet. That girl may be willing enough and have experience with brothers and sisters but it's not the same as raising a child to be a prominent member of society. Podge will be a duke someday and Nanny is raising him accordingly. You must let us help you find someone suitable, Georgiana, I absolutely insist. I did mention the Clayton-Cloughs' nanny, didn't I? Their boys have grown up. All in the army. She's probably been snapped up by now, but one can only try."

"We will select a nanny in our own good time," I said. "But so far everything is working very well. So when is the visit to Podge's prospective school planned?"

"Not until next week," Fig said. "It turns out they were busy with exams this week."

Which you obviously knew, I thought, and planned an extra week down here with good food and no gales.

"We told you we've already put his name down for Eton, didn't we?" Binky brightened up. "I had a good time there, after your mama got me away from that horrible outdoor type of school. Cross-country runs and cold showers before dawn." He gave a dramatic shudder.

"Everyone I know has enjoyed Eton," I agreed. "And make sure you find a prep school for Podge where they are kind and understanding. He'll only be seven, after all. That's awfully young."

"You British with your horrible schools," Mrs. Simpson drawled. "It's no wonder you all grow up sexually repressed and unable to express emotion."

I caught Darcy's glance and tried not to smile. We looked up as Phipps came in with some kind of letter on a silver salver. "Telegram, my lady." He offered it to me. I took it and opened it. "It's from Sir Hubert. He's coming home next week. On the new *Queen Mary*."

Chapter 6

Monday, November 2
Eynsleigh

So much for my quiet vision of domestic bliss. It seems we are to have a rather full house.

"You'll be glad to have Sir Hubert home, won't you?" I asked Mrs. Holbrook when I gave her the news.

"I shall indeed." She gave a shy little smile. She had been his housekeeper for many years and was clearly fond of him. "I'll make sure his bedroom is aired out and the fire laid ready to be lit."

She had just gone off to oversee that, when we got another telegram. It said simply, "Am bringing some people with me. Prepare for invasion."

I found Mrs. Holbrook and showed the telegram to her.

"What on earth can he mean by that?" she asked.

"I have no idea. The only person he's had to stay was that old explorer. You could hardly describe him as an invasion."

"Am I supposed to make up more rooms, do you think?" She looked really worried now. "I've already put your guests in the best rooms. There are those bedrooms at the other end of Sir Hubert's private wing. Should I make those up?"

"I think we should wait until he gets here," I said. "He's not usually inconsiderate so I'm sure he wouldn't spring a whole lot of people on us."

"You're right, my lady," she said. "He's been the most considerate of men. Maybe this is his idea of a joke."

"Let's hope so," I said.

I warned my guests that the owner of the house would be coming home and may be bringing some people with him. Mrs. Simpson was not pleased, to say the least.

"I came here for complete seclusion, not to have half the world visiting," she said. "Can you not tell him it's not convenient?"

"I can't," I said. "For one thing it's his house and for another he's on the *Queen Mary*."

"Oh, the new ship." She burst out laughing. "I thought for a moment you meant . . . What an intriguing picture that conjured up."

I didn't smile. I knew too well that she liked to make digs against the royal family.

So we waited. The next evening we received a telephone call from the station, asking Phipps to come and pick up Sir Hubert. We held our breath, not knowing what to expect. While the others sat over sherry in the long gallery I went to the front door to greet him, or was it them? The motorcar pulled up and only one man got out. Sir Hubert, looking extremely fit and tanned, ran up the front steps.

"How's my favorite godchild?" he asked, hugging me. "You're looking very well."

"So are you," I said. "You've been somewhere sunny."

"Hollywood," he said. "I was the expert consultant on a film set in the Himalayas. Not that they paid any attention to me when I pointed out things that they were getting wrong. But they did pay me a good fee. And it was quite fascinating to see how motion pictures are made."

"You mentioned that you were bringing people with you," I said. "Are they coming later? An invasion, you said?"

"That's right. They'll be arriving tomorrow."

"Exactly how many of them? Mrs. Holbrook's worried we won't have enough bedrooms."

"A couple of dozen at least."

"A couple of dozen?" My voice rose an octave.

He laughed then. "Naughty of me. They won't be staying in the house." He slipped an arm around my shoulders as we walked. "It's people I met in Hollywood. They are shooting a film about Henry the Eighth and his wives and daughters and when they learned that I live in a Tudor mansion, they begged to be allowed to shoot some of the outdoor scenes here. The crew will be staying at local pubs but I've arranged for the stars to stay at the Meadowsweet Country Club. You know it, don't you? Very swank and is known to celebrities, which is good. These people are not used to roughing it. There are some big names, I gather. I've never been much of a film buff but I expect the names will mean something to other people."

"How jolly exciting," I said. "I've never watched a film being made."

Sir Hubert froze as we approached the long gallery and he heard voices. "Do we have company?"

"I'm afraid we do. My brother, his wife and children are supposed to be staying so they can check out schools for Podge. They don't show any inclination of doing that so far." I grinned. "Oh, and we've a certain American lady. She's hiding out here."

"A certain American?" He stopped, suddenly startled. "You don't mean Mrs. Simpson?" He looked half horrified, half amused.

"You know about her, then?"

"My dear, I've been in America. The papers are full of her. It's front-page news—the love story of the century. They claim she wants to marry the king."

"She certainly intends to do so. So far she isn't common knowledge in England, but she will be soon. Hence the desire to hide out in the countryside."

"But why here for God's sake? Whose idea was that?"

"Because my dear cousin the king asked my husband a favor. He doesn't want his bride to be hounded by the press."

"Oh, of course. Your cousin. One forgets." He chuckled. "So he really does mean to marry her, then?"

"He really does."

"And how is that going to go down with Parliament?"

"Not very well, one gathers. David, I mean King Edward, is convinced he can get the British public on his side and thus force Parliament to agree."

"I can't see that happening," Sir Hubert said. "Well, it seems we are in for an interesting time. Come on, then. Better face the music and dance." He gave me a big grin and propelled me into the long gallery.

THE NEWS THAT a film crew was arriving any minute did not go down well with Mrs. Simpson.

"Are you completely mad?" she asked. "I come here to hide out until the storm blows over and now every newsman in the country will be on the doorstep hoping to get a glimpse of Hollywood stars."

"They won't be coming in the house, dear lady," Sir Hubert said. "They'll only be shooting the external scenes here. Only for a few days. And they bring their own caravans for wardrobe and makeup and the like. So there's no reason any of them should know that you're here."

"I hope you're right," she said. "Well, at least it will relieve the boredom to watch from a window."

"Clearly we should have invited a juggler or two and the Dagenham Girl Pipers," Darcy muttered to me, making me suppress a giggle.

THE NEXT MORNING I had awoken for James's six o'clock feed and had just gone back to bed when there was a tap on my door. Mrs. Holbrook came in, still in her dressing gown, her hair still in curlers. "So sorry to disturb you, my lady, sir," she said, "but the people from the film company have arrived and they want to come into the house."

"I thought they'd be bringing their own caravans and tents," Darcy said.

"They are, but they need electric cables connected and access to water."

"Perhaps you should go and wake Sir Hubert," Darcy said. "They are his guests, after all. Oh, and tell them there is a tap in the stable yard and electricity in the garage."

"Very good, sir. I'll tell them. And I'll go and wake Sir Hubert."

"That was naughty of you," I said as the door closed.

"They are nothing to do with us," Darcy said. "I'd never have invited them in the first place. Clearly your godfather is rather smitten with Hollywood, or maybe it's a particular Hollywood star?"

"Surely not? He's more sensible than that."

"He was rather smitten with Zou Zou," Darcy said.

"Well, Zou Zou is gorgeous and fun and delightful and rich," I said. "Who wouldn't be smitten? He should have pursued her more, not gone off to climb another blasted mountain."

"He's really still in love with your mother," Darcy said. "And can now accept that that's hopeless."

I sighed. "You're right. I wish she'd see the truth about what's going on in Germany and come home. But she won't."

After the interruption there was no going back to sleep. Besides, I was more than a little curious about what was happening outside. By the time I had bathed and dressed, our forecourt was a hive of activity. I peeped out of the window in the upstairs corridor to see lorries disgorging all kinds of weird and wonderful electrical equipment, caravans being towed around the side of the house, a marquee being erected on the side lawn, racks of costumes being wheeled over the gravel with difficulty.

"It's like a bloody circus," Darcy exclaimed. "Do they really need all this to shoot a few scenes?"

It was rather like watching an anthill at work, everyone scurrying and busy. But rather exciting to watch. I had no idea it took so many people and so much equipment to make a film. And not even a whole film. Just a few outdoor scenes. I presumed the indoor ones would be shot in a studio somewhere, maybe back in Hollywood.

Darcy came to join me. "So much for your quiet life," he muttered. "I had better move the car now or I'll never be able to get it out later."

"You're not going out today?"

"Have to, I'm afraid. Another meeting in Whitehall. But don't worry, I'll be back before dinner."

When I gave him a querying look he kissed my forehead and said, "That's a promise."

"Should we go and say hello and welcome them, do you think?" I asked.

"That might be a nice gesture. Let's see if any voluptuous female film stars have arrived yet."

I gave him a warning look and he chuckled as he put an arm around me and we walked down the stairs. As we came out onto the steps two men were in the process of maneuvering a tall light into position.

"You want it here, this close, boss?" one of the men called.

"Yeah. That doorway's a bit gloomy. Needs lighting up," came an American voice. I saw a large middle-aged man wearing a cap and sheepskin jacket heading for us. He had heavy jowls and an unpleasant scowl. He spotted us. "You there. Get out of the way," he called. "We're setting up a scene."

"We just came to introduce ourselves," Darcy said, in his best frosty English. "I'm Darcy O'Mara and this is my wife, Lady Georgiana. This is our front door."

"And right now we're using it," the man said. "So if you can tell your people to make sure they go out through the back way until we're done that would be great."

Darcy was looking around. "Your men have boxed in my motorcar. I'll need it later to go up to London, so please have them move that lorry," he said.

"Can't you drive it out over the grass for once?" the man snapped.

"Absolutely not. And it's not the grass. It's the Eynsleigh lawns, which remain pristine."

The man sighed. "Right. Okay. Frank! Get the truck out of the way. The guy needs his auto."

Darcy strode across the forecourt, apparently oblivious to all the comings and goings, and I watched as he drove the Daimler through the chaos so that it was facing the front gate. Then he walked back to me as if none of the intruders existed.

"You were wonderful," I said as we went inside.

"Damned cheek," Darcy said. "Ordering us around as if he owned the place." He leaned closer to me. "I could have got the car out perfectly easily by driving through the farm but I wasn't going to let that man get the better of me."

We were laughing as we went to find Mrs. Holbrook.

"I went ahead and had the breakfast prepared early, seeing as how you were woken up at the ungodly hour. Sir Hubert's already in the dining room," she said. "He's instructed us that we're not to use the front door while they are filming there. I don't know what the postman will think."

We went through to the dining room. Sir Hubert had a large plate of bacon, scrambled eggs and mushrooms in front of him and was tucking in with relish.

"A proper English breakfast for once," he said. "I can't tell you how dismal breakfast is in America. Waffles and syrup with my bacon. I ask you!"

"You are always telling us about starving on mountaintops," I said. "At least you didn't starve."

He threw back his head and laughed. "That's so true. Be grateful for what you have, eh?"

He took a bite of toast. "So have you been out there to meet them yet?"

"We met him who must be obeyed," I said. "The man shouting orders. Most unpleasant."

"Oh yes. That's the director, I'm afraid. Cy Marvin. Not the easiest of men. I was warned about him."

"So how did you get involved in this?" Darcy asked. I noticed he also had a plate piled high with eggs, bacon and kidneys.

"I met the star of the film one day in the canteen at the movie studio," he said. "And she told me they were going to England and looking for a place for the outdoor shots. When I told her I lived at Eynsleigh she was very excited, and she introduced me to the producer."

"What's the difference between a producer and a director?" I asked.

"The producer is the one who sets the whole thing up, hires the actors, gets the financing. He's the managing director, so to speak. The director is the one who brings the thing to life, the one with the vision. They are usually temperamental, so one hears."

"This one certainly is," I said.

"It won't be for long." Sir Hubert gave me an encouraging smile. "And we'll have a nice fat check to put into the estate, which we could certainly use right now, don't you think?"

"Oh, they're paying us for this?" I asked.

"Handsomely."

"In which case I suppose we can be polite for a few days," Darcy said.

Chapter 7

WEDNESDAY, NOVEMBER 4
EYNSLEIGH

The place is overrun with film people, including some very glamorous stars. I suppose it's exciting in a way but I hope they don't stay too long. So does Mrs. Simpson, who is seriously miffed about the whole thing.

Later that day, when all was set up and our forecourt looked like a giant spider's web of cables, we got our first glimpse of the actors. It seemed that the story revolved around Henry VIII's first wife, Catherine of Aragon; his second wife, Anne Boleyn; and their daughters, Mary and Elizabeth. In true Hollywood manner the script deviated from history so that Catherine was younger, Elizabeth was older, and Henry was handsome. According to this version of history Anne knows that Henry wants her killed and asks Catherine for help, making her promise to look after Elizabeth, who is an adorable four-year-old. At least this is what we could gather when we were told the story at dinner.

Yes, Sir Hubert invited them to dine with us that first night. Pierre was not pleased that he had been given such short notice.

"'Ow I cook zee superb meal wiz no ingredients?" he demanded. "Eez bloody daft." You can see that his English had improved. He had also picked up the wrong sort of words from Queenie.

"What were you planning for our dinner?" I asked.

"The sole Véronique and then the lamb cutlets," he said. "But eez only enough for six persons."

I nodded. "I can see that would be a problem. What else do we have in the larder?"

"Nothing special," he said, reverting to French with me. "I make zee plan to go into 'aywards 'eath to order my weekly supplies tomorrow."

"Could you turn the sole into a bouillabaisse if we got some shrimp from the village fishmonger?"

"Alas, I have no tomatoes, no peppers. How I make a bouillabaisse?" he demanded, waving his arms as only the French can.

I had a brilliant idea. "Make a fish pie."

He wrinkled his nose. "What eez zis?"

"Queenie makes a good one. Like a shepherd's pie but with fish. We'll send Phipps to get some tiny shrimp, then it's a cheesy sauce and a potato crust. Queenie can show you."

He was clearly not pleased with this idea. "It is food for peasants," he said.

"I agree but we'll tell them it's an old English tradition. It's not our fault if Sir Hubert springs guests on us at the last minute."

He went away grumbling and I went up to change my clothes before I had to entertain film stars. Pierre wasn't the only one who was displeased at the announcement. Mrs. Simpson was furious. "Coming to dinner? Where am I supposed to dine, then?" She gave an infuriated toss of the head. "I can't let anyone know I'm here. It won't be long before the press are swarming around and it will be all over America by morning. I'm certainly not joining you for dinner. I'll have to have my food sent up to my room."

"I quite understand," I said. "It's most inconvenient and most unlike Sir Hubert. He's usually the most considerate of men."

"He better not be making a habit of this," she said, "or David will have to come up with another idea for me."

And she did a grand exit, worthy of any of the queens in the picture.

In honor of the occasion I dressed properly for dinner. By that I mean evening gown. Jewels. Darcy arrived home as I was finishing my toilette.

"Just in time," I said as he came in. "I need you to do up the clasp of this necklace. Maisie is bathing James."

"Heavens," he said. "I presume I have to wear a dinner jacket. So we really are entertaining royalty tonight or are you helping them to get into character for their parts in the film?"

"I just thought we should do things properly for once," I said. "We've been too lax about changing for dinner when it's just us at home. We should show them how the English gentry behaves. Especially that rude director."

Darcy laughed as he came up behind me and fixed the clasp on my rubies. I was wearing my burgundy velvet gown (not the one that Queenie ironed the wrong way, but one that my mother had treated me to). It did look quite sultry on me, I have to admit, and I gave a pleased little nod to myself in the mirror. Darcy also approved. "You look very desirable in that," he said, wrapping his arms around my waist. "I'd watch out for Henry the Eighth if I were you. We know his reputation with women."

"No thanks. I want to keep my head off the chopping block," I said, laughing. "And we haven't got time for that sort of thing," I added as Darcy nuzzled at my neck.

As we headed for the staircase we met Binky and Fig. Binky always dressed for dinner, even at home in Scotland, but Fig was wearing a sort of draped black cocktail dress that made her look deathly pale. She gave a little squeak of horror when she saw us.

"You didn't tell us it was formal," she said. "I thought you'd dispensed with the whole dressing-for-dinner routine in this house."

"I just felt we should show the Hollywood types how the English behave," I said.

"Then I should go and change," she said. "I only brought one long gown with me. And the good jewelry is in the safe at home. I didn't think . . ."

"It's all right, Fig. You look fine as you are," I said. "Short gowns are quite acceptable these days. Remember my mother wore one when she was here and if anyone is up to date with fashion trends it's my mother."

"Well, if you really think so." She looked at Binky. "You should have brought your Order of the Garter sash."

"Not that formal," I said.

"So I really do look all right, Binky?" she asked.

"Frankly, old thing, if you're competing with film stars it really doesn't matter much what you wear," he said. "You're not exactly built for glamour, are you."

Darcy and I exchanged a glance as Fig gave her husband a frosty stare. Sir Hubert was already in the drawing room, where we were going to have drinks before dinner, as it was easy to heat and we were sure that Americans would feel the cold. He looked dashing in evening dress. I felt a tinge of annoyance that my mother had not stayed married to him and had chosen Max instead.

Mrs. Simpson did not put in an appearance. We had already started on the sherry and cheese straws, when Phipps announced our guests. I had been to Hollywood once with my mother so I had encountered film stars before. I expected these actors to be as glamorous as the people I had met. Instead a group of five people, looking distinctly chilly and miserable, came into the room.

"Oh, thank God. It's warm," one of the women said. She made a beeline for the fire. "We've been freezing our butts off in that poor excuse for a hotel. Country club? It's more like a country jail. Do you know they have one little radiator in the bedroom and it's only lukewarm to the touch? And a draft came in through the window. So uncomfortable." She shot a venomous glance at an innocuous little man who was dressed in a blazer and slacks with a warm scarf at his throat. "I've told Zack he needs to find us a proper hotel or we're heading back to Hollywood."

Then she looked around, spotted Sir Hubert and came over to him, holding out her hand. "Hello. Lovely to meet you. I'm Lana Lovett."

He took the hand and planted a delicate kiss on it. "Of course you are. No introduction needed. I'm Hubert Anstruther. Welcome to Eynsleigh."

"Lovely house you have here," she said. "Have you lived here long?"

Sir Hubert smiled. "It's been in my family for four hundred years." He turned to the rest of the group. "Mr. Dennison," he said, addressing the little man. "Mr. Marvin"—the blustery man we'd encountered that morning—"and of course Miss Gloria Bishop."

He repeated the kissing-the-hand gesture, this time with a little more sincerity, his lips lingering on her hand. The recipient was a beautiful older woman, dark haired and with perfect bone structure. She was dressed in gray wool with a mink stole thrown carelessly around her shoulders. They made eye contact as he straightened up and I saw her eyes twinkle at him. I watched, rather amazed. I had never thought of Sir Hubert as a woman charmer. "Perhaps you'd introduce us to the rest of your party?"

"Of course, darling." Miss Bishop had a smooth sultry voice. "I'm sure you recognize Grant Hathaway. He's our King Henry. And I must say he has the perfect temperament for it."

I had seen Grant Hathaway in a film before and stared at the man she was indicating. Then he had played a gangster with slicked-back black hair. Now his hair was bright red and he sported a red beard. He was wearing a jacket made of some kind of sleek fur—sealskin?

"Great to meet you, folks," he said. "Good of you to have us here to dinner. If the food at that place we're staying was anything to go by we'd be dead of botulism by now." He had a rich, rumbling voice with an accent that could be described as transatlantic. Was he originally English? I wondered.

"Oh dear. I am sorry," Sir Hubert said. "The country club has a good reputation. People come down from London to play golf there."

"The golf course may be exceptional," Grant Hathaway said, "but the rooms and the food remind one of an English boarding school, which I was unlucky enough to have endured for two long years."

There was a short, embarrassed silence.

"And last but of course not least our wonderful Nora." Gloria Bishop led Sir Hubert over to a plain, bony woman who stood at the back of the group, arms wrapped across her chest as if she was cold. She was wearing a navy suit that emphasized her plainness. "Nora Pines. She's Cy's secretary but we all know she waves her little magic wand and makes everything tick smoothly."

Nora flashed her a look of annoyance before she managed a hint of a smile.

"Well, welcome, everyone." Sir Hubert sounded a little too cheerful, as if he too were playing the part of the genial lord of the manor. "Let me introduce you to our lot. First of all my goddaughter, Lady Georgiana. She's cousin to the present king so you'd better behave yourselves or you might find it's the Tower of London for you."

I noted the impressed glances and gave what I hoped was an encouraging smile.

"Gee, Hubie, do you people dress up like this all the time or did you do it specially for us?" Lana Lovett asked. "I feel like we're on some kind of movie set. I'm sorry we didn't bring our evening gowns with us. We were told we were shooting some scenes at a country house for a few days and that was it."

"It really doesn't matter. Don't worry about it," Sir Hubert said. "We do usually dress for dinner, especially when we have guests, but that's just our quaint English customs." He gave an easy laugh. "So let me continue with introductions. This is Lady Georgiana's brother, the Duke of Rannoch, and his wife, the duchess. I should probably have introduced them first. I must apologize." He gave a little bow in their direction. Fig returned a "we are not amused" stare. "And rounding out the party is Lady Georgiana's husband, Mr. O'Mara. I should add that Mr. O'Mara is the heir to Lord Kilhenny, so I am the humble one here, a mere baronet."

"God, Hubert, I had no idea," the producer said. "You folks are the real deal. If we want to know how to act like royalty we just have to watch you guys."

"Why don't we have some sherry before dinner," Sir Hubert said, giving a nod to Phipps, who was waiting by the drinks table.

"Sherry? Is that what you people drink?" Cy Marvin asked. "You don't have any whiskey? I thought Brits drank nothing but Scotch."

"I can certainly offer you a Scotch if you'd like," Sir Hubert said. "Do you take it with soda or water?"

"On the rocks," Mr. Marvin said.

"Oh dear. I'm afraid we don't go in for ice here." Sir Hubert looked amused.

"You'd only need to step outside and find the nearest puddle," Lana said in scathing tones. "I'm sure it's frozen over. This was a stupid time of year to shoot the outdoor scenes."

"The script calls for bleak winter," Cy said. "We're leading up to Anne Boleyn's death." He turned to us. "It's real intense drama. Henry wanting to get rid of Anne, Anne trying to find a place where little Elizabeth will be safe, and appealing to Catherine, his first wife, to take her in and protect her."

"So you have baby Elizabeth in this picture?" Fig asked.

"Little girl Elizabeth," Cy said. "She's being played by Rosie Trapp—you know her, of course? The up-and-coming child star? You saw her in *My Sweet Honey*? She sang and danced with the dog?"

"Oh yes," we muttered politely, although I suspected none of us had seen the film.

"But Elizabeth was still a baby when her mother was executed," Fig pointed out.

"Honey, this is the movies," Cy said. "An appealing three-year-old who can cry on cue is what the public wants."

"And I'm not sure that Anne and Catherine would have wanted to help each other," Fig went on. "One of my ancestors was at the court of Henry the Eighth so we have always been interested in the relationships at that time." The stare she gave him was one of scoring a point.

Cy shrugged. "So we bend history a little when we need to. Emotion and drama. That's what the public wants. And cute kids. Rosie Trapp. She was a hit in her first film with us, so I think we might have another Shirley Temple on our hands. You mark my words, she's going to be a big star," Cy went on, wagging a finger at us as if this was a hot tip.

"Not as big as her mother wants her to be," Lana Lovett said with a catty chuckle.

"We've also got little Dorothy Hart playing the teenage Mary. You know her, right? Teen sensation? In the film with the horse? Do we have the hottest stars in Hollywood in this movie, or do we not?" He nodded to his three stars in turn, who each smiled graciously.

I wasn't sure if this was purely a rhetorical question. "Did you bring your child actors to England for these scenes?" I asked.

"Sure we did," Cy Marvin said. "They are back at that country club, or rather Dorothy is. Rosie's mother chose to rent her own place nearby. Overprotective, you know. She wanted to bring the kid along tonight but there are strict rules about child actors and going out after supper is not allowed—except for the premiere. You'll meet them tomorrow when we start filming."

"I got the feeling the kid's mother was really put out that she wasn't invited herself," Lana Lovett said with a wicked smile. "If you want an example of a pushy stage mother, she's it. She'd do anything for that kid."

"We have to be nice to her, Lana, sweetie," Zack Marvin said, "because her daughter is going to bring us in the big bucks. She may turn into a little walking gold mine as you very well know."

Drinks were handed around. Cy knocked back his Scotch without ice.

"Are these all the actors, apart from the children?" Fig asked in her most clipped and frosty voice. "Don't pictures usually have a cast of thousands these days?"

Cy Marvin grinned at this. "We've shot all the big scenes back home at the studio. We're only doing the intimate scenes at Catherine's house here. We'll need a few extras but I guess we can find them locally." He looked up as if he had an idea. "Say, you've got a houseful of servants. Why don't we just use them? Saves having to mix with the locals, deal with a few crazies, huh?"

I opened my mouth to say our servants were fully occupied and we didn't exactly have a houseful of them, just enough to keep the place running, but before I could speak Sir Hubert said, "Why not? I'm sure they'd love it and we can muddle through for a day or two, can't we?"

"Just don't borrow our cook," I said, "or we'll all starve."

We chatted in polite fashion until a gong rang in the foyer. Grant Hathaway had also opted for Scotch and I noticed he'd held the glass out for a refill several times. He came over to me. "So what's a gorgeous young thing like you doing in a backwater like this?" he asked and he placed one hand on my lower back. I tried to recoil in surprise. "You should be up in London, or New York, where the bright lights and the action are."

"Actually I've just had a baby, so I'm pretty much tied to the house," I said, "but I enjoy country living anyway. My husband is rearing pigs. You must let us show you when you have a moment." I looked across and caught Darcy's eye. He winked at me.

"Shall we go in to dinner?" Sir Hubert asked. I think the rest of us breathed a sigh of relief. As was required by protocol Binky and Fig automatically led the procession. I should have followed but Lana Lovett and Cy pushed ahead as if it was the most natural thing, as I suppose it was in their world. She was a big star. She was used to going first. It was only on the way to the dining room that I had a moment of panic. What if Chef hadn't managed to make anything acceptable for dinner? What if the sole was not enough for a fish pie, or Queenie refused to show Pierre how to make one? Or worse still, what if Queenie had ruined something?

"Oh my, this is fancy," Gloria Bishop said, looking around at our walls decorated with family portraits and the long mahogany dining table, now adorned with two silver candelabras and sparkling silverware. "I can get right into character sitting here, can't you, Grant?"

I noticed she was quick to secure the seat beside Sir Hubert at the top of the table.

"You must please be tolerant of what we're about to eat," I said as they took their places at the table, without being told where to sit. "We were only given short notice that you'd be dining with us so our chef didn't have time to go into town to order more food."

"That's okay. I'm on a diet anyway," Gloria Bishop said. "I have to watch my figure." And her gaze went to a certain gentleman. I noticed she had been very attentive to Sir Hubert during the sherry hour. Did she fancy herself as lady of this manor when her acting days were over? She had to be close to forty and that normally spelled doom for movie stardom, didn't it?

I slid into the seat beside her. Wine was poured. Sir Hubert proposed a toast to our guests. Then a lentil soup was brought in. It was smooth and rich and I saw nods of approval. Clever old Pierre, I thought. He's filling them up with soup so they won't be too hungry.

"So how long have you lived around here?" Gloria asked me when our host had turned to chat with Cy Marvin on his other side.

"Only about a year," I said. "The house belongs to my godfather, Sir Hubert, but he invited us to make our home here after our marriage as he's away so much and I will inherit the house one day."

"Lucky you," she said. "Although I imagine a house like this takes a lot of upkeep and a lot of money."

"It does," I said. "My husband and Sir Hubert are trying to make the estate self-sustaining. They have got the home farm up and running and are putting the land to good use. We've brought in several lads from the village and they are working out splendidly. You should ask to be shown around when you're not working."

She nodded and I could see her thinking that walking through a muddy farmyard would not be right for the type of shoes she wore. "Yes. That would be interesting," she said. "To meet the locals." She paused, then asked, "So you're not originally from this part of the world?"

"Oh no," I replied. "I grew up in a remote castle in Scotland. My brother still lives there." I nodded to Binky, who was looking rather shell-shocked at being vamped by Lana Lovett. "His son will inherit one day and become the duke."

She paused, digesting this.

"Do you have children?" she asked. "Oh, that was rather rude of me, wasn't it, since you're newly married."

I smiled. "We've been married just over a year," I said, "and we have a baby son."

"A little boy. How lovely." A wistful look came across her face.

"How about you?" I asked. "Do you have children?"

"No," she said. "No children. None at all. What's this we're eating now?"

I examined my plate. It appeared to be quenelles of sole. So I wasn't sure what would be going in the fish pie or if Chef had managed to concoct something quite different.

"I think it's sole," I said.

"It's very good."

"Our chef is excellent," I replied.

"I can't say I'm too fond of American food," she said, scraping her plate for the last of the sauce. "Too fatty and enormous portions."

"You're English originally, aren't you?" I asked. "Have you been in Hollywood long?"

"Too long," she said with a sigh. "But yes, I grew up in England. Not the fondest memories. I hated feeling trapped in a petty little life. Couldn't wait to get away and make something of myself. I miss it sometimes. Life in Hollywood is . . . well, you know. It has its pros and cons. Always being in the spotlight is not fun."

"I imagine," I said. "Do you know this part of England at all?"

"I do. I grew up not too far from here," she said. "So green. That's what I remember. I wish we'd come in summer. I've been meaning to come back for some time."

"So, young lady, they tell me you're related to the king?" Grant Hathaway asked from the other side of me.

"You're really related to the king?" Lana looked skeptical.

"He's my cousin," I said.

"Her great-grandmother was Queen Victoria, no less," Sir Hubert said.

"Gee, are we supposed to curtsy and call you Your Highness?" Lana asked.

I couldn't tell whether she was being funny or not.

"Absolutely, or she might send you to the chopping block at the Tower," Darcy said, chuckling.

"Related to the king, huh? Perhaps you can give me pointers on how to play Henry. Some private coaching, maybe?" Grant Hathaway said and to my annoyance I felt his hand on my thigh.

"I'm afraid the current king doesn't chop off too many heads," I said, "but I could persuade him to if necessary," and got a laugh from those around me. I brushed his hand from my leg and gave him a warning look.

"But he still intends to marry the Simpson woman, doesn't he?" Lana Lovett asked. "That's what we hear in the US."

"I think he does."

"About time he married someone," Cy Marvin said. "He's supposed to produce the heir, isn't he? And he's getting past it."

"Well, *she* certainly can't produce the heir," Lana said. "Darling, she's older than me—although I only admit to being thirty."

I tried not to make eye contact with Darcy, and just prayed that Fig would not blurt out that the lady in question was actually hiding in her bedroom in this very house. Luckily the conversation moved on.

Phipps and Sally removed the plates and I waited with bated breath to see what might come next. Phipps put a plate in front of Sir Hubert and muttered something into his ear. Sir Hubert glanced down at the plate, then looked up with a bright smile. "Chef said that he thought you might enjoy a classic English mixed grill."

A plate was put in front of me. It contained a lamb cutlet, a sausage, a rasher of bacon, tomatoes, mushrooms and fried potatoes. I saw all the guests with pleased expressions on their faces.

"Now, that's more like it," Grant Hathaway said. "That's a meal you can get your teeth into."

I looked around the table as they ate. Gloria taking tiny nibbles, Grant, Zack and Cy tucking in. So were Binky and Fig. And poor Miss Nora Pines, the secretary, sitting at the far end of the table, ignored, her eyes darting around as she watched everyone else.

The pudding course was one of Pierre's masterpieces, the floating island, the light meringue floating in a rich custard with strands of spun sugar like a spider's web over it. It was also met with approval.

"Gee, Hubert, old man, we'll have to come eat here every night," Cy said, slapping him on the shoulder. "It's better food than the Ritz."

"Certainly better than the ghastly country club with its freezing cold dining room," Lana said.

"Our chef is very good, I do admit," Sir Hubert said. "Georgiana found him in Paris."

I gave a modest smile as if I popped across to Paris to find chefs all the time.

Fortunately they left early, since apparently shooting a film always starts early in the morning.

"Thank God they've gone," Fig said. "Weren't they awful people? That Lana woman sat beside me and kept telling me how much she spends on her clothes. And she kept glancing at mine as if she didn't approve." She glanced across at Binky. "There's nothing wrong with my dress, is there? Just because it isn't this year's fashion. I told you that you should have brought your royal regalia to wear. And I should have put on my tiara. That would have shut her up."

As the others lingered over coffee I popped down to the kitchen to congratulate Pierre. "That was a stroke of genius," I said.

He shrugged. "They're Americans. They would not know haute cuisine anyway," he said.

Chapter 8

Thursday, November 5
Eynsleigh

Now our house has been turned into a film set. It's entertaining to watch in a way but also annoying. At least Binky and Fig are finally going to look at a school, and Mrs. Simpson is hiding away in her room, so there is a plus side to this.

The next morning filming got underway in earnest. When I looked out from the upstairs window I saw actors in period costume, including the two queens looking absolutely magnificent. I also caught my first glimpse of the child actors. A pretty little tot with springy curls holding hands with Anne Boleyn and a serious older girl walking through the grounds holding a prayer book. Elizabeth and Mary. Then I thought of Jacob and the dogs. If he hadn't been warned and had taken them for their usual walk, the dogs would come rushing around the house, probably knock over a couple of arc lights and put muddy paws on Tudor costumes. I hurried downstairs and slipped out through the French doors at the back of the house. It was a misty morning with the trees in the woodland looming as indistinct shapes, and cold enough that my breath came out as white steam. I should have stopped to put on my overcoat.

There was no sign of Jacob and the dogs so I kept walking until I came toward the farm. I heard the sound of voices and traced them to the chicken run. Jacob and another lad called Donnie were scattering corn and scraps, surrounded by eager birds. They looked up when they saw me.

"Is something wrong, my lady?" Jacob asked.

"Not at all. I came to warn you about the filming, but I see you're not walking the dogs."

"No, my lady. Mrs. Holbrook said I should keep them indoors in case they did damage to all that equipment. My goodness, that's some setup, isn't it? All that stuff just to film a couple of scenes. Donnie and me thought we'd go and watch when we'd finished the morning chores."

"Make sure you stay out of sight," I said. "That director doesn't have the best of tempers if you get into a shot by mistake."

"Don't worry. We'll be careful," Donnie said. "Perhaps they'll discover one of us and make us into a film star, eh, Jacob?" And he gave Jacob a nudge.

"Not you, that's for sure," Jacob laughed. "I'm the handsome one. Born with good looks."

"Get away with you!" Donnie laughed too and gave him a shove. "But perhaps they'd use us as extras."

"Who knows? They might." I shivered. "I'd better get back inside. It's bitter today, isn't it?"

"We're used to it, ma'am," Donnie said. "We've been working outside since we were twelve."

"And it's a darned sight better now that we're living in the cottage," Jacob said. "Warm and cozy and enough to eat. We didn't get that before, did we, Donnie?"

"We slept over the stables. It were freezing at night. We're ever so thankful you took us in."

"You were both orphans?" I asked. "Did you go from the orphanage to work on another farm?"

"I was," Donnie said. "He lost his family quite young and came to the orphanage. And then we both went to work on farms."

I glanced at Jacob's face and saw the pain. "Well, I'm so glad things are looking up for you now," I said. I gave them a big smile and hurried back inside.

I came back into the house to hear Mrs. Holbrook's voice, sounding a little tense, coming from the entrance hall. Intrigued, I went to see what was going on. She looked up as she heard me coming.

"Oh, my lady," she said. "I'm glad you're here. This lady wants permission to use the house."

I looked past her to a woman I hadn't yet seen. She was bundled in a long fur coat of indeterminate nature. Certainly not mink. She had brassy blond hair set into tight waves and wore too much makeup, not applied with great skill.

"You're the owner here, are you?" she said in a gravelly American voice. "Thank God. Look, we need to get into the house.

We have a trailer to go to between scenes but it's simply too cold for my daughter. She's delicate, you know. If she catches a chill the whole filming will be put on hold. She's the star of the picture."

I saw then that the little girl was huddled against her, a blanket wrapped around her. Underneath I caught a glimpse of a long blue gown, richly embroidered. She did look extremely cold and miserable. As I made eye contact with her she said, "I'm so cold, Mama. I can't feel my feet. Do you think I'll get frostbite?"

"These costumes are quite wrong for the climate here," the mother said. "We're used to California temperatures."

"You'd like a room in the house where you can come to warm up, is that right?" I said. "Of course. What do you think, Mrs. Holbrook?"

"In the servants' quarters, my lady?" Mrs. Holbrook said, eyeing the woman frostily.

"No, how about the little reception room at the front here? It should be easy to heat that quickly if Sally gets a fire going. Then they won't have to walk through the house."

"Very good, my lady," Mrs. Holbrook said.

"We'll have a room set up for your use," I said. "Let me show you."

She stepped inside, looking around in wonder and making me realize she was not used to this kind of house. "Gee whiz, Ma. This is like a palace," the little girl said, staring openmouthed at our staircase going up. "It's like the stairs where Cinderella lost her shoe."

Her mother was also staring. "So this is a real house? You actually live here, all the time, do you?"

"We do," I said.

"How many people in a house this size?"

"Usually just my husband and me. And our son. Sir Hubert when he's home. And the servants. At this moment we have my brother and his family staying with us."

"We're getting a house built in Beverly Hills," she said. "Not as big as this, but fancy. With a swimming pool. Just as soon as Addy is finished with this picture."

"Addy?" I reacted to the name as it wasn't a usual one.

"That's my real name," the little girl said. "Addison Rose Trapp. But now I'm known as Rosie to my public. They thought Rosie sounded better for a movie name."

"My niece is called Addy too," I said, "only she's really Adelaide. She's staying here at the moment. Perhaps you'll have time to play with her. She's about your age, I think."

"I'm nearly six," the girl said.

"Oh golly. I thought you were . . ." I broke off, embarrassed.

"She looks younger, doesn't she?" Addy's mother said. "That's why she's so perfect for the movies. She can play a little tot but she can read and follow directions."

I opened the door to the sitting room. It had that cold, unused feel. We were rarely in it as there were nicer spaces in which to sit. It was supposed to be a room into which a visitor would be shown while the lord of the manor was notified. We had a larger sitting room behind it that we seldom used. Actually we preferred the morning room, with its view over the grounds and sunshine most of the day. I saw her shudder. "It's not much warmer in here than in our trailer," she said. "Don't you folks have heating?"

"Only when we light a fire," I said. "The maid will be in right away to light one here. It should soon warm up."

"Every place we've been in this damned country is cold," Mrs. Trapp said. "That was one of the reasons I refused to stay with the rest of them at that country club. Freezing cold rooms. And then I felt that Rosie would be too exposed with all those other people coming to play golf. Not just germs, you know, but all that publicity. She'd be hounded by adoring fans and she's such a shy little girl. I'd rather nobody knew she was here, just to be on the safe side."

"So where are you staying?" I asked.

"I rented us a small house outside the nearest village," she said. "I thought it would be nicer and much closer but it's kind of primitive. Still at least it's warm with a big stove in the kitchen."

"Does it come with a maid and cook to look after you?" I asked.

She shook her head. "I didn't want strangers looking after my daughter. She's only used to my cooking, but don't worry. I don't mind hard work. We were poor until Rosie hit the big time."

"I have to be back on set, Mom." Rosie Trapp tugged at her mother's coat. "It's coming up to my scene."

I got the feeling she didn't like being ignored.

"Feel free to come back in when you are done," I said. "And I'll bring Addy down to meet you. She'd love that."

"Where is she?" the girl asked.

"Up in the nursery with her nanny," I said. "Children stay up there most of the day."

"You keep the kids shut away? That's so cruel," Mrs. Trapp said.

"Gee, that's boring," the girl said. "No friends over? No trips to the soda fountain? I'd hate that. Come on, Ma, let's move it."

"Of course, sweetheart. Whenever you want."

They went back out into the cold. I hurried to the breakfast room, where I found the rest of the family assembled and in the middle of breakfast. I related my encounter with the child star and her mother.

"You want to watch it," Fig said. "It's the thin end of the wedge."

"What do you mean?" I asked.

Fig gave a knowing look. "First they want to get inside because it's cold and use one room. Then it will be a room that's bigger and warmer and before you know it they'll have taken over the whole place."

"You may be right," Darcy said. "They are certainly aggressive enough. But as Sir Hubert says, it's only for a few days."

"I just met the little girl. She is also called Addy," I said. "I thought our Addy would like to meet her namesake and watch the filming."

"What a lovely idea," Fig said. "We were planning to leave her here while we tour the schools with Podge. Send one of the servants up to let Nanny know when to bring her down."

I felt that I had scored a rare point. It wasn't often that Fig approved of anything I had done or said.

Chapter 9

November 5
Eynsleigh

It seems that the film people are going to be here longer than we thought. Oh golly. I wish they'd hurry up and go.

If I had thought that having a film shot outside our house would not inconvenience us in any way, and might actually be fun, I was wrong. My first mistake was when I peeped out through the window of the little sitting room when I came to check on the fire being lit.

"Cut!" shouted an angry voice. "Get the hell out of the way." And I saw Cy Marvin was waving an angry fist at me. It seemed my face had appeared in his shot.

Then Queenie let the dogs out by mistake and they did exactly what I feared they'd do: bounded up to everyone and jumped all over them. We had to apologize profusely and promise it wouldn't happen again. Sir Hubert invited them to dinner again, which I thought privately was going too far with the apology, but they accepted readily and I had to rush down to the kitchen to warn Pierre.

"Eez no problem," he said. He went on to say that he enjoyed showing off his skills for a big party and would create something worthy tonight. I was tempted to suggest escargot followed by frogs' legs in the hope that they wouldn't want to eat with us again, but of course I didn't.

"Nothing too fancy," I said. "As you mentioned they are American and seemed to like the plain food last night."

"I could whip up a jam roly-poly if you like, missus," Queenie said. "Everyone seems to like my jam roly-poly."

Pierre gave her a withering look. "If I am known to be the chef the dinner must have my touch to it, you understand. And Pierre does not create zee jam roly-poly."

"Have it your way, ducks." Queenie shrugged. Then she remembered that this was the man she was sweet on. She smoothed down her apron over her impressive chest. "Of course your puddings are better than mine," she said coyly.

I looked at her with surprise. I had always thought Queenie was too thick to act with guile.

"You could make a few little scones and cakes for their tea, Queenie," I suggested. "Your cakes are always appreciated."

She brightened up at this. "And I could carry the cakes out to them, couldn't I? I saw that Grant Hathaway out there. He ain't half handsome, although I don't like him with that red beard. And Rosie Trapp. We've got Rosie Trapp outside our own house, imagine that. If I write and tell my mum and dad they'll never believe me that I'm hobnobbing with film stars."

"You're not exactly hobnobbing with them," I said, "but at least you can say that you served them scones."

"Bob's yer uncle, missus," she said, a big grin on her face.

Mrs. Simpson had not put in an appearance since the previous afternoon, not even to telephone His Majesty from the foyer. I felt concerned and asked Mrs. Holbrook about her.

"She hardly touched her breakfast," she said. "She wanted to know how much longer those film people would be here, but of course I couldn't tell her. I don't think she's doing very well, my lady. She is certainly not pleased."

"Well, there's nothing we can do about it," I said. "We didn't invite her. We're doing the king a favor."

"The king, why is that?" she asked, and of course I realized that I had nearly put my foot in it. She had no idea who the lady was and what her connection was to the king.

"She's a friend of his," I replied. I wondered when he'd make the big announcement and whether we'd be besieged with newspapermen immediately afterward. So much for peace and quiet.

I debated whether I should pay Mrs. Simpson a courtesy call to see if she needed anything, but then a wail from my bedroom drew me to see what master James wanted. He was awake and also not happy this morning. No sign of Maisie. I supposed she had more to do than usual if Mrs. Simpson and Fig were both expecting her to be their maid. I picked up James and changed a very nasty nappy. I had resisted getting a nanny but doing this made me realize that I was very glad when someone else did it.

As I came downstairs again I met Fig, leading Addy down the stairs.

"Binky has taken Podge to see a school that's nearby," she said. "I thought a woman might be out of place in such a manly environment."

"I'm going to meet another girl called Addy." Addy skipped excitedly beside her mother, her face alight with excitement. "Perhaps she'd like to play with me."

"I don't think she has much free time," I said. "She's acting in a film. She's pretending to be Queen Elizabeth when she was a little girl."

We reached the foyer.

"Why don't I leave her to you, then?" Fig handed over her daughter. "I'll go on down to the morning room. Coffee should have arrived by now." This small attempt at motherhood was obviously too much for her.

We came into the little sitting room and found that Rosie Trapp and her mother were happily ensconced there. The fire was burning brightly and the room was delightfully warm. What's more there was a tray with hot chocolate and slices of cake, brought in by one of the kindhearted servants—or maybe Queenie had done it as a chance to meet the famous Rosie Trapp. Mrs. Trapp was smoking and a fug hung in the air.

"Here's our Addy come to meet you," I said to Rosie, who was trying to eat cake without smudging her makeup. She had a white cloth over her costume to catch the crumbs.

"Hello," Addy said, running straight up to Rosie. "I'm Addy

too. We have the same name." She went to hug her but Rosie flinched away.

"Watch my makeup," Rosie said, "and don't get too close because of germs." She went back to eating cake. "You can have my autograph if you like later."

Addy gave her a bemused look, having no idea what an autograph was or whether she'd want one.

The door opened and Dorothy Hart, the older girl who was playing the teenage Mary, came into the room. Her face lit up. "Oh, how lovely, a fire, and hot chocolate," she said. "They said we could go in here to warm up and I'm freezing."

Unlike the others she sounded like any well-bred English schoolgirl. She warmed her hands in front of the fire.

"Would you like me to pour you a hot chocolate?" I asked.

"Oh, yes please. Thank you so much." She beamed at me. Her cheeks were red from the bitter cold and her eyes were very bright. Such an attractive girl. I handed her the cup.

"Is this your house?" she asked me. "It's really beautiful."

"Thank you," I said. "I agree it is a lovely house. It belongs to my godfather but I'll inherit it one day. Where is your home?"

"In Los Angeles," the girl said. "My parents moved there after I got the part in *Race of Her Life*."

"Do you like living there?"

She made a face. "I miss England. We lived in Cornwall. Everyone was so friendly and nice. In America it's all rush and people are quite rude. And I would have gone to boarding school with other girls. I would have liked that."

"Watch yourself, Addy, you're getting cake on your face," her mother snapped, grabbing a napkin and wiping savagely at her daughter's cheek. "We won't have time to do full makeup again. They'll be mad at you."

"Too bad," the child said. "I heard them say they were lucky to get me for this picture."

"You're right, sweetheart. You are the star of this picture," her mother said.

Rosie Trapp turned to my niece. "I'm a big star," she said. "I have to have a bodyguard to protect me."

"What's a bodyguard?" Addy looked up at me.

"It's like we have servants to help us out," I said.

"Why do you need a bodyguard?" I asked. "To keep the fans away?"

"After the Lindbergh baby kidnapping she could be held for ransom," Mrs. Trapp said. "You can't be too careful." She tapped her cigarette into the ashtray.

"Have you had any threats?" I asked.

"Not yet, but you can never be sure in these days of gangsters."

"But you didn't bring a bodyguard with you over here?" I asked. "I'm sure England is quite safe from gangsters."

"It's okay. I got my mom to watch over me here," Rosie said. "And we're way out in the country." She reached out and took another slice of cake. I noticed she was young enough to still have her appealing baby fat, in contrast to her mother, who was painfully thin.

"And it's only a few days," Mrs. Trapp said. "We figured the whole cast is watching out for her. And I'm her official chaperone. It's required for child actors."

"Do you have a chaperone too?" I asked Dorothy.

"I'm supposed to have one until I'm nineteen," she said. "My mother chaperones me at home but she's not very well at the moment so Mrs. Trapp said she'd look after me."

I studied the contrast between the two girls, one quite natural and unspoiled and the other acting like a little princess, thanks to her mother. My niece, Addy, was gazing at Rosie Trapp in awe.

"You have a lovely dress on," she said. "Are you allowed to keep it?"

"No, silly. It's wardrobe," Rosie said. "But I have plenty of lovely dresses. I have a dressmaker who makes things just for me. And lots of people send me clothes as presents too."

She examined Addy, who was wearing a kilt and hand-knit jumper. "You'd look quite pretty if you had better clothes," she said. "Perhaps you could be in movies and make a ton of money." Then a big smile crossed her face. "Hey, Mom. I got a great idea. She could be my stand-in. Then I wouldn't have to get cold until the actual take."

"You know what, bunnykins? That *is* a great idea." She put a hand under Addy's chin. "Say, would you like to be part of the movie too? And get to wear the dresses?"

"Oh yes. I'd like that." Addy looked up at me, waiting for me to agree.

"I don't see why not, but we'd have to ask your mother," I said. "You're stuck in the nursery while your parents are looking at schools. It might be fun for you."

Mrs. Trapp got up. "I'll go and have a word with Cy. But listen, kid, you'll have to do exactly what you're told if you're Rosie's stand-in. Understand?"

Addy nodded solemnly. I decided I would be her chaperone to make sure nobody shouted at her.

"So don't you ever get to play?" Addy asked.

Rosie shrugged. "Not much. If I'm not filming it's photo shoots and meeting people and interviews and trying on clothes." She moved closer to Addy. "It's kinda boring, if you want to know."

"So you don't have any friends to play with?"

Rosie shook her head.

"Neither do I," Addy said. "We live in a castle a long way from anywhere. I have my brother but he thinks I'm too little to play with him."

"You really live in a castle? No kidding? Like Cinderella, you mean?"

Addy nodded. I noticed Rosie's expression had changed from supercilious boredom to being interested.

"I really do. It's really, really old and there are ghosts, right, Aunt Georgie?"

I nodded. "That's right. They do say there are ghosts. I've never seen one. And the rooms are so big that it's horribly cold and drafty too. But I also grew up there and it's very lonely with no one to play with."

Rosie was examining us both now. I suspect it was the first time that she'd been impressed or intrigued by anyone. Normally she was used to being the center of adoration.

"You know what," Addy said, gaining confidence now, "you could ask them if you could play with me and I could take you and show you the witch's cottage and the farm animals."

"Witch's cottage?" Rosie's eyes opened wider. "There are real witches in England?"

"It's not really a witch's cottage," I said, smiling at her. "It's the farm cottage on our farm but it was built long ago and it does look as if it belongs in a fairy tale."

"Do you want to come and see it?" Addy said, jumping up and down with excitement now. "Uncle Darcy took me there and we saw the baby pigs and the chickens and there are sheep too. It's a lot of fun. We could ask Uncle Darcy to take you too."

"That would be swell." Rosie's expression was wistful. "I never got to see a baby pig. Could I go with her, Ma, do you think?"

"There's not going to be time for that, honey. We're only filming here for a couple of days and we have to get all the scenes done." She glanced down at her watch.

"Come on, Rosie. You're due back on set," she said, yanking her daughter away from the cake. Rosie stood up reluctantly and followed her, glancing back at Addy as she went. Addy and I were left with Dorothy.

"It must be a funny life for you, away from other girls," I said.

"It is," she said. "Sometimes I wish I was just ordinary and could go to school and play sports and things. But I realize the money I earn is helping my family. We didn't have much money in England. But I did have a pony. I was a good rider. That's how I was chosen for my first film. They saw me win a gymkhana and took me to Hollywood. It's all been very strange ever since."

I smiled at her, thinking how alike our lives had been in many ways. I'd grown up away from other children in our Scottish castle, wishing I could go to school. The only difference was that she now had lots of money. I had been penniless.

"But you enjoy the acting part?" I asked her.

"Oh yes. I really like that. It's the people. . . . I don't like being shouted at, and not all the other actors are nice." She paused. "Mr. Hathaway. I don't like him." She shuddered. "He . . . pretends he's being friendly but he touches me." She was looking at me as if she was begging me to understand without having to explain further.

I reached out and put a hand on her arm. "He was a little too friendly to me too," I said. "I've met his type of man before. You have to let him know that it's not okay."

"But he's a big star. I don't like to make a fuss," she said.

"I think you'll find that the other actresses are on your side," I said. "Most women have encountered men who don't want to take no for an answer." I leaned closer to her. "Next time he behaves in a way you don't like, say, loud enough for everyone around you to hear, 'Please take your hand away. It's making me uncomfortable.' I guarantee you'll have instant support."

"Really? Gosh. Thank you," she said.

From the foyer came the sound of the grandfather clock striking eleven. She jumped up. "I should be back on set," she said. "So nice to have met you."

And she ran out.

Chapter 10

November 5
Eynsleigh

Handling Mrs. Simpson plus the film people really is getting to be a bit too much! What was Sir Hubert thinking when he invited them here?

Mrs. Trapp returned and wanted to take Addy to meet the director. I popped up to the nursery to get her winter coat. Nanny was sitting there, mending socks, and didn't seem at all impressed. "Just as long as it doesn't give her any strange ideas," she said in her soft Scottish accent. "She's inclined to be a bit of a show-off as it is."

"It's only for one day, Nanny," I said. "She'll just see it as an adventure."

Then I found Fig to tell her what was being suggested. She

didn't appear overly interested. "Anything that keeps her occupied and out of Nanny's hair," she said. Then a thought came to her. "I presume they will have to pay her for being a stand-in?"

"I expect they will."

"In that case why not." She gave a satisfied little smile.

Addy and I stepped out into the bitter wind. Dark clouds swirled above us but there were so many lights working that the area looked quite bright. Addy was taken into one of the caravans and I watched while a lovely Tudor dress was put on her. It was cream-colored brocade with a burgundy surcoat, making her look like a miniature adult, which I suppose was the style in those days. She certainly wouldn't have been able to play much in it.

"Now, you will behave well and not let the family down, won't you?" I whispered. Addy was not always the best behaved of children. "Exactly like at my wedding." She had been a flower girl and the king and queen had been present. For once she'd been an angel.

Addy nodded, examining herself in the mirror with great satisfaction.

She was led out onto the step and instructed on where to stand and then she had to run to Lana Lovett, who was her mother. She did it perfectly the first time, then the second time. Before the third time she announced, "That's enough. I'm getting cold."

The director seemed to agree. "Okay, folks. Break for lunch. We'll shoot this scene when we come back. Get Rosie back on set."

I helped Addy out of the costume and into her own clothes

and we walked back toward the house. "I did it well, didn't I?" she asked.

"You certainly did. Podge will be very envious."

She skipped happily beside me.

As we returned to the house I heard someone shouting from outside the front gates. I stared down our long driveway and saw a mass of cameras with long-distance lenses on them. So the gentlemen of the press had discovered what was going on here. I wasn't surprised. Nothing remains secret for long in a small village. The maids at the country club would have told their relatives who was staying there, and they would have passed this along in the pub and pretty soon the newspapers would have learned about it. I saw that the gates were closed and there was a crew member standing guard to make sure the press didn't get any closer.

The film people were going to get food from their food tent. As they filed past I spotted faces I knew. My three farmhands. What's more they were dressed in Elizabethan garb.

"Jacob?" I called.

"Oh, good day, my lady," he said, turning back to me. "How do you like the outfit?"

"You're part of this film?"

He grinned. "The director wanted extras so Sir Hubert said they could use us. We've a scene this afternoon, so don't worry. The animals won't be neglected."

"I'm not at all worried," I said. "I hope you enjoy it."

"Where would I find Sir Hubert?" Cy Marvin came up to me. "I need to speak to him right now."

"Why, is something wrong?" I asked.

"The actors are saying they don't want to eat in a freezing cold tent and I gather you've set up a room in the house for the kid. So how about you find our people a place to eat? It's okay, you don't have to feed everyone, we've got the chuck wagon making our food, but is there a room we can borrow?"

Exactly what Fig had said about the thin end of the wedge.

I took Addy back to her nanny, then went to find Sir Hubert. "A room for them to eat in?" he said. "We can do that, can't we?"

"You don't want them to use our dining room, do you?" I asked. "All those strange people coming in and out of the house and walking past us?" My thoughts went instantly to Mrs. Simpson. She'd have a fit if she encountered any of them.

"Oh no, absolutely not," he agreed. "But they could be fed in the servants' hall. It's not as if we have a huge number of servants here. That table seats at least twenty. And they can come in through the servants' entrance."

I nodded in agreement. "Just as long as they don't expect Pierre to cook for them."

He went out to pass along this news to Cy, while I went down to break it to Mrs. Holbrook.

"Coming in the house now, my lady? Oh, I don't think I like that. But as you say, it's just for a few days. I'll go and warn the servants."

We sat down to our own lunch and I wondered if there might be chaos and rebellion going on downstairs.

"Have the film people come in to eat in the servants' hall?" I asked Phipps.

"They certainly have. A rude bunch if you ask me. One of

them told me to fetch her the salt. And I heard that one went into our kitchen and asked Chef what he was cooking as it smelled good. Then they asked if there was a spare bowl of soup." He paused, then grinned. "Pierre told them he cooked for the family only."

"Oh dear," I said. "I hope there won't be trouble."

"The girls don't mind at all," he said. "Waiting on film stars? You should see Queenie hovering over that Hathaway bloke."

I smiled. I could picture it. If anything made them decide that being in the house was not a good idea it would be Queenie pestering them.

I told Fig how successful Addy had been.

"We mustn't let it go to her head," Fig said. "She just happened to be the right size, that's all." At least Fig would never be a doting stage mother.

After lunch I did go up to see Mrs. Simpson. I was greeted with "Go away. I have a headache."

"It's Georgiana," I said. "May I come in for a minute?"

"I suppose so," came the weary reply.

She was lounging on her bed giving a good rendition of the Dame aux Camélias about to expire. She looked up. "Are those awful people still here?"

I told her they were, but she was welcome to come down and join us in the sitting room.

"I may join you for tea," she said. "And I really have to telephone the king. He must be so worried that he hasn't heard from me for a whole day. You haven't seen the newspapers, I suppose? No news yet about what Parliament is saying?"

"Not in the morning papers."

"How long is this damned thing going to take?" she snapped. "He's the king, for God's sake. If he wants to change the law, he should be able to. It's those petty little politicians who are against me because I'm American. Petty and prejudiced. But we'll show them!"

I warned her that we were entertaining the stars at dinner again that night so she might want to continue eating in her room. I then suggested that she come down to make her telephone call now. "They're all outside still filming," I said. "I'll stand guard at the front door while you make your telephone call."

"You're a sweet kid, Georgiana," she said. "When I marry David I'm going to see that you and Darcy are properly rewarded. I might suggest that I take you on as a lady-in-waiting and Darcy can be an equerry to the king."

"That's very kind of you," I said. "But I have a new baby. My first duty must be to him. I'm not going to be one of those mothers who leaves the child-rearing to a nanny, so I couldn't give you the attention you deserve. Neither could Darcy at the moment."

"I suppose not," she said, and I could see that it hadn't crossed her mind that children might get in the way of her plans. "Well, at least I can see that Darcy gets some sort of title."

"He'll be Lord Kilhenny when his father dies," I said. "But I hope that's not for a long time."

"Well, I'm sure David could make him a duke or an earl or something before then. It's not right that he comes across as less important than you."

"I don't think Darcy minds," I said. "He's not that sort of

person. Come on, then, if you want to make that phone call while you won't be disturbed."

I went ahead of her down the stairs. As I came into the long gallery I saw a strange man standing there. Mrs. S gave a gasp of horror and I heard her high heels retreating back upstairs.

Chapter 11

November 5
Eynsleigh

A night of great excitement.

I walked toward the man, who was examining the weapons hanging on the oak-paneled walls.

"Can I help you?" I asked.

He didn't look the least bit guilty as he turned to me. "This stuff is all real old, right? Not fake?"

"It's all really old," I agreed. "But what are you doing here? Did Sir Hubert send for you?"

I wondered for a moment if he was some kind of appraiser. He still went on examining the walls and actually touched a shield. "I think we could use this room for some interior scenes. It's got that great Tudor feel to it."

"Who are you, exactly?"

"Larry Roper. Assistant director. Is it the old titled guy who runs the show here?"

"If you mean is it Sir Hubert's house, it is," I replied.

"Are you his secretary, honey?"

"I am Lady Georgiana, his heir," I replied, my voice now giving a good imitation of my great-grandmother Queen Victoria, as it sometimes did when I was stressed. "I also live here."

"Great. Then can you go find him and tell him that we'd like to shoot some scenes in here? It's starting to rain."

"I will find Sir Hubert for you," I said, in my most frosty tones. "Please wait here."

I looked in his study but he wasn't there. Then I suspected he might have gone down to the farm. He was showing a keen interest in everything that went on there. I put on my coat and hat and hurried out. Sure enough he was standing admiring the piglets. "I'm wondering if they'll be warm enough, now that winter's coming," he said as he spotted me. "Should we arrange some sort of heater in their sty, do you think?"

"I think you better leave the pigs and come with me," I said. "There's a man from the film who wants to shoot a scene in our long gallery because it's raining outside. You don't want that, do you?" I really hoped Sir Hubert would say no, but he seemed quite amenable. "A scene this afternoon?" he said. "I don't see anything wrong with that. They can pay us extra, of course. Help to feed these pigs!" He chuckled.

We walked back together. "Are the boys still off being extras?" I asked.

He looked around. "I presume so. Nice little pocket money

for them. They're good boys. Hard workers. I don't mind letting them have fun. Oh, and I agreed to let them have the bonfire tonight."

"Tonight?"

"Guy Fawkes," he said. "Had you forgotten?"

"Oh, of course. One forgets which day it is out here," I replied, noticing now that a huge bonfire of sticks, leaves and old cardboard had been built in the meadow, with an effigy of a man, stuffed with straw, sitting on top. That was the guy, part of the rather gruesome tradition. "Are they going to let off fireworks? I bet Podge and Addy will love that."

We went into the house and I heard Sir Hubert saying, "But I don't want the family inconvenienced. We use the long gallery to access the morning room and the far staircase."

"Don't worry, we'll be in and out before you notice," the man said. "And we'll make it worth your while."

Again I remembered Fig's comment about the thin end of the wedge. Soon they'd be wanting us to make up bedrooms for them. Binky and Podge had returned from their school visit. I warned everyone that we'd have tea in the drawing room, since it would be well out of the way of the film crew. Queenie came in, pushing a well-laden tea trolley.

"Oh, Queenie," I said. "What are you doing serving the tea? Where's Sally? It's usually her job."

Queenie's face looked like thunder. "She's off being an actress in that film," she said. "Her and Maisie both of them. Going to be ladies-in-waiting." There was an ominous pause. "That man said he didn't want me. He said I was too big."

"Well, of course you are," I replied and watched her misery

deepen. "You see, in those days, in Tudor times, women were tiny. So a tall girl like you would be quite out of place. They couldn't have a servant being nearly as tall as Henry, could they?"

"Oh, I see what you mean," she said. "Yeah, I am quite tall, aren't I? And them two girls are little shrimps."

"Absolutely," I said. "There are some advantages to being tall like us, and some disadvantages. At least we can see over heads at a procession."

She laughed then. "That's right. You ain't half a card, missus."

"Those cakes look jolly nice, Queenie," Binky said. "You've outdone yourself today."

Anyone else would have blushed and muttered. Not Queenie. "Well, I had to make something special for the film stars, didn't I? I left a plate for them in the little sitting room and told them I'd bring them tea when they were ready."

So now it appeared it would not just be the child stars who would be warming up there. Addy and Podge were brought down by Nanny to join us for tea, as was the custom, and Podge tried to tell us about the school. He sounded excited. "And they have lots of fields for sports," he said. "And an indoor swimming bath and we start learning Latin and French and one of the boys said the food was decent."

I realized then that anything would be more exciting than being alone in a Scottish castle. I remembered feeling the same way as a child, wishing I too could go to school.

Any further conversation was hindered by loud shouts from the long gallery. "Action! Cut! No, not your right hand. Your left. Don't you know your right from your left, you moron?" I wasn't sure whom this was aimed at but I would not have liked it. I hoped it wasn't our maids. I also hoped he wasn't going to yell at Addy if they used her again. Although I suspected she was a tough little soul and probably wouldn't care.

By the time tea was over the film people had finished shooting, but I could hear voices coming from the sitting room we had offered them and as I passed, Lana Lovett came out and hailed me.

"Oh, hi," she said. "You don't mind if we stick around here and don't dress up for dinner, do you? None of us wants to go back to that country club place in the rain. And if you've a room handy where we can change and freshen up?"

What could I say? I was just about to answer when Sir Hubert appeared behind me. And Gloria Bishop came out of the sitting room at the same time.

"Hi there," Lana said, her voice becoming sultry as she turned on the charm. "I was just asking this young lady if there might be a room where we could freshen up for dinner here."

"Hi, Hubie," Gloria said, giving him a big smile. "You wouldn't want us to have to drive back to the hotel in the rain, would you? Since we're about to have dinner here."

"Of course not," he said. "Georgiana can arrange for a room for you."

"We really don't want to inconvenience you," Gloria said, sidling up to Sir Hubert now, "but it's so cold and wet and miserable out there. We're all frozen to the marrow."

"It's not trouble at all," he said. "We do have nineteen bedrooms, if I remember correctly. Not counting the servants' bedrooms, of course."

Oh golly. Now they know we have enough rooms for them to stay the night! I went off to find Mrs. Holbrook, who was not at all pleased. "What next, your ladyship?" she said. "They'll be wanting to stay here."

"I know, Mrs. H, I feel the same way but Sir Hubert is easy prey for those female stars. Just make sure the bedroom is not heated," I said, giving her a knowing grin.

"One of the north-facing ones," she said. "Down at the end of the hall. It's got a nasty draft down the chimney." She returned my grin and departed.

"I'm so sorry but we weren't given any notice that this room was needed," I heard her saying as they went up the stairs. "You may find it a little chilly but there would be little point in lighting a fire now as it wouldn't warm up the room in time."

They came down from getting dressed rather rapidly, I felt. In fact Lana commented, "Do you people actually sleep in rooms like that? No wonder the British are so repressed in their sex lives."

They had suggested eating early since they had to be up for filming at crack of dawn. So we found ourselves entertaining them again. We served them sherry and Scotch in the drawing room.

"You people don't drink any cocktails?" Lana asked. "You couldn't make a sidecar?"

"I'm afraid I have no idea what a sidecar is apart from something attached to a motorbike," Sir Hubert said.

Lana gave a dramatic sigh. "Then I guess it will have to be sherry, I suppose."

Suddenly there was a loud explosion. Our guests leaped up.

"Somebody's shooting!" Cy shouted.

"Gangsters," Lana shrieked. "They knew we'd be here. Oh my God. What do we do?"

"Where do you folk keep your guns?" Larry Roper looked as if he was ready to hide behind the sofa. I looked out of the window to see a red glow in the darkness. And I remembered.

"It's only Guy Fawkes night," I said. "Bonfire and fireworks. Binky, go up and get the children. They'll want to watch."

"What the hell is Guy Fawkes night?" Cy asked.

"It's to celebrate the execution of the man who tried to burn down the houses of Parliament," Sir Hubert said. "We make a stuffed effigy of him and burn it on a bonfire."

"How primitive," Lana said.

"Oh no. It's fun," Gloria said. "I remember it from my childhood. Let's all go out to watch."

They hastily put on coats and we all traipsed out to where the giant bonfire was burning merrily. On top of it the straw-stuffed figure had already burst into flame. The three farmhands were in the process of letting off fireworks. A rocket shot up, leaving a trail of sparks. Over on our left there was a loud bang from a squib. And then a Catherine wheel spun a trail of fire from a post. Nanny had both children by the hand, but Jacob came forward with sparklers for each of them and they grabbed them with delight. I showed them how to make circles and patterns of light in the darkness.

"It's a pity the kids aren't here," Cy said. "They would have liked it. But I guess they'll see fireworks where they're staying."

Then Jacob came around with sparklers for the adults. "Oh,

no thank you. Keep away from me. You're going to singe my mink," Lana snapped.

"Don't be such a killjoy." Grant Hathaway reached out to take a sparkler, waving it with reckless abandon. He took a second one and held it out to Gloria Bishop. "Here. Want one?"

"Sure." She went to take it, then hesitated, looked up, frowned and shook her head. "Uh. Not now." And she backed away.

From all around us came answering explosions and flashes of color as all the families in the village celebrated. We heard distant shrieks and applause.

"We should have arranged to have bangers out here," Darcy said.

"Aren't there enough bangs already?" Larry Roper asked. "My head is quite throbbing. I'll get one of my migraines." Again he looked nervous.

I laughed. "'Bangers' means sausages. We should have had some sausages to cook on sticks around the fire. And baked potatoes too."

"It's a tad chilly to stay outside to eat food," Lana said. "Remember we are not as hardy as you guys seem to be. We're used to air-conditioning and California weather." Of all of us, she was the one wrapped in a long mink coat. "I say we go inside for supper." And she headed back toward the house.

It seemed we had exhausted our supply of fireworks so one by one we made our way back. Podge and Addy lingered on with Nanny and Binky, still wanting to watch the bonfire and the remains of the burning figure until it toppled and collapsed. As I moved forward to catch up with Darcy I saw Gloria and Grant

Hathaway walking together. Her voice floated back to me. "I'm telling you now, stay away from that sweet child."

"Sweet child? You mean little Dorothy? I'm just being a friendly uncle. You know me. I'm the friendly type."

"I do know you. Too well, unfortunately. And I wouldn't trust you further than I could throw you. So keep your hands off her or I may have to spill the beans about you-know-what."

"You're threatening me?" He laughed. "Sweet little Gloria is threatening me?"

"Maybe I've been too sweet for too long," she said. "I've just realized a few things. Things I've done that I'm ashamed of. I need to make them right."

HAVING HAD TIME to prepare, Pierre had cooked a wonderful meal. It started with mock turtle soup, then roast leg of lamb with crispy roast potatoes, tiny brussels sprouts and mint sauce, followed by a sweet soufflé and cherry compote. The guests were extremely impressed. There was loud chatter around the table. Even Fig sounded animated and normal for once. She had obviously succumbed to Grant Hathaway's devastating charm, having not had much opportunity to have been seduced in her life. I heard a girlish giggle coming from her, and "Really, Mr. Hathaway, you are naughty!"

I met Darcy's amused glance. He winked at me.

The only one who was not having a good time was Gloria. She sat, quiet and withdrawn, picking at her food. I suspected that whatever confrontation she had had with Grant Hathaway had somehow upset her.

Everyone praised the chef at the end of the meal.

"I guess the food makes up for the cold rooms," Lana said.

We escorted them to the front door.

"Let's hope that those vultures from the press have called it a day and are not waiting around for us," Gloria said.

"Darling, I thought you were the one who usually lapped up chances for publicity," Lana purred.

Gloria shot her a swift venomous glance. "There are limits," she said. "But apparently you don't have any."

"Meow." Grant chuckled. "I say the more press here the better. We need more exposure in other countries, you know. Over here we're competing with British films."

"As if they could compete," Cy said with a derisive sniff. "They're small potatoes. They can't compete with Hollywood. And when we get color going properly . . . well."

We stood at the front door until the lights of their motorcars vanished along the drive. I suspected they would not encounter any news photographers. Nobody could be desperate enough to linger at the gate in this weather for a chance to spot a film star.

"Well, that's that, thank God," Darcy whispered to me, and we went to bed in our perfectly warm bedrooms. I gave James his ten o'clock feed, then snuggled down next to Darcy.

"That went off rather well, didn't it?" he said. "Who'd have thought famous film stars would be impressed with humble old us?"

"When have you ever been humble?" I asked, nudging him.

"Or you, for that matter? I've heard the Queen Victoria tones coming from you in the past couple of days." He started to tickle me.

"We are not amused," I said.

We were woken at first light by the sounds of the film crew arriving. Shouts, crashes, sounds of engines revving. I was going to stay in my warm bed until Maisie brought up the tea but the sounds woke James, who demanded to be fed instantly. Outside the window it didn't look like the kind of day I'd have enjoyed filming. A bleak mist hung over the estate, making the trees in the distant woodland look like strange bony figures. I took James back to bed with me and was still nursing him when Maisie brought in the tea.

"It's a miserable old day, my lady," she said. "I don't envy those ladies in their silk dresses out there."

I was just enjoying my tea and about to get dressed when there was a knock on our bedroom door. Mrs. Holbrook came in, her face white and worried.

"I'm so sorry to disturb you, my lady, but the American lady has gone."

Chapter 12

Friday, November 6
Eynsleigh

I'm not sure what we're going to do next. It's all very worrying. I hope nobody blames us.

"Gone?" I reached for my slippers. "Do you mean she's left without telling us?"

"I'm not sure, my lady," Mrs. Holbrook said. "I'm not sure where she is."

Darcy scrambled to put on his dressing gown. I hastily tied my robe, asked Maisie to keep an eye on James, and we followed Mrs. Holbrook along the hallway.

"I sent Sally up with a cup of tea for her," she called back breathlessly as we continued at a great pace, "and she came back and said the lady wasn't there. I said I expected she was in the bathroom but Sally said no, the bathroom door was open. So I went up and looked and there's no sign of her."

"Out for a walk maybe?" Darcy said.

"Early morning walks in the cold fog? That doesn't sound like her," I replied.

"Perhaps she's had enough of being cooped up here and not adored and she's gone back to the king," Darcy said.

I shot him a warning look. He'd forgotten that the public did not know about Mrs. Simpson yet. Luckily Mrs. Holbrook was already barging ahead and didn't hear this.

We pushed open her bedroom door. Mrs. Simpson was clearly not the tidiest of women. Perhaps she usually relied on a maid to keep things in their place and Maisie had not had time to visit her this morning. There were clothes draped over the end of the bed and a chair. A pair of silk stockings lay on the floor. Her silver-backed hairbrush lay on her dressing table, as well as her makeup equipment. An open box of powder and a puff had spilled a thin coating of powder onto the glass top of the dressing table. It did seem logical that she might be in the bathroom. Perhaps she found the nearest bathroom too cold for her or someone else was using it. We looked in the other bathrooms. No sign of her.

"She hasn't simply gone down to breakfast, has she?" I asked.

"No, my lady. I checked the breakfast room before I came to you. And she's had her breakfast sent up to her room every day so far. Nobody's seen her this morning."

A cold dread crept over me. I remembered our guests mistaking the fireworks for gunshots last night and talking about gangsters. What if the unthinkable had happened and Mrs.

Simpson had been kidnapped, or even killed? My imagination raced away with me. Someone connected to the government who had decided that Mrs. S was a threat to the Crown and needed to be disposed of? But how could that happen in a houseful of servants and guests? Then I remembered that we had all been outside at the bonfire last night. The house would have been empty, the doors unlocked, nobody to see someone spirited away.

"Mrs. Holbrook, would you ask the rest of the staff if they saw the lady last night, or heard a vehicle of any sort?"

"Very good, my lady," she said. "But the lady wouldn't have left without her things, would she? Her room looks as if she was in the middle of getting ready for bed."

"It certainly does," I agreed.

As she hurried off, down the back stairs, I turned to Darcy. "What do you think?" I asked.

He ran his fingers through that unruly mop of dark curls, something he always did when facing a perplexing puzzle. "Beats me," he said. "It could be a perfectly simple explanation. Perhaps she's visited Sir Hubert in his wing, asking for his help with transportation maybe?"

"Oh, of course. That would make sense," I said.

We went along the corridor in the other direction to the east wing just as Sir Hubert was emerging from his study.

"You're up bright and early," he said. Then he noticed our faces. "What's wrong?"

"We can't find Mrs. Simpson," I said. "She wasn't in her room when the maid took up her morning tea. We've been up there now and she's not in a bathroom either."

"Well then, out for a walk, I expect. She likes to keep fit."

"Would you want to walk in this weather?" I asked. "Besides, she's afraid of bumping into one of the film crew and being recognized."

"That's true," he agreed. "So might she have decided to leave without telling us? She's obviously not having a good time, hiding away in her room while the film people are around. Perhaps she called a taxi in the middle of the night and off she went."

I remembered her horror when she almost encountered the assistant director in the long gallery. "I'd think that was a good explanation except that all her things are still in her bedroom, clothes strewn everywhere, makeup on the dressing table."

My godfather put a hand on my shoulder. "Let's not get too excited about this. I'm sure there's a perfectly reasonable explanation. We'll have the servants search the house."

Mrs. Holbrook called for the servants and they were given instructions to search the whole house. I saw puzzled looks on their faces.

"The lady hasn't left her room since those film people came," Maisie said. "Each time I've been up to see if she needs help with anything she's been most shirty with me."

"Why does anyone think she'd be somewhere in the house where the fires haven't been lit?" Sally asked. "You know how she hates the cold."

All this was true. "Nevertheless we need to find where she might have got to," I said. "It's disconcerting when a guest simply vanishes."

Clearly this made an impression on them. They nodded solemnly before they divided up the sections of the house between them and off they went. I felt compelled to search with them.

No sign of her in any of the downstairs rooms. Sally was lighting the fire in the small sitting room and Rosie Trapp's mother came in just as I was questioning Sally.

"My God it's horrible out there today," she said. "My poor kid. She's got some big scenes. Be an angel and get your niece down here to stand in again so Rosie won't have to be in that damned cold all the time. I can't risk her catching a chill. She was outside last night to watch those stupid fireworks. I didn't want her to go out there but she begged and begged. She doesn't have much of a normal life so I thought why not? And then when we were out watching fireworks with all those bangs and explosions I started to think it would be a perfect time to kidnap her, so I dragged her back inside. Oh, did she give me an earful! She likes to get her own way, that kid."

She turned to Sally, who had now stood up from the crackling logs. "Honey, go get me a coffee."

Sally glanced at me. I nodded.

"Just make sure you bring it and not that creepy girl."

"Creepy?" I asked.

"The big one with the goofy smile. She was all over Rosie yesterday, following her around, breathing all over her, telling her how wonderful she was, asking for her autograph. She scared the kid."

"Oh, that would be Queenie," I said. "She's quite harmless. But Sally will get you the coffee."

"Black. No sugar. Got it?" She barked out the order.

Sally and I exchanged a glance before she hurried off.

"I'll go and find Addy and see if she wants to join you today," I said.

I could hear the servants still opening and closing doors as I went up to the nursery floor to find Addy. Addy was eating a bowl of porridge for breakfast. She sprang up when she saw me. "Are we going to play at princesses again?"

"If you want to."

Nanny was much against the idea. "Have the wee bairn standing outside in this raw weather in those flimsy clothes? That can't be right," she said.

"It will only be for a short while, Nanny. I'll make sure she doesn't get too cold," I said.

"I want to do it, Nanny." Addy tugged at her apron. "It's fun. I'm a princess."

Nanny rolled her eyes. "Well, who am I to say? If her mother is fine with it then I'll have to agree, but I hope you have some good broth made up and a mustard plaster for when she gets a chill."

With that admonishment I left Nanny with instructions to bring Addy down when she was ready. As I came out into the corridor I heard the sound of doors opening and closing as the servants searched the upstairs rooms.

"Any luck?" I heard my godfather's voice.

"No sign of her, sir," came a female response. "We've looked in every room."

I felt I had to be part of this. I hurried in the direction of the voices and I met Sir Hubert heading back to Mrs. Simpson's bedroom.

"She can't have left," he said, shaking his head. "All her things are here." He looked up at me. "She wouldn't be hiding to play a trick on us, would she?"

"I don't think she's the type of woman who would think a trick was funny," I said. "She doesn't strike me as having a great sense of humor."

"It doesn't make sense." He picked up the robe from her bed and let it fall again. "Is her coat in the wardrobe?"

I opened it. "I don't see her mink," I said.

"Ah. Then she did go out. We must have the gardeners search the grounds."

"But why would she want to go out into the grounds?" I asked. Then I stared at her dressing table and froze. "Her jewelry case is gone," I said.

"Are you sure?"

"Yes. It was there when I came to talk to her yesterday. I noticed it was open and I could see the sparkle of diamonds inside."

"Dear me." He scratched his head. "This might be a matter for the police. A robbery? Surely she couldn't have been foolhardy enough to chase after a thief. . . ."

My heart was racing. I couldn't come up with a rational explanation. Mrs. Simpson's jewels meant a lot to her. Might she have chased after a robber? And?

"We should call His Majesty immediately," I said. "He might know where she is. And he'll be able to call more resources than a country police station."

"Good idea." He nodded. "Will you do it? You actually know him. I don't."

At that moment Darcy came into the room. "Well, we've searched the whole place," he said. "Do we know if her outdoor clothes are missing?"

"Her mink is gone, but so is her jewel case," I said. "I think we should telephone the king."

"Of course," Darcy said. "It's up to him what he does. It's not as if she was a prisoner here. She can come and go as she pleases."

"But not leaving all her things behind," I said. "And not telling anyone."

Darcy took a deep breath. "I'll go and ring him," he said. He glanced at the clock. "Perhaps wait a little while. He's not known to be an early riser, is he? Let's have some breakfast first. Who knows. She may come strolling in from her morning walk."

I didn't think this was very likely but agreed that breakfast would be a good idea. As we headed for the dining room I had a brief flicker of memory: last Christmas at the estate in Sandringham Mrs. Simpson had gone missing and it had turned out that she had been knocked out by a falling ladder from the ceiling. Could anything like that have happened to her again? But then the whole house was being searched and why on earth would she have gone to an unheated part of it? The fact that her jewel case no longer stood on her dressing table was what worried me. If she had left she would have taken it with her. But when she arrived she had made such a big fuss about not having all her things brought up to her room immediately and now she had apparently left everything behind, including her makeup. Her appearance mattered a lot to her. She couldn't have just gone and abandoned all her belongings. Something must have happened to her. Oh golly.

Chapter 13

Friday, November 6
Eynsleigh

It appears we have lost Mrs. Simpson. I should be glad, I suppose. I really didn't want her here in the first place, but I do feel responsible for her and I certainly wouldn't want anything to have happened to her. Where can the wretched woman be?

I hurried upstairs and dressed hastily in warm clothes in case I was obliged to do more searching outside. We had just settled down to kedgeree and coffee when Nanny tapped at the door. "Sorry to interrupt, my lady, but the wee girl is ready now. I've put on her wool vest to keep out the cold."

I got up and took Addy's hand. "Let's go and find Rosie and her mummy, shall we?"

She skipped excitedly beside me, tugging impatiently for me to go faster. Outside there was the usual chaos of a film set. Men wheeling great cameras around, laying yards of cable. Gloria Bishop stood wrapped in a mink cape over her costume. Rosie's mother emerged from the wardrobe trailer.

"Oh good. You came. Rosie will be grateful she doesn't have to spend the whole morning freezing in that costume. Let's get you dressed. Come on." She grabbed Addy's hand and yanked her into the trailer.

I decided I had a few minutes' grace to finish my breakfast. Fig had arrived and was working her way through kidneys and bacon.

"Your daughter has gone out to be a film star again," I said. "I suppose that's all right with you. It is awfully cold out there."

"I only hope it doesn't go to her head," Fig replied. "You know she can be a bit of a show-off. But the money will come in handy. Binky has already gone with Podge to look at another school. You should see what they charge for fees these days! It would be cheaper to stay at a hotel like the Dorchester. And this school they are visiting sounds most unsuitable. They specialize in art and drama and all that kind of bosh. Oh, and languages. I said that Podge only needed to learn English since we rule half the world. And I told Binky it will not prepare Podge for his future in the army."

I looked up. "Why do you think he wants to go into the army?"

"Not wants to, but has to, Georgiana. All the men in my family go into the army. My father, my uncle, my brother."

"I didn't know you had a brother."

"I did. Killed on the northwest frontier in India."

"And I'd never heard you talk of your father."

"Killed in the Boer War. All the men in my family died fighting."

"And yet you want Podge to do that?"

"Of course. It's an honorable way to go."

"Perhaps he'd rather not go at all," I said. "I certainly wouldn't want James to have to go and fight somewhere."

"Darcy might have other ideas. It's what men do." She gave me a little smirk, then stopped, listening. "What is all the commotion about?" she asked. "I keep hearing running feet and slamming doors."

I told her Mrs. Simpson had gone missing. "Of course she hasn't," Fig said. "She's bolted because she doesn't like it here. We're not paying her enough attention."

"I hope you're right," I said. "But she's left all her things as if she'd be back any moment. I'm just worried that something might have happened to her."

"Such as what?"

"I've no idea. Kidnapped?"

"Who would possibly want to kidnap her?" Fig said, reaching for another piece of toast. "Obnoxious woman. We're well rid of her."

"I agree except I feel responsible. The king did ask us to look after her."

"Georgiana, it really isn't your fault if the woman has no manners."

At that moment Darcy came into the room. "Time to face the music and call the king," he said. "I hope we don't get sent to the Tower for losing his ladylove." He grinned, then became serious again. "Not funny, is it? I wonder what can have happened to the damned woman."

I heard him go out into the foyer and his clipped "get me Buckingham Palace."

Curiosity got the better of me. I put down my fork and went to the door of the dining room. I saw Darcy waiting impatiently as he was passed from one layer of palace official to the next.

"Yes, it's important," he said, growing increasingly annoyed. "Yes, Mr. O'Mara. The king's secretary will know what it's about. Lady Georgiana's husband. That's right."

Finally I heard him say, "What do you mean, he's not there? He's not attending an official function at this hour, is he? What? Then put me through to where he is right now." A long pause. "You must know where he is. He must have told you where he was going. Look, this is very important. He'll want to hear what I have to say."

Another long pause. Then he said, "Really? This is most inconvenient, and worrying for you, I'm sure. When you do trace him could you please give him a message? Could you tell him that our houseguest seems to have left without telling anyone? Yes. He'll know what that means."

The receiver was replaced. Darcy came over to me, frowning. "Bloody woman," he said. "Your bloody cousin."

"What's happened?"

"Apparently his secretary has no idea where he is. He left the palace without telling anybody last night."

"Aren't they worried?"

"I don't think this is entirely unusual for the king. He doesn't seem to take his responsibilities too seriously and doesn't like being tied down by protocol. His secretary thought he might have gone out to the fort to get away."

"The fort?"

"You know. Fort Belvedere. His bolt-hole in Windsor park."

"Oh, of course. I see." I considered this latest news. "Do you think it's possible that they've gone off together somewhere? The king and Mrs. Simpson?"

"Very possible," he said. "But you know what? We're not going to waste any more time looking for her. She's a grown woman. What she does is up to her. If she has the bad manners to leave our house without saying good-bye and thank you, then there's nothing we can do."

"But what about her things? They're all still in her room."

"She'll probably send for them with an imperious note at some stage. Until then we go about our normal lives." He gave an exasperated sigh. "I hope your cousin knows what he's getting into if he marries her."

We notified Sir Hubert and the staff. Mrs. Holbrook shook her head. "That was most unthinking of her, my lady. I don't care if she is a friend of yours. That's not how a true lady behaves. She had all my staff worried and rushing all over the place looking for her. I think the boys at the farm are still out scouring the woodland. Someone had better tell them to stop searching."

"I'm really sorry, Mrs. Holbrook," I said. "It wasn't our idea to have her here, I can assure you. And we can be thankful that she's gone."

"Now, if we can just get rid of those awful film people we can go back to normal," she said.

"Let's hope that's soon." I gave her an understanding nod. "Oh, and please tell Queenie to stop bothering the film people. I gather she's been a bit of a pest."

"I can imagine," Mrs. Holbrook said. "She's starstruck, that's what she is. Babbling on about them all the time. The only good thing is that she's forgotten to flirt with Pierre, for which he's truly grateful."

We were both chuckling as I left her. I went back to the dining room for a more peaceful cup of coffee. Darcy came in to say he was heading up to London. "If I can run the gauntlet of all those newsmen," he said. He glanced out of the window. "Thank God they never discovered Mrs. S was staying here. We'd never have got rid of them."

"They'll obviously think you're a film star too with your good looks." I stroked back a wayward curl that had fallen across his forehead.

"Naturally." He gave a cheeky grin. "Perhaps they'll discover me and whisk me off to Hollywood and I'll make us a million dollars."

"I'm not having you doing love scenes with any of those female stars," I said. "That Lana Lovett has already been making eyes at you. I saw her at dinner last night."

"And what about Grant Hathaway?" He raised an eyebrow. "I saw him getting rather friendly with you."

"I know," I said. "I think he gets too friendly with any female within reach. Don't worry. I resisted temptation. Actually I found him quite repulsive."

"Glad to hear it," he said. "Otherwise I'd not want to go up to London and leave you alone with him."

"I'm glad to know you're jealous." I shot him a grin as I got up. "I'll see you off. I should go out and make sure that Addy is being looked after properly. She should have her costume on by now."

I waited while Darcy put on his greatcoat and scarf, and put on my own coat before I went out. The air that greeted us was raw. Fog swirled across the grounds so that the caravans looked like crouching animals. The arc lights only enhanced the fog, creating an eerie glow, but filming was still going on in spite of the weather. I heard Cy Marvin's shouted directions and saw Lana coming toward us, holding Addy's hand. When she got close to where the director was sitting she bent and kissed Addy, taking her face into her hands. I couldn't hear the words but it was clearly a tender scene of good-bye—or would have been. Addy shook her head and pulled away.

"Cut!" the director shouted. "You're not supposed to move."

"I don't want that lady to kiss me," Addy said emphatically. "I don't like being kissed."

"It's only playacting, honey," Lana said. "You're the little princess, remember?"

"I don't want to be a princess anymore," Addy said. She pulled away from Lana. "I want to go back to Nanny."

"Okay," Cy said. "Take her away and get Rosie out here. I want this scene shot before the fog lifts."

I took Addy's hand and we headed for the house. "I didn't like being a princess," Addy said. "That lady smelled of perfume. And her long fingernails dug into my cheeks. I didn't like it."

"I understand," I said, trying not to smile.

"We know real princesses, don't we?" Addy said, brightening up as we came up the steps. "They don't dress like this. They wear normal clothes. I play with Margaret when she comes up to their house near us."

"That's right. The princesses do come up to Scotland in the summer."

"Margaret's fun," Addy said. "I like her. She's a bit naughty. We played a trick on their governess. But Elizabeth told us not to do it. She said we'd get in trouble. She's a goody-goody."

"She's probably going to be a queen one day," I said. "She has to be well behaved."

"I don't have to be well behaved, do I?" Addy said. "Podge is going to be a duke, isn't he? And he'll have to be well behaved. But I'm not going to be anything."

"You still have to behave well so that you don't let the family down," I said, trying not to smile. "Remember our cousin is the new king."

I could see her pondering this. We entered the house. "We'll get Nanny to take the costume off and Mrs. Trapp can return it to them when she takes Rosie out."

I waited while Nanny undressed Addy, tut-tutting all the time. "And feel how cold she is. I'll have to make her a nice hot cup of Ovaltine. Such nonsense."

"I didn't like being a princess," Addy said. "A lady tried to kiss me."

"I certainly wouldn't like it either," Nanny agreed. "Most unnatural to go around pretending to be something you're not."

She handed me the costume. I went downstairs with it and opened the door of the small sitting room. A pall of cigarette smoke hung in the air. Mrs. Trapp sat there alone, puffing on a cigarette, a cup of coffee in one hand.

"They are ready for Rosie now," I said.

She stubbed out the cigarette on our fine bone china. "What do you mean? She's already out there."

I glanced out of the window. "I don't think so. She wasn't a moment ago."

"But she was. I looked out and watched her. She was doing a scene with Lana."

"That was our Addy," I said. "Rosie wasn't there."

Mrs. Trapp jumped up. "What do you mean? She hasn't been in here for hours. Then where the hell is she?"

Chapter 14

November 6
Eynsleigh

Now we really are in a pickle. It seems we've lost two people in two days. I have to think there's a logical explanation but if there is not . . . golly.

Mrs. Trapp rushed to the front door, flung it open and dashed toward the area where they were now filming.

"Where is she?" she screamed. "Where's Rosie? Where's my daughter?"

"Cut," Cy Marvin shouted. He glared at Mrs. Trapp. "Your daughter isn't out here. We've been waiting for her. We had to go ahead with the next scene because she didn't show up on time. She must be somewhere playing truant."

"Rosie?" Mrs. Trapp screamed. "Rosie, where are you?"

There was no answer.

"My daughter's missing!" Mrs. Trapp was hysterical now. "Don't just stand there. Start searching for her. Somebody call the police."

"I think you're overreacting." Nora Pines came over and put an arm around her shoulder. "She's a little girl. She wandered off. Why don't you go back indoors? We'll find her."

"I'm not going inside. I want to find my daughter." Mrs. Trapp took great gulps of air between words. "Something bad has happened to her. I knew it would. I had a premonition."

"We were all here," Nora said. "We would have noticed an outsider."

"Not in this fog. She'd only have to have wandered a few yards and someone could have grabbed her."

"Why would anyone do that?" Nora still attempted to sound calm and reasonable.

"Why, for money, of course. Look what happened to the Lindbergh baby. Rosie is a valuable commodity. We have to get her back before it's too late."

"We'll search all the trailers," Nora said. "She might be playing a trick on us and hiding. Little kids do things like that, you know."

I didn't like to interfere but watched as crew members went first into one trailer, then another. I began to feel a bit sick and scared. Two people disappearing in one day? That couldn't be a coincidence, could it? We were assuming that Mrs. Simpson had bolted during the night with the king, but what if she hadn't? I tried to calm my racing thoughts and be sensible. There must be a perfectly reasonable explanation for all of this.

Suddenly a thought came to me. I went over to Mrs. Trapp and Nora. "If you remember the other day when we told Rosie about the witch's cottage and the baby animals, she wanted to see them. And you told her she had no time. Maybe she decided today would be a good time to slip away."

Mrs. Trapp turned watery eyes on me, dabbing with her handkerchief as she spoke. "You may be right," she said. "Yes. She did want to see those animals and the witch's cottage. She talked about them that evening."

"Do you want me to send some of the servants to look for her?"

"No!" She shouted out the word. "I want to go myself. I have to find my daughter. Show me where this damned place is."

"It's quite a walk," I said.

"I don't care. Take me there now."

We set off, Mrs. Trapp, Nora and a couple of crew members following us. We came around the side of the house to the formal gardens at the back, the lawn surrounded by herbaceous borders, a rose arbor and then beyond an expanse of meadow. Mrs. Trapp hurried forward, stumbling through the wet grass. I noticed she was not wearing the type of shoes for long wet grass and her heels wobbled as she walked. Soon after we left the vicinity of the house we were swallowed up in the mist. It swirled about us, deadening sound and making it hard to pinpoint direction. I was glad when we picked up the path leading to the kitchen garden.

"Rosie!" she shouted. "Rosie, where are you? Come to Mama right now."

The words sounded muffled, swallowed into the fog. At last

the shape of the cottage could be made out. In this weather it looked even more like something from a fairy tale with its pointed roof, gables and twisted chimney pot. We passed the chicken run. The birds had decided it was too cold to be outside and were all inside their house. We heard the sounds of gentle clucking.

"Might she have gone in there?" one of the crew members asked.

"Oh no. She's afraid of birds," Mrs. Trapp said.

"Besides, she couldn't reach the bolt on the gate," I pointed out.

The pigsty was on our right. As we approached we saw someone moving around in there.

"There you are. Just as we thought," I said.

"Come out at once, you naughty girl," Mrs. Trapp said, rushing forward now.

Instead Bill, one of our farm boys, stood up, holding one of the piglets. "What's wrong, missus?" he asked.

"She's looking for her daughter. Little girl of five. You haven't seen her this morning, have you?" I said.

"I haven't seen anybody," Bill said. "Of course in this murky weather she could have walked right past and I'd never have seen."

"Have you been out here long?" I asked.

"Not right here, my lady. I was helping Jacob load up the cabbages onto the cart until he told me and Donnie that more firewood was needed for the house. So we stopped what we were doing and went up to the woods. But after a while I left Donnie to it because I remembered that one of the piglets had been poorly and needed her medicine. So I came back to check on her."

"So Jacob's gone off to deliver vegetables and Donnie is still up in the woods?"

"That's right, my lady."

"What about the little house?" Mrs. Trapp said, eyeing it through the swirling mist. "She was keen on seeing that, wasn't she? She might have gone in there."

"Oh no, missus. I'm sure she didn't. The lock on the door is quite high up. I don't think she could have opened it by herself." He put down the piglet and came over to intercept us.

Mrs. Trapp ignored him. She walked up the path to the front door of the little house and opened it. I could see why Bill wasn't keen for us to go in there. The house was clearly occupied by three unmarried young men. There was only one main room downstairs with a cast-iron stove on the back wall, a Welsh dresser holding crockery on one side and a scrubbed pinewood table in the middle. It was not exactly tidy, with the remains of a meal, unwashed cups, cigarette stubs and a beer bottle all sitting on the table. It smelled of unwashed clothing and last night's fried food.

"Rosie? Are you there?" Mrs. Trapp called.

No answer. She crossed the room and peered up the stairs.

"She'd have no reason to stay here, once she'd seen inside," Nora said, leading her away again. "It's not exactly appealing, is it?"

Mrs. Trapp turned away. "That's right. She wouldn't like an untidy place like this. She'd tell me it smelled bad. She has a very acute sense of smell."

We closed the front door and waited uncertainly. Mrs. Trapp was still looking about her with a terrified, bewildered expression on her face.

"Where are these damned woods he was talking about?" Mrs. Trapp said. "Could she have gone there and gotten herself lost?"

"She'd be a brave little girl to wander into the woods alone," I said. "They are rather frightening at this time of year, especially in the fog."

"Rosie's such a daring child. She's not afraid of anything," Mrs. Trapp said. "She might well have gone over there."

I stared at the murky outlines of bare trees. "We do have a herd of deer in the woods. Perhaps she saw a fawn or a rabbit. Bill," I called him over. "Go and find Donnie, and the two of you search the woods for the little girl. Her name's Rosie. Keep shouting."

"I will, my lady." He nodded. "But Donnie's been working there all morning. Surely he'd have heard someone blundering around with all those dead leaves underfoot."

"We must call the police." Mrs. Trapp's hysterics had returned. "Before it's too late. She's been kidnapped, just as I feared."

"Oh, I don't think so," I said. "Not out here in the country, in the middle of England."

"Maybe American gangsters followed us over here. And you must have criminals too. They learned about Rosie and she's easy pickings out in this godforsaken place."

"Calm down, Mrs. Trapp," Nora said. "I'm sure it's going to be all right."

But Mrs. Trapp shook her head. "No. We have to act quickly. The kidnappers can't have gotten too far yet. And the press. They'll help us, won't they? They'll get the news out in the evening edition. Then the whole country can be on the lookout for her."

I was tempted to tell her this was maybe premature, but she broke into a run, heading back in the direction we had come.

Chapter 15

November 6
Eynsleigh

Oh dear. More drama. Actually quite worrying this time. I don't know what to think.

As we tried to keep up with her Nora fell into step with me. "I'm sure there's a perfectly reasonable explanation for this," she said. "The child might have slipped unnoticed into your house. Perhaps she wanted to find your little girl and have someone to play with. She may have gotten herself lost with all those rooms."

"Possibly," I said, "except we were just searching the house for a missing guest."

Her expression changed. "You have a missing guest? Another person has gone missing?"

"We couldn't locate her, but now we have to assume she left

without telling us," I said. "I'll have the servants do another thorough search, just in case Rosie got herself shut in a cupboard or something."

"These film people tend to overreact," Nora muttered, staring at the scene ahead of us, where we could see Mrs. Trapp waving her arms and others milling around her. "They live in this unreal world where they are used to being the center of attention and everyone adores them. And most of their day is spent playing someone else's quite unreal life. No wonder they lose their grip on reality."

I stared at her. She was not much older than me. Maybe in her thirties and the sort of plain woman who is overlooked. "I wonder why you chose to go into this profession if you are so cynical about it," I said.

"Because I'm interested in the process of filmmaking," she replied. "My father was one of the first filmmakers. He came out to Hollywood when there were just orange groves, and he was responsible for a lot of innovations we take for granted now. I wanted to follow in his footsteps, learn the ropes and become a director one day. But it seems women are destined to the role of secretary no matter how good they are. Still, I'm learning by observing."

"Could your father not help you get a better position?"

She shook her head. "My father died some years ago. He was filming action scenes in the desert for a cowboy movie when he was killed. He was the sort of man who always liked to take risks. My mother is something of an invalid, so the role of breadwinner pretty much falls to me. I'm all she has."

"I'm sorry," I said. "My father is dead too. But I do have a lovely family around me."

We reached the chaos of the movie set.

"I already searched the wardrobe trailer," someone was shouting. "I told you, she's not there."

"Somebody let the newsmen in, so I can tell them," Mrs. Trapp said. "I want the whole country searching for my little girl."

"I don't want newsmen walking all over my set," Cy said. "Just calm down and we'll decide what to do."

"I really think we'll find her." Grant put a hand on her shoulder. "After all, we're on an estate. The gates are shut. Someone is guarding them. There's no other way out, is there?"

He looked around and spotted me, turning to me for confirmation.

"Actually there is an unpaved track out from the home farm," I said. "Otherwise there is a wall around the whole estate."

"You see!" Mrs. Trapp screamed. "There is a way out. She went up to see those damned pigs and someone grabbed her and has run off with her."

"Let's be reasonable," Cy Martin said, his voice commanding attention. "Who would know that she might want to go and see some damned pigs? Who even knows she's here at this house, for God's sake?"

"Those newspapermen know," Mrs. Trapp said. "Why do you think they're all here? And she was spotted in the village when I took her to see the fireworks last night. I heard someone say, 'Isn't that Rosie Trapp? She's staying here? In our village?'"

"That doesn't mean that people immediately get an idea to kidnap her," Cy said. "At the most they'd want her autograph."

"Then where the hell is she?" Mrs. Trapp demanded, her voice rising to a scream. "Why hasn't anyone found her?"

"Why don't we call the police?" Lana suggested. "They can bring in dogs and things."

"You're welcome to use our telephone in the house," I said, "but the village only has one policeman. They'd have to bring in help from Haywards Heath."

"What about Scotland Yard?" Mrs. Trapp asked. "Isn't that where the big guns are? I want the best police searching for my daughter. I want detectives who can find her."

"We'll call our village bobby and he'll have to make the request," I said. "Do you want me to telephone him?"

"I guess," Mrs. Trapp said. "And while you do it I'm going to talk to those guys at the gate. We have to do something quickly, while there's still a chance of finding her alive."

"Of course she'll be alive," Grant said, in a voice that didn't sound too sympathetic. "If she's been kidnapped for ransom money they'll want to keep her alive, won't they? Or they won't get paid."

"Not the Lindbergh baby." Mrs. Trapp sounded perilously close to hysterics again. "Look what happened to him. That's all I can think of. My poor little Rosie . . ."

Nora tried to comfort her but Mrs. Trapp shrugged her off and ran for the gate. She was swallowed into the fog before she reached the newsmen standing there but I could hear the raised voices, the buzz of excitement. I thought I saw the flash of camera attachments. I hurried back into the house and had the operator put me through to the local police station.

"One of them film stars, you say?" the bobby asked in his soft country voice. "Oh, we've heard all about them in the village. Everyone's talking about nothing else. So you say one of them got herself lost in the fog?"

"That's what we think but her mother is worried she's been kidnapped."

"Kidnapped? Why would anyone do that?"

"She's a little girl, just like Shirley Temple."

"Even so, this is Sussex," he said. "People don't go kidnapping in Sussex."

"I think you're right, but I'd like you to come out and see for yourself. Maybe you should notify the big police station in Haywards Heath too."

"If you say so, my lady," he said. "I'll come right away, but I can't guarantee how quick I'll get there. My old bike isn't working too well in this cold weather."

I put down the receiver and went back to the assembled group. "The local bobby is on his way," I said.

"I don't know what you think he can do," Cy said. "Come on, folks. We need to get back to filming. Each day here is costing me money. How about persuading your kid to stand in again so I can get the long shots?"

I thought this was pretty callous. "I'll ask her," I said.

As I went back to the house I had a brilliant idea. The dogs. I'd kept them shut away inside but perhaps if I took them out onto the estate they might be able to locate Rosie. Not that they were trained bloodhounds or anything but they did have good noses. It was worth a try. First I found Mrs. Holbrook and told her to have the servants search the house again, this time looking for the little girl. She didn't seem too thrilled with this idea.

"Are we to have no peace, my lady? How can the maids get on with their work if they are continually to be going through the house looking for missing people?"

"I know, it is annoying, Mrs. Holbrook," I replied, "but the little girl has vanished. Her mother is frantic and the police will be here soon. We'll want to say that we've given the whole house a good search."

"Very good, my lady."

"And perhaps ask Phipps to search the stable block, although I don't know why she'd be there."

She nodded and headed off to round up the staff. I went up to the nursery floor to see if Addy would come down to play princesses again. Nanny peered out of the window. "The fog's not lifting," she said. "I'd say it's not good for her chest."

"I think it would only be for a few moments, Nanny," I said. "But it's up to Addy." I turned to her. She had been playing with blocks, building a house for her dolls. "Would you want to come down and play princesses again for a little while?" I asked.

"No thank you," she replied. "I didn't like that lady. She was scary and she smelled perfumy."

"All right. I'll tell them." I came down, pausing to check on my son. He was sleeping with a sweet smile on his face. I found I was smiling too as I went down the second flight of stairs. Thank heavens for my husband, my son and my own peaceful life. Then suddenly a feeling of dread swept over me. What if that had been James and he were missing? I could understand how frantic Mrs. Trapp must feel and vowed to do anything I could to help find Rosie.

"What's going on?" Fig's face appeared around the morning room door. "People running around and doors slamming every five minutes. Is everyone still looking for the Simpson woman? Are we to have no peace?"

"The little girl in the film is missing now," I said. "Her mother is frantic. She's terrified the child has been kidnapped. We're searching the house just in case she came in here and might be hiding."

"The child is missing?" Fig's voice rose. "Oh my goodness—Addy. She's not out there, is she?"

"She's not. She's safely back in the nursery," I said. "She really didn't enjoy acting in the film. It's too cold for one thing."

"Oh, thank God." Fig looked as if she might cry. This was most unusual. I'd never thought of her as the motherly type. "If this child has been kidnapped then they could easily have taken my daughter by mistake. That poor mother. I should go out to her."

"What's this?" Sir Hubert came along the hall. I explained to him. He frowned. "This is most irregular. Two people vanishing from my house in one morning. I don't like it at all. Have the police been called?"

"I telephoned the local station and the bobby said he was going to call Haywards Heath."

"I think I'd better have a word with them myself," Sir Hubert said. "We can't let anything bad happen while these people are with us. Maybe the child's just hiding, playing a trick."

"That was my initial thought," I said. "The servants are

searching the house again now, just in case. I thought I might take the dogs out to look for her."

"As if those dogs could find anything other than food," Fig said in scathing tones. "Untrained brutes, that's what they are."

"They're only puppies, Fig. And you know that Labs take two years before they settle down and grow up. But they do have good noses. It's worth a try, isn't it?"

"I'll get my coat," Fig said. "That poor woman will need comfort."

I thought that Fig would be the last person I'd want if I needed comforting, but I was touched that she actually wanted to help.

I went through the baize door and down the stone steps to the servants' quarters, trying to swallow back my feeling of dread. Surely the policeman was right. People didn't go around kidnapping in Sussex. It wasn't Chicago or even Los Angeles. But that didn't mean there weren't dangers. There were occasional tramps who poached game from our woodlands. There were sometimes burglaries in local houses. Certainly there were men who took their chances and didn't always obey the law. Might one of them have been tempted to make some money when he saw a little film star was staying in our neighborhood? A little girl who had wandered off at the wrong moment?

But how did that tie in with Mrs. Simpson? And the king? If his secretary didn't know where he was, shouldn't we be concerned about that? What if this was part of something bigger, like a communist plot or even our own government trying to rid the country of the wrong man on the throne?

Chapter 16

November 6
Eynsleigh

We're still looking for Rosie. I don't know whether to be annoyed or scared. I simply can't believe that anything bad could have happened to a little girl on our estate.

I opened the door to the servants' dining hall and was met by two very shamefaced Labradors.

Instead of bounding to greet me with great delight, they slunk toward me, heads down.

"What have you two been up to?" I asked.

"We didn't mean it, Mum. It was too tempting," their eyes were saying. I looked and saw that the film crew chef had brought over a platter of some kind of cake or biscuits. At least I suspect that was what it had been once. A few telltale crumbs lay on the floor, along with the platter. I realized that one of my staff had shut the dogs in here, not knowing that an outsider had brought in food. An honest mistake except I now had two overfed labs who would probably throw up in the most inconvenient of places and my own cooks would have to come up with replacement food.

I went through to the kitchen. "Have the dogs been in the dining hall all morning?" I asked.

"No, missus," Queenie said. "They weren't allowed out for their normal walk so they were being terrible rambunctious and Chef told me to put them away somewhere so I shut them in next door."

"Without looking, I suppose?"

She stared at me with that vacant cowlike expression I knew so well. "Looking for what, missus? It's where we shut them when we need to get on with things."

"Except there was a big plate of food on the table, ready to feed the film crew."

"Bloody 'ell," she said. "How was I to know that?"

"You weren't," I agreed. "And it wasn't my idea to let the film crew come in and eat here. Certainly nobody gave them permission to bring in food in advance. Never mind. I'm taking the dogs out now." A thought struck me. I remembered Rosie's fondness for cake. Could she have seen the platter being carried across to the house and come in here to investigate? "I don't suppose you've seen the little girl down here, have you?"

"Little girl? You mean Rosie Trapp? The one what's like Shirley Temple? Only I think she's prettier than Shirley, don't you? Ever so pretty. Lovely 'air."

"Yes. Rosie Trapp. Has she been down here at all?"

Chef Pierre looked up from something he was stirring on the stove. "I would not allow strange children to come to my kitchen," he said. "I would tell to go away pretty sharpish."

I tried not to smile at his English that always seemed to have a hint of Queenie's speech in it.

"All right." I sighed. "Queenie, perhaps you could whip up a new pudding for their lunch. Something simple."

"Like meringues or maids of honor? Yeah, I can do that. And then I can help serve them and I can say that I've cooked for film stars." She had a big grin on her face.

"Queenie, there have been complaints," I said. "You must not bother the film actors. They have work to do."

"Bob's yer uncle, missus. I won't bother 'em. But I'll have to be close to them when I serve them their pudding, won't I?"

"Make some sort of pudding they can help themselves to. They won't want you around when they're eating."

She glared at me. "That ain't fair. If I cook it, then I bloody well get to serve it." And that was that as far as Queenie was concerned. I decided that if she ever tried to get a job with any other household she wouldn't last a week. But it was no use trying to teach her. She didn't want to learn.

I called the dogs and off we went. As I opened the scullery door the dogs bounded ahead of me, as usual. Unfortunately there was a tense scene being filmed, with the two actresses in fur capes meeting under a big beech tree, holding hands and about to hug each other. The dogs saw fur capes and presumably thought it was intruding animals who needed to be driven off. They came flying across the lawn, barking furiously, then realized there were people inside the animal skins and jumped up at them, wagging tails.

"Cut!" the director screamed. "Get those goddamned brutes out of here."

"Sorry." I ran to retrieve them. "I brought them out to see if they could help in locating the little girl."

"Okay, I guess." He gave an exaggerated sigh. "We have to try everything, don't we? We went on with the filming because the weather is just perfect for this scene and it might not happen again. But the police have been called and now Mrs. Trapp is down there giving the scoop to all the journalists who've been hanging around." He wrapped his scarf more tightly around his throat. "I don't know where the damned kid can have got to. It's not like her to go wandering off. Usually she's an absolute little pro."

"Let's see what the dogs can find," I said. I didn't like to admit that probably all they'd find was some kind of dead animal or some mess to roll in. But it was worth a try. I could see Mrs. Trapp still at the front gate. A large crowd seemed to have gathered there and we could hear raised voices through the fog. Cy glared in that direction and sighed again. "How am I supposed to shoot a scene with that row going on? Someone get that woman away and send off those newsmen to telephone in their stories. She seems to be milking it."

I called the dogs and we set off, retracing steps to the farm. The dogs ran ahead, tails in the air, sniffing the ground. They found a rabbit and chased after it but it got away. We reached the farm. None of the boys was there, as I had sent them to look for the girl in the woods. I paused outside the farmhouse to think. If there was the remote possibility that Rosie had been kidnapped, then the only way a kidnapper could have come in was along the track that led from the farm to the outside world. I went past the pigsties to see if there were any fresh tire prints from a motor vehicle. There had been plenty of rain and the track was a succession of muddy puddles. There were horseshoe prints and the wheels of the cart in which Jacob had taken the cabbages this morning. But no obvious motorcar had been here since the van that came to collect produce and eggs once a week.

I turned away. This was a wild-goose chase. None of it made sense. If Rosie had wandered up here she could have easily seen the outline of our house through the fog and found her way back. If she had gone into our house one of our servants would have spotted her. And if someone had tried to grab her she could have cried out and someone would have heard it. People don't vanish into thin air. I was still inclined to think that the child was playing a trick on us. Rosie clearly adored attention. I suspected she'd wait until we were all absolutely frantic, then reappear saying, "I had you all worried, didn't I?"

Then I looked down, stepping around a large puddle, and froze. In the mud was a child's footprint. Of course it could have been Addy's. She had come to see the bonfire; she had been to the farm with Darcy. But what if Rosie really had come this way? I looked around for more prints but a lot of big boots had walked around this area and I couldn't find another clear print. I looked over the empty parkland to the outline of the trees, lurking in the fog. Was it worth taking the dogs over there to see what the boys might have found? But why would a little girl go alone into the woods? If I'd been that age I wouldn't have wanted to be far from safety and people I knew, especially on a bleak and foggy day like this. Rosie was definitely more confident and grown up than most children but even so . . . I shook my head again. None of it made sense.

Chapter 17

November 6
Eynsleigh

I was sure we'd have found her by now. I can't believe something terrible has happened here at our estate. It has always felt so safe and welcoming.

The police, in the person of PC Barnes, arrived from the village. When the man guarding the gate let him in some of the newsmen managed to sneak in too and were already pestering the cast and crew.

"Now then, you lot, off you go," PC Barnes said. "Leave these poor people alone. And if you want to do anything useful then go looking for the little girl yourselves. She must be somewhere around. She can't have got that far."

"What are you going to do to find my child?" Mrs. Trapp demanded.

Clearly the PC hadn't the slightest clue. "I put in a telephone call to Haywards Heath," he said, "but the inspector was out investigating a break-in last night at a local chicken farm."

"A chicken farm?" Mrs. Trapp shrieked the words. "My child is a hell of a lot more important than chickens." Then she wagged her finger at him. "You see, there are criminals in the area. I knew it. You must call this police station again right away. We need every police car in the area driving around looking for my daughter and we need it now."

"Sir Hubert is telephoning the police in Haywards Heath again," I said. "Our servants are searching every corner of the house. I'm not sure what more we can do."

Fig had arrived, now wearing gum boots and a large sheepskin jacket, and her head tied in a scarf. "Which one is the poor child's mother?" she asked.

I pointed her out. "Now, this child of yours, is she used to playing silly tricks?" Fig asked.

Mrs. Trapp took a step back at Fig's commanding tones.

"Of course not," Mrs. Trapp said angrily, "and who are you, anyway? Are you the farmer's wife?" I had to agree that Fig did look like a farmer's wife at the moment.

"Certainly not. I am the Duchess of Rannoch," Fig said in her most duchessy voice. "It was my daughter who was standing in for your child, so I know how you must be feeling. But don't worry. You're in England, where people are sensible and safe." She took Mrs. Trapp's hands. Mrs. Trapp was too startled to pull them away. "Come inside the house, my dear woman," Fig said to Mrs. Trapp. "Your hands are freezing."

"But I can't leave. I have to help find her. I have to be ready in case the press want more information. We must get the word out before it's too late." Mrs. Trapp tried to pull away but Fig was bigger and stronger.

"Nonsense. There's nothing you can do at this moment. A hot cup of tea is what you need." She half dragged a protesting Mrs. Trapp toward the house.

"Call me if there is any news," Mrs. Trapp shouted.

"I don't know about her hands. I'm freezing all over," Lana Lovett said. "This is insane, Cy. We've been standing around so long we're just too cold to keep filming. Let's call it a day."

"She's right," Gloria Bishop chimed in. "I can't speak properly with my teeth chattering. None of us can settle until Rosie is found anyway. We'll go back to the country club and then the crew can join in the search." She started in the direction of one of the caravans. Lana followed.

"Hold on a minute, ladies. We've a schedule to keep to," Cy Martin called after them. "Time is money, you know. But I get that it's too cold to shoot out here. Let's see if we can move any more scenes into the house. I'm sure that Sir Hubert guy won't mind." He put an arm around Lana's shoulder. "Come on, sweetie. Let's get back to work."

I noticed that he hadn't thought to ask me for permission to use the house. In his mind I was clearly not the person who counted.

"If you want us to keep filming we need to change for the Hampton Court scene," Gloria said. "That's the only one coming up that doesn't include Rosie."

"Yeah, right, the Hampton Court scene. We'll go get set up and you change to the ball gowns."

The actors headed back to their trailers while Cy went toward the house. PC Barnes just stood there, holding his bicycle, unsure what to do next.

At that moment Sir Hubert came out, a worried frown on his face. "I've talked to your superiors in Haywards Heath," he said to the police constable. "A team of men will be coming as fast as they can and they've put out an all-points bulletin to nearby stations."

"There's not much I can do here now, sir, is there?" the constable said. "Me and my old bike can't exactly comb the neighborhood."

"I suggest you'd be most useful at crowd control." Sir Hubert glanced at the gate, where the crowd seemed to have grown, even though I was sure the newshounds had already headed to the nearest telephone box to call in their stories. "The natives seem to be getting restless."

"Hey, Hubert," Cy Martin called. "I need to talk to you." A conversation followed that I couldn't hear, then Cy slapped him on the back, turned to bark out a lot of orders before walking toward the house with my godfather. The crew sprang into action. I watched cameramen dismantling leads and crew members staggering with lights. It was as if Rosie didn't exist and they were just moving on without her.

I stood there feeling sick and useless. There had to be a rational explanation. Was it ridiculous to think that anyone might have kidnapped Rosie? For one thing how would they know that she might wander off into the fog and be unattended? Would anyone lurk on the grounds, awaiting their chances? It seemed so much more probable that she was hiding, but where? The dogs were sitting at my feet, obedient for once, or perhaps alarmed by things that looked like snakes being dragged across the grounds. I whistled and we started back toward the woods to see if the boys had found anything. The dogs bounded ahead as they saw the boys coming out of the trees with a load of firewood.

"Any luck?" I called.

They shook their heads. "We didn't see nobody or nothing," Donnie called back. "I don't see why a little kid would come up here in the fog. It's spooky enough for us in those woods. There was a fox barking this morning. Sounded quite eerie, didn't it, Bill?"

Bill nodded. "We must get this firewood to the house, my lady," he said. "My arms are about to drop off."

Donnie still looked worried and hesitated. "I don't know what else we can do," he said. "Do you want us to keep looking after we've taken this wood inside?"

"I'm not sure," I said. "I know more police have been called. You might come and offer your services to them. When do you expect Jacob back?"

Donnie glanced at Bill and grinned. "He's probably got delayed talking in the village."

"Delayed?" I asked. "Why?"

Bill was grinning too. "He's quite sweet on that Joanie in the newsagent's."

"Ah, so that's why he's keen to take the produce." I felt relieved. Of course I hadn't suspected Jacob, but it was an odd time to choose to take the cabbages into the village.

The boys set off toward the house with their firewood. The dogs followed them. They were fond of the boys, I suspect because they got food scraps from them.

"Make sure the dogs are put away and don't bother the film people," I called.

"Don't worry, my lady," Donnie called back.

I arrived back to chaos. Somehow the gates had been opened and newsmen were surrounding the film crew as they tried to work. PC Barnes was attempting feebly to corral the interlopers but flashbulbs were going off and the burning, sulfury smell hung in the air. I noticed too that a number of local spectators had also managed to worm their way in and were gazing in awe at the trailers, waiting for the stars to emerge from them. They spotted me and some of them came over to me.

"It's true, is it, your ladyship?" one of the women asked. "That little girl Rosie Trapp has been kidnapped?"

"She is missing, that's all. There's no sign she's been taken away. I suspect we'll find her hiding in the house somewhere. There are plenty of good places for a child to hide."

"Are the other film stars still here?" another woman asked. "Someone said it was Lana Lovett and Gloria Bishop."

They were all looking at me with keen, excited faces.

"That's right," I said.

"See, I told you, Sarah." The woman nudged the woman beside her. "Ooh, and that Grant Hathaway. I like him, don't you? Such a handsome brute. Sexy."

"And she's lovely, isn't she? That Gloria Bishop." The first woman turned to her friends, then to me for confirmation. "We loved her last film, didn't we, Sarah?"

"But not very friendly," the one called Sarah responded. "When their car stopped in the village and someone went for a packet of cigarettes she hid herself in the backseat. Pulled her hat down over her face so that we didn't recognize her, but of course we knew who she was, didn't we, Gladys?"

"She may just be shy," Gladys said. "Some actresses are. They don't like the attention."

"I don't know why you'd be an actress with your face all over the posters if you don't want attention." Sarah looked puzzled. "Do you think we'll see them? I'd dearly love their autographs."

"I don't think now is a good time," I said. "They're going to be filming in the house in a minute. As you can imagine everyone is pretty worried about the little girl too. So please, if you want to be helpful, go back to the village and ask if anyone might have seen Rosie there."

"What would she be doing in our village?" one of them asked.

"She might have been spotted in the back of a motorcar." Not that I had seen any motorcar tracks but you never knew.

"Being carried off, you mean? So you do think she was kidnapped."

They were looking at me in horror and bewilderment.

"We really don't know anything but if she has been taken, then the swifter the police can act the better." I paused, looked around at the crowd that seemed to have swelled around me and then added, "So please go back to the village now, and persuade the others to leave with you. The film director is going to get really upset at people hanging around his set. He can't film with everyone here. And I'll try to arrange a good time for the film actors to sign autographs for you if you help us now."

This bucked them up. "Right you are, my lady." The women nodded agreement to each other.

"You better get going anyway before your husband sees you hanging around film stars." One of them chuckled and gave her companion a friendly nudge.

"Your husband wouldn't even notice. He'd be down the pub no doubt."

They were chuckling as they set off toward the gate. "Come on, you lot. Get moving. We've work to do to find the little girl," one of them shouted. "It's no use hanging around here. You're not going to see any film stars today."

"Just do what the lady says, there's good people." PC Barnes stepped up. "Come on now. Off you go. Or she'll have to set the dogs on you."

I tried not to smile at this. The worst Holly or Jolly would do would be to lick them to death. A few minutes later the women had gone and several local men were starting to move toward the gates as well.

"Hold on for a moment, there, you blokes," PC Barnes called after them. "Why don't you wait around a bit. We might need your help. We have more policemen coming and they may want to organize a search party over the grounds."

The group of men halted and turned back to the policeman. I was interested to note that they all seemed to be local farmers or farmhands, in their ancient tweed jackets, cloth caps and big boots. Not the usual admirers of film stars, I thought. But I supposed anything for a bit of excitement in the dull life of a village.

"Right you are. We're willing to help any way we can. Poor little girl," one of the men said in his gravelly local accent. "I don't mind hanging around, do you, Bert?" He nudged a big burly man in a tweed jacket and cloth cap. "I'd quite like to set eyes on some good-looking women. Make a change after thirty years of the same old bag serving my dinner. And she weren't no oil painting to start with." He chuckled, then added, "And you'd better not repeat that to her neither. I'd never hear the last of it."

The man beside him was scowling. "I don't hold with women flaunting themselves or showing off their bodies. You know what the Bible says about loose women. I reckon these film stars are headed straight to the fires of hell."

"Then what were you doing coming to have a gawp at them?"

"He's checking up on his missus, that's what he's doing. Scared she's going to run off with one of them male film stars," a third man shouted from the back of the group.

There was laughter and banter as they followed the policeman.

I saw no reason to stay outside any longer. In my haste I had forgotten my gloves and my hands were freezing. This made me pause and think about Rosie. It was bitterly cold outside. If she had run off to the farm or the estate she would soon have been unbearably cold and not wanted to wait around. If she was hiding anywhere it would more likely be a linen closet in the house, where it was snug and warm.

I came back inside to find Sir Hubert on the telephone in the front hall. He finished his call and put down the receiver. "No luck, I suppose?" he asked.

I shook my head. "But there were a lot of local people outside, hoping to see the film stars. I sent the women back to the village to ask if anyone might have spotted the child. But there are some local men waiting around to see if the police might need them."

"Good thought." He nodded. "That was the chief inspector on the phone. He's on his way now and wants to interview everyone."

"The actors are getting changed before they start filming in the long gallery again," I said. "Cy Martin is determined to press on. He said time was money."

Sir Hubert smiled. "I suppose that's true," he said. "When you are paying all those people to stay in hotels the costs must mount." He looked at me critically. "You're awfully cold," he said. "Go and warm up by the fire. I'll handle the film people and make sure they don't take over the entire house."

I didn't need telling twice. My face felt like a block of ice and I couldn't feel my fingers. I went into the little sitting room by the front door and found Fig now sitting with Mrs. Trapp.

"The police are on their way and they want to interview everybody," I said. "And they're going to organize a search party."

"What the hell good would that do?" Mrs. Trapp snapped. "What they should be doing is driving around the whole neighborhood, questioning everybody to see if they've seen my child. My poor little Rosie . . . I can't believe it." And she broke down, sobbing. Fig put a tentative arm around her. I was impressed. I don't think Fig had ever hugged anyone before.

Chapter 18

November 6
Eynsleigh

It's all too horrible and unbelievable. Mrs. Simpson and Rosie Trapp vanish on the same morning. They can't be linked, can they? Oh dear. I wish they had never come.

I suddenly felt the need to see James. To know he was safe and all right. I almost ran upstairs, and found him blissfully asleep in his cot, his thumb in his mouth. Then another thought struck me. I went up the next flight of stairs to the nursery. Addy was now playing happily, having a tea party with the stuffed animals.

"Would you like some sugar, Mrs. Elephant?" I heard her saying as I came in.

Nanny was sitting in the rocking chair, mending a sock.

"She's not going down again to do that acting and that's final," she said firmly. "The poor wee mite was a block of ice. We'll be lucky if she doesn't come down with a chill."

"They've stopped shooting outside for now," I said, my brain toying with the word "shooting." I remembered the explosions from last night that we assumed were Guy Fawkes fireworks. People didn't go around shooting other people in England but what if American gangsters had followed the film people from America? I had seen on newsreels how casually they mowed people down. Surely this was too far-fetched. It belonged in a film, not in real life.

"Addy, I need your help," I said. "We can't find Rosie and we wondered if she might be hiding. You've played hide-and-seek in this house, haven't you? Do you want to come and show me your favorite places?"

"Rosie is playing hide-and-seek?" She jumped up and took my hand. "I want to play too."

She dragged me around the top floors, pointing out a cupboard under the stairs, the linen closet and a big oak chest in a spare bedroom. We even opened wardrobes but to no avail. It seemed clear that Rosie Trapp was not hiding anywhere in the house.

"Rosie's a very good hider," Addy commented.

"She might have decided not to play anymore and gone back to her mother," I said, not wanting to worry the child with the truth. I deposited her in the nursery and came downstairs. As I came into the front hall I saw that several police vehicles had now arrived. A smart-looking man in a well-cut overcoat was coming toward the house, accompanied by a younger man and a constable in uniform. I opened the front door to them.

"We're here to see Sir Hubert," the man said. "Be a good girl and let him know we're here. I'm Chief Inspector Harlow." And to my surprise he handed me his hat and gloves.

Realizing that finding a little girl was more important than making a fuss at this moment, I was about to accept them meekly when Sir Hubert appeared in the foyer. "Ah good. You've arrived. I'm so grateful," he said, stepping forward to shake the policeman's hand. "I see you've met Lady Georgiana."

I must say I enjoyed watching the chief inspector's face turn beetroot red.

"What? Oh yes. Of course. Delighted to meet you, my lady."

I placed his hat and gloves on the side table and gave him a polite nod.

"I can't take you to the morning room right now," Sir Hubert said. "Those film people are shooting a scene in our long gallery so we can't get through to that part of the house."

"The little sitting room by the door is nice and warm," I said. "The child's mother is already in there. I'm sure you'll want to question her."

"Good idea," the chief inspector said. "But first I'd like to fully understand what we are doing here and who exactly is missing. You have an outside film unit using your house and grounds, correct?"

"Quite correct," Sir Hubert said. "I met them in Hollywood and when they found out I owned a Tudor manor house they jumped at the chance to shoot some scenes here. They came over with me on the *Queen Mary*."

The chief inspector nodded. "And there is a child actor who has now gone missing?"

"Rosie Trapp," I said. "I gather she's quite a rising star."

"Never heard of her," the man said, "but then I'm not one for the pictures myself." He gave me a hard stare. "You say she's missing? For how long? Has anything been done to locate her?"

"I presume she was here with her mother at the start of the day's filming," I said. "I only know that her mother asked my niece to stand in for her because it's too cold to keep working out there. And when my niece was finished and they were ready for Rosie again she had vanished."

"Vanished?" He looked around. "I'd say this was quite a big house and it wouldn't be hard for a child to hide."

"We thought that too," I responded, "but we've had the servants search the house. I even asked my niece to show me where she might like to hide when they were playing hide-and-seek. Children are so creative about such things. So we've checked the place from top to bottom. We've looked in the woods. We also went up to the farm because Rosie had shown interest in seeing the piglets. But the farmworkers hadn't seen her although . . ." I paused. "I did see a small footprint in the mud. But that could have been Addy's."

"Addy?" He frowned.

"My niece. Adelaide, daughter of the Duke of Rannoch."

He gave a sigh. "Before I interview the mother, who is bound to be hysterical, do we have any reason to suspect any kind of foul play?"

"The mother did seem worried about kidnappers," I said, "although we've not seen any sign of outsiders and anyway, how would they know when they might catch her alone and unsupervised? She would either be on the film set or with her mother in the sitting room."

"I see." He nodded. "I think I'd better have a chat with the mother, then. Which room is she in?"

We ushered him to the sitting room and opened the door. Mrs. Trapp and Fig were sitting together on the sofa. Mrs. Trapp looked up hopefully.

"You've news for me? You've found her?"

"I'm afraid not, madam," the chief inspector said in a grave voice. "We've only just arrived and we would like to start by asking you a few questions." He nodded to the constable, who took out a notebook and pencil.

Fig stood up. "We should leave them to it," she said. I saw then that Dorothy was also in the room. In the chaos I had forgotten about her. She was dressed in street clothes and looked like any other schoolgirl. She gave me a half smile as she got up.

"Are you part of this film lot?" the chief inspector asked, eyeing Fig critically.

"I am not," she replied. "I am the Duchess of Rannoch, visiting my sister-in-law. I was merely trying to comfort this poor, distraught woman."

"And this is your daughter?" He indicated Dorothy.

"This is Dorothy Hart, she's another of the film actors," I said.

He shook his head in annoyance. "It's all getting too complicated. Perhaps you'd be good enough to make me a list of who is who, just so I don't put my foot in it again."

"Of course." Sir Hubert gave him an understanding smile.

"Do you want people rounded up so that you can question them?"

"That would be helpful, sir," the chief inspector said. I noticed he no longer had that arrogant tone. As he said, he had put his foot in it too often.

"Should I get a search party organized, then, sir?" the younger policeman asked. "We don't want to wait too long."

"I think you'd better," the chief inspector said. "We've got the bloodhound, haven't we? Perhaps her mother can supply an item of the child's clothing?"

"Her clothing? Surely if she's lost somewhere in the grounds she'll hear us calling her."

The chief inspector exchanged a glance with Sir Hubert. "Do you have any traps in your woods against poachers?" he asked.

"Mantraps? Certainly not," Sir Hubert said.

"So if she's fallen and hurt herself and she's still alive one has to assume she will hear us."

Mrs. Trapp gave a gasping sob. "You don't think . . . you're not suggesting . . . that we may be looking for her body? No. That's too horrible. Who would ever do such a thing . . . ?"

"We have to rule out that possibility, madam," the chief inspector said. "Do you have any item we might use to help the dog?"

"Her scarf is here on the table." Mrs. Trapp picked it up. "She left it here when she went to wardrobe to get changed."

I was instantly alert. "So was she wearing her costume when she disappeared?" I asked.

"She must have been," Mrs. Trapp replied.

"I thought Addy was wearing the costume," I said.

"They would have put just any costume on the stand-in," Mrs. Trapp said. "It's only to get the angles of the shots correct. All I know is that I left my Rosie to get changed."

This made it even more complicated. It would be difficult enough to kidnap a child in daylight. There had been no recent tire tracks. I found it hard to imagine someone running off with a child in Elizabethan costume tucked under his arm.

I left the room and followed Fig and Dorothy. "Where are you going?" I asked.

"I thought the morning room was simplest," Fig said.

"You can't get there. They are filming in the long gallery."

"How utterly annoying," Fig snapped. "Really, Georgiana, you should have put your foot down in the first place and not allowed them to come here."

"Fig, it was not my decision. I only live here. I don't own the place."

I looked across at Dorothy. She seemed close to tears. "Come on, sweetheart," I said. I took her hand. "Let's take you down to the kitchen and get you a hot drink."

She allowed herself to be led. "Do you think something awful has happened to Rosie?" she asked. "Do you think she has been kidnapped?"

"I really don't know what to think," I said. "Her mother was certainly terrified of kidnappers. But who would get into our grounds, then lurk around on the off chance that they found her alone? There are so many people around all the time. If someone wanted to kidnap her they'd have a better chance in the cottage at night, wouldn't they?"

Dorothy shuddered. "Poor little Rosie. I bet she's terrified."

If she's still alive . . . I tried to push the unbidden thought out of my mind. This was England, safe, orderly, rational . . . but there were occasional deranged people, tramps who wandered the countryside, travelers who it was reported stole children. I handed Dorothy over to Mrs. Holbrook, then went up to feed James. Outside my windows I heard shouts and a barking dog. I looked out to see a line of men working their way across the estate. I shivered, and held James tightly. When he had drifted off to sleep and I had put him back in his bassinet I could no longer see the search party. They must have reached the woods.

Suddenly I couldn't sit idly doing nothing. I went downstairs. From the long gallery came the sounds of the scene being acted.

"Henry, you betrayed me and now you betray her. We are both mothers of your children. Have you no pity? No heart?"

Gloria Bishop was good, I thought. I heard the real emotion in her voice.

I was going to see if the drawing room fire was lit but as I approached the door I heard the sound of a man's voice. Presumably the detective was interviewing people in there. Instead I checked the small sitting room. Fig had gone back in there by the fire, but there was no sign of Mrs. Trapp.

"What happened to her?" I asked.

"She wanted to go back to her little cottage. She couldn't bear to be here any longer. So we sent her back in one of their motorcars." She looked up. "Poor woman. She was quite distraught. I must admit, Georgiana, that it has shaken me to the core. All I could think was what if a kidnapper had mistaken

Addy for this child? It made me realize how precious one's children are."

I nodded. "I feel the same way. When I was nursing James just now I found it hard to put him down again."

"Of course if you insist on having him beside you in your bedroom he will grow up horribly spoiled," she said, reverting to the old Fig. "While we are here I'll make it my mission to find you a proper nanny so he can be up in the nursery where he belongs."

Having a lecture from Fig was one thing too much. "I'm going out," I said.

"You're going out? When everyone is trying to find this child?" She sounded as if this were a mortal sin.

Then I realized that Darcy had taken the motorcar to drive to the station. "I thought I might walk into the village and see if anyone might have spotted Rosie there."

"Walk? On a day like this? Isn't it miles?" She glanced up at the clock on the mantelpiece. "Besides, it's almost lunchtime."

"Oh. Right. So it is." I realized I had no idea of time. The morning had rushed by in a blur. Also now that I thought about it I wasn't so keen to walk the mile and a half on a day like this. But I didn't want to sit with Fig either unless absolutely necessary.

"When do you expect Binky and Podge back?" I asked her.

"Who knows? They may even choose to have luncheon at the school so that they can sample the food," she said.

"That should put Podge off forever." I smiled. "I don't think there has ever been a school known for its haute cuisine."

"Good solid nourishment. That's what boys need," she said.

"Now you've a son of your own I can show you how to raise a boy. And the first thing is no namby-pamby mothering. Our sons are being brought up to rule, Georgiana. They must be strong, fearless and completely without emotional attachment."

I did not point out that her own son was sweet-natured and not at all fearless. Of course she only saw him for half an hour each day when he was brought down from the nursery at tea-time. I had spent more time with him and found him a lovely little chap. But then Binky could not be described as strong and fearless either. Fig was the only one without emotional attachment. She should have been a boy and ruled the empire.

"I'll see you at luncheon," I said and made a hurried exit. I wasn't quite sure what to do. There was no sign of my godfather. I put on my coat and went out. The men had not returned from the far reaches of the estate yet. There was no sign of life around the caravans. I wondered where everyone was until I saw the kitchen door open and realized that their lunch must be being served. It occurred to me to wonder if all the caravans had all been searched thoroughly. There might be places for a child to hide in one of them, but what child would hide for several hours? Rosie clearly liked her food. She'd be hungry by now. I tapped on the door of the first caravan and went in. It was the makeup room, now empty. And with no place to hide. I went on until I came to the caravan being used for wardrobe. Now here would be a great place to hide among the racks of costumes. I moved between them, pulling the costumes aside. Nobody there. Of course it would have been searched. But at the front of the rack I saw Rosie's pretty little dresses hanging in a row. I fingered one, wondering if there was one outfit missing, the one she was wearing today. There were no empty hangers. . . . Having no answer, I was just about to leave when the door opened and a woman came in. She froze when she saw me.

"What are you doing in here?" she asked, eyeing me suspiciously. She had a strong American accent and must have come over with the crew.

"I was trying to see whether Rosie might be hiding somewhere."

"All this time?" She shook her head. "Besides, I've been in here all morning."

"When did you see her last?" I asked.

She thought about this. "I don't think I did see her at all. Her mother came in to get her first outfit and took it over to their trailer to get her dressed."

"Was that before filming started this morning?" I asked.

"That's right."

I came out, puzzled. Hadn't our Addy been asked to stand in quite early after shooting started? So wouldn't she have been wearing the costume? And Mrs. Trapp had said that Rosie went to wardrobe to get dressed, but the wardrobe mistress said the mother took her outfit over to her trailer. Who was right? And why was there this confusion? Nothing made sense.

Chapter 19

November 6
Eynsleigh

Bloody woman! Yes, I know a lady does not swear but this warrants it.

Fig and I ate lunch although neither of us seemed to have much of an appetite. I finished my bowl of soup but toyed with the turbot in parsley sauce that followed. I even found it hard to swallow the baked apple and custard, which was normally one of my favorites. The search party had returned having found no trace of the girl and no clues. The police had questioned everybody and apparently learned nothing. All that was certain was that two people had vanished from our house in one morning. I wished Darcy would come home.

I went up to my bedroom, gave James his two o'clock feed

and then took him onto the bed with me, feeling the comfort of his soft warm cheek against my neck as I lay there. I suppose I drifted off for a while, because I awoke with a start as he objected to being held and let out a protesting cry. I changed him, then took him downstairs with me. I didn't feel like leaving him alone at the moment and I didn't care what Fig said or thought. There was no sound from the long gallery, indicating they must have finished filming there for now. When I glanced outside, taking care not to move the curtains and thus get yelled at, I saw that the grounds were empty. Everyone had left and the caravans stood parked in a row. The only sign of life were two police constables standing at the gate.

On entering the drawing room I found that Binky and Podge had returned. Binky, usually so easygoing, was bright red in the face. "I've had the biggest insult of my life, Fig," he was saying. "The police pulled me over, made me get out of the Rolls and demanded proof that Podge was my son. The indignity of it."

"Well, I suppose they are on the lookout for any car with a small child in the backseat," Fig said, showing her usual lack of sympathy. "Potential kidnappers, don't you know?"

"I don't think too many kidnappers drive around in a Rolls," he said. "I had to be quite firm with them. 'Do you know that I'm the Duke of Rannoch?' I said. 'I am the king's cousin and I'm staying with my sister at Eynsleigh.'"

Podge gave me a secret little grin as if he was enjoying this.

"They asked me where I lived," he said, "and I told them we had a castle in Scotland and a house in London. Then they got embarrassed and apologized."

I returned Podge's grin.

"So it's true, is it? The little girl in the film has disappeared?" Binky asked.

"I'm afraid she has," Fig said. She glanced up at me. "Georgiana, put that baby down. It isn't good for him to be held all the time, you know."

"The way things have been going today I don't want to leave him in a room alone," I said. "Maisie has other chores to carry out, you know. She can't always be with him."

"But you can't think there is actually danger in this house?" Fig demanded with an exaggerated sigh.

"I don't know what to think," I said. "It makes no sense that anyone could have had the opportunity to snatch Rosie, but she hasn't been found anywhere on the estate."

"Well, at least I suppose they're doing a good job stopping every car with a child in it," Binky said. He looked around the room. "Has anyone rung for tea yet?"

"It's only three thirty," Fig said, horrified.

"Yes, but Podge and I are starving," Binky replied. "We stayed for lunch at that school and frankly it was inedible."

"It was horrid, Mummy," Podge said. "It was meat with big lumps of chewy fat in it and slimy cabbage with lots of stalk, and then it was lumpy rice pudding. Daddy and I couldn't eat it."

"So I guess that school is no longer on the list?" I asked.

"I didn't want to go there anyway," Podge said. "They have to have cold showers every morning and the boys didn't seem friendly. And the lower school have to be servants to the boys in the top class and clean their shoes and things. And get beaten." He shot me a horrified look.

"Little boys need toughening up, Podge," Fig said. "You may be a general in the army someday."

"I want to be a farmer and have lots of cows and sheep," Podge said. "Anyway, I'll be in charge of our castle one day when I'm a duke, won't I, Daddy?"

"One day," Binky said, giving his son's hair a friendly ruffle. "Not for a long time, I hope. I don't want to face an early demise."

"I'll ring for tea," I said. "And we ought to have Addy brought down if Podge is here. She can tell you all about her brief brush with stardom."

"She did more acting today?"

"She did," Fig said.

"Only she objected to being kissed by a strange woman," I said. "That was when they discovered that Rosie was missing."

"Oh, I see." Binky's face was thoughtful.

"I know. It's all been quite awful," Fig agreed, reading his expression. "I kept thinking that they could have mistaken our daughter for this girl. Addy had a narrow escape."

"Poor little thing," he said. "Yes. Bring her down now. She needs her parents."

"And her brother," Podge said. "If I'd been here I'd have looked after her."

He came over and sat beside me, smiling at James, who responded with delighted squeaks. Such a sweet child.

Sir Hubert came in to join us.

"No news on Mrs. Simpson yet?" Binky asked him.

He shook his head. "At least I suppose we can be thankful that the press hasn't cottoned on to her staying with us. I was cross-questioned today about the little girl who is missing, but think how much worse that could have been if they'd found out Mrs. Simpson had gone missing too."

"I say." Something had just dawned on Binky. "You don't think there's a connection, do you? Some blighter hanging around our grounds grabbing people?"

"At least the police have now given the grounds a thorough search," Fig said. "And so far they haven't turned up any bodies."

I shuddered at the cold, dispassionate way she said this. She only had the briefest flash of motherliness.

"But you have to admit it does seem odd, two disappearances in one day, doesn't it?" Binky frowned. "Almost as if they must have something in common."

"You can rest assured that Mrs. Simpson did not run off with the child," Fig said, giving a malicious grin. "We saw just how fond she was of children last Christmas, didn't we?"

Addy was brought down by Nanny and entertained us with a dramatic rendering of the part she had acted. She was rather good. Did we see an acting career for her in the future (although she was not descended from my mother)?

The cakes served to us at tea were especially good again. I suspected Queenie had made them to impress the film actors, not us. By now James had fallen asleep in my arms. I carried him upstairs and laid him in his cot. As I looked out of a window on the way down from our bedroom I saw Darcy pulling up in the Bentley and went out to greet him.

"What on earth's going on?" he asked, coming up the steps into the house. "There are people milling about all over the village, news vans and police motorcars. And no film people here. Do we know what's happened?"

"The little girl, Rosie Trapp, has vanished," I said. "We've had a search party here, we've looked in every nook and cranny of the house so we can only assume it's foul play of some sort."

"Good God," Darcy said. "So that was the headline on the afternoon newspaper billboards in London. Child star kidnapped? That's what it said. It never occurred to me it could have anything to do with us. They don't really think she was kidnapped, do they?"

"Her mother does. She's been paranoid about kidnapping ever since she got here."

"And how do they think this was accomplished?" He shut the front door and took off his overcoat. "Aren't there enough people around to watch her all the time on that film set?"

"Her mother wondered whether she sneaked away to look at the farm animals. She had expressed an interest in seeing them."

"And a kidnapper just happened to be lurking at the farm?" He shook his head. "That's not very likely, is it? Weren't the boys all working up there?"

"There might have been a window of opportunity," I said. "Two of them were in the woods, stocking up on firewood for the house, and Jacob had gone into the village with a load of vegetables."

"So has anyone checked for tire tracks?"

"I did," I said. "There were no recent ones that I could see. But I did spot a small footprint. That could have been Addy's, of course."

"She could hardly have been kidnapped by someone on

foot." Darcy hung his coat on the hall stand. "No one could have carried her half a mile to the nearest road."

"That's true," I said. "I don't know what to think, Darcy. My common sense tells me there are no kidnappers in rural England and that we'll still find that she has wandered off and got lost."

He paused, thinking. "Anyway, we'll know soon."

"What do you mean?"

"If she has been kidnapped it will be for money. The mother will get a ransom note."

"Oh golly. Yes. Of course. And with all the headlines in all the evening papers the whole country will be looking for her. I just wish it would happen and we could breathe easily again. I feel so sorry for the little girl. Such an unnatural life to start with." Then I remembered the other big question hanging over us. "Any news on Mrs. Simpson? Did you have a chance to ask anybody in London?"

"Oh yes." He gave a grim smile. "I had a chat with HM's secretary at the palace. And you won't believe it. It turned out that Mrs. Simpson telephoned the king in the middle of the night and said she couldn't stay here for another minute with the press and public milling around and he had to come and fetch her right away. And knowing how infatuated your cousin is, he did just that, apparently. He drove himself to pick her up in the small hours of the morning and he's whisked her across the Channel to France. She's now installed in a château."

"Bloody woman," I said, hardly realizing that I was swearing. "All of us frantic about her and she didn't even think to leave a note. So what happens to her things? Are we supposed to ship them to her?"

"I suspect she's taken the items that are important to her."

"Her jewelry box and her mink," I said.

"And she probably doesn't care about the others. She'll just buy new clothes in Paris. But I suppose we should have the rest of the stuff boxed up, just in case we are instructed to send it on to her."

"I don't see why we should pay to send it on," I said. "David can send someone to pick it up if she wants it."

"You should rejoice that we're rid of her." Darcy reached out and stroked my cheek.

I nodded. "Yes. Thank heavens that's all explained," I said. "At least we can breathe more easily about one of our mysteries. Let's hope we get an equally good explanation for the other one soon."

But as it turned out the explanation wasn't so good.

Chapter 20

Saturday, November 7
Eynsleigh

Oh dear. Things are getting worse and worse. I can't stop worrying. Why, oh why did it have to happen here, on our estate? Surely a local person couldn't be involved.

When we came down to breakfast the next morning the film crew were setting up again in our long gallery. As Fig had predicted, we were gradually being taken over. The front door was open, letting in an icy draft and stirring the tapestry on the wall. From outside I could hear the murmur of the crowd at the gate that seemed to have grown even larger since yesterday. I looked out. From what I could see every newsman in England must now be out there. Maybe newsmen from America as well. I didn't envy the policeman stationed at the gate.

We ate porridge accompanied by clatter and shouts. Sir Hubert was already tucking into his breakfast when we arrived but there was no sign of Binky or Fig. I had just started on smoked haddock when Lana Lovett and Gloria Bishop came in. They paused in the doorway.

"Sorry to disturb you but they are not ready for us yet and the fire hasn't really warmed up that little sitting room," Lana said. "So we looked in here and . . ."

"Oh, smoked haddock, how lovely," Gloria said. She was already wearing a richly embroidered burgundy Elizabethan dress with a high collar and fur-trimmed cape over it. She looked the part of a former queen. Lana's dress was more provocative with a low-cut neckline. The screen version of Anne Boleyn.

"Do help yourselves and join us," Sir Hubert said before I could say anything.

"So kind." Gloria gave him her beaming smile. From the look that passed between them I wondered if they had been carrying on the flirtation and getting to know each other better without my noticing. The women both took generous plates of everything.

"Really the food at that so-called country club is not up to snuff," Lana said. "Their idea of breakfast is greasy bacon and greasier fried egg. And something awful called fried bread."

"Oh, I remember fried bread from my youth," Gloria said. "In those days I used to love it. I suppose it was one way to give us enough calories to keep warm in the winter when the houses had no heat. Now we have to watch our figures all the time."

I thought the plate in front of her did not exactly look like diet food.

They pulled up chairs at the table beside us.

"There's no news on the missing girl?" Sir Hubert asked.

"Not that we've heard. I haven't even seen Mrs. Trapp since yesterday. They aren't staying with us anyway," Gloria said. "They've rented a cottage nearby, so we gather. I thought that was a mistake at the time."

"Why was that?" Sir Hubert asked.

"Well, you don't want to be isolated in the middle of the country when you know nobody, do you? I'm not sure they are even on the telephone. The mother is always so protective and now look what's happened, poor woman."

"What about Dorothy?" I asked. "Does she stay at the country club with you?"

"Oh yes. She's with us. I imagine she's in her trailer right now getting dressed. Lana and I only came in because the first scene is scheduled to be shot in your house with just the two of us."

"So you're going to go ahead with filming in spite of the little girl being missing?" I asked.

Gloria sighed. "You know Cy. Money before anything. He wants to get every scene that does not include Rosie shot before we leave here. And now that we have access to the lovely rooms in this house he's filming some of the scenes that would have been shot on the set in Hollywood. Cy is thrilled about the real feel of this place." She spread a piece of toast with butter and took a tiny bite. "For myself I can't wait to get back. This place is quite unnerving, even before Rosie went missing. Oh, I don't mean your lovely house and your hospitality, Hubie dear. But the villagers . . . the way they stare. And they've found we're staying at the country club so we've had them lurking around and even looking in windows."

"I don't mind being looked at," Lana said. "But at least in Hollywood people are used to seeing movie stars everywhere. They don't look at us as if we are creatures from another planet as they do here. Frankly some of your locals look as if they'd murder you in your bed in a heartbeat. Not quite all there, you know. Too much inbreeding, I suspect."

"I think you'll find our local people are all good, solid, hard-working farmers," Sir Hubert said.

Phipps came into the dining room. "The morning post, Sir Hubert," he said, holding out a silver salver with the letters on it. Sir Hubert took it, glanced at the letters, then frowned.

"This one's for Mrs. Trapp," he said. "Didn't you just say she's not here?"

"We haven't seen her this morning," Lana said.

"I should drive it over to her cottage, then," Sir Hubert said. "A fan letter, do you think?"

Darcy reached out and touched his arm. "Careful. You should open it. It could be a ransom note from the kidnappers."

Sir Hubert shot him a startled look.

"Wait. Don't touch it," I heard myself shouting. Sir Hubert froze, staring at me. "There might be fingerprints on it."

"Oh. Right. Good thinking." He took out his handkerchief and carefully held the envelope as he slit it open with his knife. Then he extracted one sheet of paper.

"Good God," he exclaimed. "I'm afraid you're right."

I got up and went over to him, peering over his shoulder. It was one sheet of flimsy notepaper and on it was printed in big black uneven letters:

WE HAVE THE GIRL. LEAVE 10,000 POUNDS AT THE CROSSROADS NEAR THE BIG HOUSE AT MIDNIGHT TONITE OR YOU'LL NOT SEE HER AGAIN. BAD IDEA TO TELL THE COPS.

"That's terrible." Lana jumped up. "What do we do?"

"Of course we must tell the police," Sir Hubert said.

"But if they find out or see any kind of police presence they could kill her," Lana said.

"That wouldn't achieve anything," Sir Hubert said. "It would be just as simple to let her go at that point."

"Not if she could identify them or even give the police any clues to find them," Lana said.

"Mrs. Trapp spoke of the Lindbergh baby," I said. "That kidnapping did not end well. They offered the ransom money but the child was not returned. He or she was never found, I believe."

"His body was found months later," Gloria said. "Killed with a blow to the head."

I shivered. "And they never found the kidnapper?"

"They arrested a German immigrant, and he was sentenced to the electric chair but he always claimed he didn't do it," Lana said. "I believe the FBI thought members of the household might be involved, including the nanny herself. But they never proved anything and nothing more has happened."

"But what has this to do with Mrs. Trapp?" Sir Hubert

asked. "Did she have any reason to fear her daughter was in danger?"

"She seemed to," I said, thinking about this. "In fact she was rather paranoid about it. She has hired a bodyguard at home in California so perhaps there has been an attempt before?"

"So Mrs. Trapp should do exactly what the note tells her," Gloria said. "Ten thousand pounds is a small price for the safety of a child."

"I'm surprised it's so little," Darcy said. "If you go to the trouble of kidnapping why not make it fifty thousand?"

"Perhaps they thought the mother couldn't raise that much in another country," Sir Hubert replied.

"True. Then I suspect it might be a humble person for whom ten thousand seems like a fortune," Darcy said.

"So should we involve the police?" I asked. "It seems like taking a terrible risk."

"That would be up to Mrs. Trapp. I'll go and fetch her right now." Darcy stood up. "Where is this cottage?"

"On the right between this house and the village. We picked Rosie up the first morning," Gloria said. "Rose Cottage. Her mother said she picked it because of the name."

"I know where that is," I said. "I'll go." I got up but was still putting on my coat when the front door opened and Mrs. Trapp herself came in.

"Is there any news?" she asked, grabbing at my arm. "I have spent the worst night of my life. Not a second's sleep. Hoping for the best but picturing the worst. Is it in the morning papers, do you think? Will people be looking for her?"

"It was already in the London papers yesterday evening," I said.

"Well, that's good. Maybe we'll soon have her back, do you think?"

I put a hand on her shoulder. "Mrs. Trapp, I'm afraid we've had news. You've been sent a ransom note. You'd better come in and sit down."

She stumbled like a sleepwalker into the dining room and gave a heartrending sob when she saw the note. "Oh no. What am I going to do? How will I ever get ten thousand pounds this quickly?"

"I could advance you the money from my bank," Sir Hubert said. "They know and trust me. And let's hope it will be recovered when they arrest the kidnappers."

Mrs. Trapp waved her arms frantically. "We can't go to the police. We simply can't. We have to do exactly what these people say. I'll take the money myself to the crossroads and leave it there. Do you understand? Nobody else. It's my daughter's life that's at stake. I'm not risking it for ten thousand pounds." She stopped, considering. "How much is that, by the way?"

"About fifty thousand dollars," Darcy said. "Quite a lot of money."

"It sure is," Gloria said.

"Not for my daughter's life. I'd give my life savings for her."

We sat her down and gave her some coffee. I even offered breakfast but she turned it down. "I can't swallow a morsel," she said. "I can't think about anything else for one second."

Nobody felt much like eating after this. My haddock was

cold now. So was my coffee. The actresses were summoned to the film set. Darcy stressed upon them that they should not mention the ransom note to anybody.

"It could mean the child's life if the kidnappers panic," he said.

Sir Hubert suggested he go with Mrs. Trapp, to try to obtain the ransom money. Mrs. Trapp was adamant that they should not take the ransom note to show to the police in Haywards Heath.

"They can't know. Absolutely not. It's not your child whose life is at stake," she said.

As they went out of the room I remembered what we had been discussing. "Mrs. Trapp," I called.

She turned around, eyeing me suspiciously.

"You mentioned your fear of kidnappers when we first met you. You said Rosie had a bodyguard. Did you have some idea that this might happen? Have there been threats?"

"Not exactly," she said. "But I got suspicious. There was this guy, hanging around outside our house in Beverly Hills. Oh, we get plenty of crazy fans wanting to see Rosie, but he looked different. Long overcoat. And a beard. I told Mr. Trapp I didn't like the look of him."

So there was a Mr. Trapp! That was the first we'd heard of him.

"And what happened?"

"Mr. Trapp told Rosie's bodyguard and they went out to speak to him. They said he was quite harmless but a bit simple. But you never know. He could be working for a gang."

"But you never received any written threats?"

She shook her head. "Although Rosie gets a ton of fan mail. Some of those letters are weird . . . saying how they'd love a little daughter like her. How their own child died. Always made me nervous. I wouldn't show them to Rosie."

"Well, this is clearly a kidnapping for money and nothing else," Sir Hubert said. "I say the first thing we do is obtain that money, and then we can go from there."

He went to pick up the note, then looked at Darcy and me. "Should I leave this with you for now? You probably know what we should do with it better than me."

"Yes. Leave it," Darcy said. "We'll have to consider the best course of action."

Sir Hubert nodded, then sighed. "Come along, then, Mrs. Trapp. Let's go and get your money."

Chapter 21

November 7
Eynsleigh

Darcy said we could trust our servants and I was so sure, but now I don't know what to think.

I was left alone with Darcy. There was still no sign of Binky and Fig.

"We shouldn't talk here," Darcy said. "That was a bad idea. You never know who might be listening." He picked up the note and envelope, using his handkerchief. "We shouldn't leave these around for prying eyes."

"What do you mean?" I asked. "We're in our own house. Surely we can trust our servants."

"I expect we can," Darcy said, "but don't forget the film crews are coming in and out. We've just had those two actresses in here. We can't let the word of the ransom note get out."

We left the dining room, realized that we could not get to the morning room with the filming going on, so we headed back upstairs to our bedroom. James was still sleeping in his cot although it was almost time for his ten o'clock feed.

"What do you think we should do?" I asked as Darcy closed the door behind us. "I never thought something like this could happen in rural Sussex. England's green and pleasant land!"

Darcy put the letter down on the little desk in the corner. "I don't know what to think, or what we should do. In the end it's up to the mother. If she doesn't want the police involved then we have to respect that. But I tell you what . . . I think I might go to the crossroads and station myself there long before midnight."

"Darcy, that might be terribly dangerous," I said.

He actually smiled. "Not compared to some of the things I've done in my life," he said. "Besides, I do have a revolver and I'm quite a good shot, so I wouldn't worry for my own safety, only about making the wrong move and putting the child in danger."

"Oh golly, you're right," I said. "If you step in and arrest the kidnapper, or nappers, they may never tell you where Rosie is. And she could be locked up somewhere and die of starvation."

"Precisely. So maybe I'll watch and stay hidden and hope to follow them, or at least observe enough to allow the police to move in later."

I went over to him. "Oh, Darcy, this is so awful, isn't it? Why did it have to happen at our house?"

"The question is actually, How did it happen at our house? I have to think that someone here has to be involved. It's an inside job, as they say."

"Someone here? One of our staff, do you mean?"

He shook his head. "I can't believe that one of our staff would do anything so stupid. But we have recently employed those boys at the farm. We don't know all that much about them."

"The boys? But they are lovely. They would never do . . ." I paused. "Although it was strange that Jacob took the vegetables at the same time that the other two were in the woods."

"Almost as if it was planned that they should all be gone at the same time?" He nodded, considering this. "I suppose it is just possible that someone paid them a sum of money to be away at the same moment."

I toyed with what he had just suggested. "But how would they know when Rosie might want to visit the farm?"

"We have to consider that one of the film crew might be involved. Their cameramen and electricians came with them from America, didn't they?"

"I think so," I said. "I haven't actually spoken to any of them but they sounded like American accents when they were setting up just now."

"So what if one of them had criminal connections and saw the opportunity when this child didn't have her bodyguard around? It would be easy enough to lure her up to the farm when the boys weren't there."

"I suppose it would on such a foggy day, especially when filming was going on and everyone was occupied. We need to get a list of everyone working here and hand it over to the police."

"Not the local police," he said. "They wouldn't have an idea.

They'd botch it all up. I'll take it up to London and run it past my connections."

"Yes. Good idea," I said.

He was still frowning. "I'm afraid there's another thing we have to consider. The boys were extras on the set the other day, weren't they? Maybe one of them was paid to ask Rosie if she wanted to visit the piglets with him while her stand-in was filming."

I stared at him, trying to picture sweet-natured Jacob or easygoing Donnie or shy Bill luring a little girl to be kidnapped. But then they had grown up in an orphanage and had hard lives. If they had been offered enough money, who knows what they might do?

"Jacob did take the pony and trap into the village," Darcy reminded me. "What if the little girl was hidden among the vegetables?"

"Jacob would never do a thing like that," I said angrily. "He's such a sweet boy. Always so helpful."

"Money is a great seducer," Darcy said. "And we must accept that they are simple boys, not much education. Perhaps the kidnapper had not divulged what he planned to do. If he'd said it was some kind of publicity stunt?"

"We should go and talk to them immediately," I said.

"I presume the police questioned them yesterday." Darcy walked over to the window and stared out. Today the fog had lifted and frost sparkled on the grass. It looked like the perfect country scene and it was hard to believe that something so horrible could have happened here.

"And probably put the wind up them," he went on. "So now they'll be on their guard and not tell us anything."

"If they were tricked into helping with this without realizing what it was, they'll be terrified now," I said. "Maybe they'll be happy to talk to us and get it off their chests. Especially if we let them know that we'll speak up for them and let the police know that they didn't mean any harm."

"If they didn't mean any harm," he said. "Georgie, we don't know. They seem like nice boys but with their backgrounds, who knows?"

"I can't believe it," I said firmly. So firmly that James whimpered, opened his eyes and looked around.

"Now you've done it." Darcy smiled as he went over to the cot, made faces at James and was rewarded with a giggle. "I guess someone is going to want to be fed any moment."

I glanced at the clock. "You're right. So a visit to the boys will have to wait."

"I think that's wise anyway." Darcy scooped up James, giving him a kiss. "Let them think they are not suspected of anything but then keep an eye on them. You might pay them a visit later with the children, and just casually let them know that Rosie hasn't just wandered off, but she has been kidnapped. Watch their reactions."

"Good idea," I said. "And you?"

He handed James to me.

"I'll get a complete list of all those who came across from America and are working on the set, then I'm off to Scotland Yard with the ransom note. They can dust for fingerprints and analyze the letter writing. . . ."

"But it's only printing, and very bad printing at that."

"They have profilers. They can sometimes tell what kind of person would print in that way. Oh, and the envelope . . . did you see where it was posted?"

"No. I didn't look," I said. "Sir Hubert opened it." I went over to the desk and looked at the envelope. "There is a stamp but no postmark," I said. "So either the post office forgot to frank it, or . . ."

"It never was posted in the first place but somehow deposited with the rest of the post."

Darcy frowned. "You know what that means, don't you? It was written by someone here. Someone who had the opportunity to slip an extra letter into the postman's bag or even put it on the salver before Phipps brought us the post."

"That means one of the crew or someone in our house," I said.

"Or . . ." Darcy paused, wagging a finger at me as the thought struck him. "One of those people who've been lurking around the front gate. The newsmen. The local admirers. That would be easy enough. The postman arrives and has to wait while the policeman guarding the gate opens it for him. And while he waits someone slips in the letter."

I stared, my mouth open. "So you are now suggesting that the kidnapper was among that crowd, not one of us at all."

"It's possible." He gave an impatient sigh.

"Which puts us back to square one, doesn't it?"

"Not quite. It would still require someone to take Rosie when nobody was looking. My bet is still someone on the set, or one of our boys." He picked up the note and envelope again. "I'll get a big envelope from my desk downstairs to put these in and I'll be off to London, then."

Before I could say what I intended to do James let out an impatient wail.

"I know what I'll be doing next," I said, and carried him over to my nursing chair.

Chapter 22

November 7
Eynsleigh

I don't know what to think. This feels like the longest day of my life.

James seemed to pick up my tension, nursed only fretfully and then didn't want to be put back in his crib. I carried him down to the drawing room. Voices came in from the long gallery, Gloria's sexy melodious tones and Dorothy's clear, high voice.

"Mother, you can't let him take her. She's done nothing wrong."

"She's the daughter of an adulteress, a whore. She's a bastard in the eyes of the church."

It seemed that nobody else was thinking about Rosie. Fig wandered in soon after I had settled with James.

"Oh, Georgie, you haven't brought that child down again, have you? Don't you realize how spoiled he will become? There must be rules. There must be a routine." She settled herself in an armchair near the fire across from me.

"He was upset this morning, probably because I am upset," I said. "I'm not leaving my baby to cry alone."

"You have a nursemaid of sorts. Let her deal with it."

"She's had more than enough to do, acting as maid to Mrs. Simpson and to you, as well as everything she has to do for me."

"That odious woman," she said. "I wonder if she'll ever send for those things she left behind. She does dress well, doesn't she?"

I sensed what she was hinting. Maybe she and I could help ourselves to items left behind. I had to chuckle. "Fig, she is the skinniest woman I've ever met. You and I have had children and those clothes would never fit. Besides, I'm sure she'll want them eventually."

"Nonsense. She'll get *him* to buy her more, the way he buys her jewels. I note she took the jewel case with her. Valuable stuff in that. If someone had tried a robbery to get their hands on those jewels, I'd understand. But any sort of other crime is preposterous."

"Not so preposterous," I said. "This is to go no further but Mrs. Trapp has had a ransom note."

"Good heavens. Are you serious?"

I nodded. "Money to be left at the crossroads at midnight."

"That sounds ridiculously dramatic. Almost like a pantomime."

"You're right." A log shifted on the fire and I stared at the sparks dancing up the chimney. "It does sound overdramatic."

"It has to be a first-time kidnapper trying his hand, having seen kidnappings on the newsreels or in the cinema."

"It does seem that way," I said. "All the same, she may be in equal danger—more so maybe as an amateur might panic if he thought the police were closing in."

"So what are they going to do? Have the police been told?"

"Mrs. Trapp was adamant that they weren't involved. Sir Hubert's gone to try to get the money from his bank."

"Brave man. He may never see it again." She sniffed. "You can't see me doing that out of the goodness of my heart."

No, I can't, I thought.

"And Darcy has gone up to London to see pals at Scotland Yard. They'll test for fingerprints and analyze the writing. And Darcy plans to be at the crossroads watching and waiting."

"Isn't that awfully risky?"

"He says he'll stay hidden. Observe the vehicle. Get a description of the man or men."

She sighed. "Let's hope it works out satisfactorily. That poor child. Probably locked in some dark cellar or something."

"I know. I can't stop thinking about it." I bent to kiss James, who was now gazing at me contentedly.

Fig was staring out of the window, frowning. "I still can't see how it was done. Surely someone noticed the child being led away, or slipping away on her own? All those people standing around out there . . . not all of them working at one moment. One of them must have seen her."

"You'd have thought so, wouldn't you? Where's Binky, by the way? Off to another school?"

"No, he's up with Podge. They are going through the schools they've seen so far, what they liked about them and what they didn't. I told him that he didn't need Podge's opinion. Parents know best what is right for the child. You can't choose a school because the child liked the dormitory or the cricket pitch. But you know Binky—far too soft."

"I think he remembers his own horrible experience at that school in Scotland before my mother rescued him and sent him to Eton."

"That school might have done wonders for him. Toughened him up a bit. That's what he needed."

"Fig, not everybody needs to be tough. Darcy loved his school. He wants James to go there."

"Well, Darcy was good at sports, I imagine. Anyone good at sports loves their school. Binky was an absolute duffer, as you can imagine. Not good at anything much, bless his heart."

She gave an impatient little sigh. "So I suppose all we do is sit and wait today. I just hope they don't have the nerve to ask to use Adelaide again in place of the missing girl."

Binky and Podge came in as she was speaking. "What-ho, old bean," he said to me. "And look at young Jamie. Isn't he growing splendidly?"

"What's Podge doing down here at this hour?" Fig asked, frowning at her son. "I hope we're not slipping into bad habits by watching Georgiana."

"We thought we'd take a look at another school we heard

about yesterday," Binky said. "It's near Brighton. Good sea air, don't you know."

"Brighton?" Fig's tone was damning. "Not the sort of place I'd wish for my son and heir. It's the place people go for a dirty weekend, isn't it?"

"It's not exactly *in* Brighton, Fig. On the cliffs outside the town."

"And not that close to Georgiana either. I'd want the children to be able to go to their relatives' for half terms. You couldn't expect Darcy to drive to Brighton to pick them up."

"It's not that far, Fig," I said. "We love driving into Brighton sometimes. And not for a dirty weekend."

"What's a dirty weekend, Mummy?" Podge asked.

"Nothing that you should know about," she said, "and nothing that either of your parents has ever done or would ever do."

Binky put an arm around Podge's shoulder. "Come on, then, son. Let's be off."

"Bye, Auntie Georgie," Podge called as they left the room.

"What was wrong with the school that Podge liked the other day?" I asked.

"Too lenient for my taste. And lots of art and that kind of bosh. What's more it's horribly expensive."

"I expect they all are," I said. "I plan to keep James at home until it's time for Darcy's school. I'm sure there are some excellent day schools nearby. Besides . . ." I glanced down at my now sleeping baby. "Seven is awfully young to go away from home."

I stood up carefully so that I didn't wake him and carried him up to bed.

THE MORNING PASSED painfully slowly. I waited for a telephone call from Darcy. I wished I could talk to Granddad. He'd been in difficult situations like this. He'd have good ideas. But alas he was not on the telephone. He refused to have such luxuries installed. In an emergency I could ring the pub at the end of his street and they'd pass on a message. I was tempted, but I knew he wouldn't come back here while Fig was in residence.

I waited for Sir Hubert and Mrs. Trapp to return. It wasn't until just before luncheon that he came back.

"Well, that's done," he said. "What a tricky situation. My bank manager wanted to know what I needed the money for in such a hurry and you know how I hate to lie. I had to bluster and say it was a private matter so that now he thinks I'm paying off a woman or something. Anyway, I finally was given the money. It's in a suitcase and it's with Mrs. Trapp at her cottage."

"Is that wise?" Fig asked. "All that money and no man to guard her. Any thief worth his salt wouldn't have to wait until midnight at the crossroads. He could just break in and take the money."

Sir Hubert nodded. "I felt the same way. I offered to stay with her but she didn't want me there. She was adamant she had to handle it alone. Almost pushed me away." He sank onto the sofa on the other side of the fire. "Poor woman. I suppose I can understand what she's going through. I asked if I should telephone her husband and she said no, I shouldn't. He couldn't know. It would drive him crazy."

"I've been wondering about that husband," I said. "She only

mentioned him once in passing. Are they happily married, do you think? Or . . ." I broke off. "Golly. You don't think her husband could have anything to do with the kidnapping, do you? He doesn't have custody of Rosie, or he wants a share of Rosie's money and is not getting it?"

Sir Hubert sighed. "Who knows. I wish I'd never invited the dratted people in the first place. It's been nothing but trouble."

"Darcy has taken a list of all the Americans up to London, where his pals can check on their backgrounds. Presumably they'd know if there had been a dispute between the Trapps and if they were now separated."

"We can't spend every minute worrying about it, Georgie." He put an arm around my shoulder. "Come on. Let's go and have some lunch."

We ate lunch in silence. Filming in our long gallery had apparently ended and they were setting up for another scene on our front steps. This meant having the front door open again, letting in more cold air. James would want his two o'clock feed soon and I had promised Darcy that I would pay a visit to the boys at the farm. I decided to do that right away. I went up to the nursery to ask if Addy would like to join me. Of course she jumped at the chance. Nanny made her take her wellies to wear outside and bundled her up in her coat, hat and scarf. We picked up James and took him down to his pram, tucked him in warmly, then set off, the pram bumping over the frozen grass, which he seemed to enjoy. I tried to locate that little footprint again but couldn't see it this time. I expect big boots had walked over it. But I did notice that Addy wore her wellies. I had to assume she wore them every time she visited the farm. It would not have been her print, then. So Rosie did come up here.

I looked around, then heard laughter coming from the cottage. I went over and tapped on the door. There was the sound of chairs being pushed back, scrambling, and then Jacob opened the door. He looked shocked when he saw me.

"Oh, your ladyship," he said. "We were just finishing up our dinner. We were running late today, on account of that filming and everything."

"I don't want to keep you from your meal, Jacob," I said. "I just brought the children up to look at the piglets and the chickens since it's a nice day for once. Not like yesterday. That fog was pretty bad, wasn't it?"

"It was, my lady," he agreed. "Cold and damp and most unfriendly."

"I expect you got pretty chilled going into the village with that pony and trap."

Did I detect a wary look crossing his face? "I did. That's right. But those cabbages had to be delivered when I promised them."

"Of course." I noticed he hadn't invited me in, but then he probably didn't want me to see the state of the place. I peered past him and saw Bill and Donnie both staring warily at me from the table.

"Excuse me, my lady," Donnie called, "but there's no more news about the little girl, is there?"

"I'm afraid not," I said, not mentioning the ransom note. It would be interesting to see how much they knew without being told. "I presume the police asked you questions yesterday?"

"They did." Donnie got up and came over to join Jacob at the door. "They fair grilled us. Of course we told them that Bill and me were up in the woods all morning and didn't hear or see nothing. And Jacob was gone into the village."

"So if the child had come up here to see the farm there would have been nobody around?"

"That's right, my lady."

"I suppose none of you noticed any outsiders at the farm recently? Any tramps?"

"The only outsiders were those film people," Donnie said. "Some of them came up and took a look around to see if there was anywhere worth using for their film."

"When was that?"

"The first day they were here," Donnie said. "And then some of them came up for the Guy Fawkes bonfire, didn't they?"

"Yes, they did."

So plenty of them knew the lay of the land up here.

"How was it acting in a film, then?" I asked, apparently changing the subject and lightening the mood. "I hope you got paid."

"They've promised to pay us all right," Bill said from the table.

"Did you enjoy it?" I looked at Jacob.

He blushed. "I didn't," he said. "I wish I hadn't said I'd do it."

"Oh, why was that?" I asked innocently.

His face was still beet red.

"He got teased in the village about wearing tights," Donnie replied, giving Jacob a nudge. "His girlfriend called him a sissy."

"Robin Hood wore tights and he was an outlaw," I said. "That's what they did in those days."

James decided he'd had enough of lying in his pram when it was now his feeding time. He let out a loud cry of indignation. Addy had wandered over to the chickens.

"I should be getting back," I said.

"Did you come up here for a reason, my lady?" Jacob asked.

"Only to give the children some fresh air. I didn't see anyone around and just wondered where you were."

He nodded. "I see." He shot me another brief stare.

"Jacob, when you went into the village, you didn't notice anything strange then, did you?"

"Strange?"

"A motorcar parked somewhere? A delivery van? Anyone along the lane?"

"Can't say that I did, my lady. To tell the truth it was so darned cold that I just wanted to get to the village and get it over with."

"I can imagine." I smiled at him. "But if any of you remember anything that might help find this little girl, you will come and tell me, won't you?"

"Do you really think she's been kidnapped, then?" Donnie asked. "That someone's taken her?"

"We do," I said. "And it's possible her life might be in danger."

"No! Surely not," Jacob said. "I wish these darned film people had never come here. They've been nothing but trouble from the first day."

I gathered Addy from the chickens and we made our way

back. Jacob knew something, I was sure. He had hardly said a word, when usually he was the spokesman for the three. And the pain on his face when I mentioned kidnapping . . . Had he been lured into being part of it? Had he really taken Rosie into the villages hidden among those cabbages? And now he'd be terrified to own up because he'd be complicit. Poor boy . . . I stopped, thinking. Or was he a poor boy? Had he been part of the plotting of this?

Chapter 23

November 7
Eynsleigh

Now it seems that yet another complication has entered our lives!

This was all I needed.

I did a lot of thinking while I fed James. The bad printing on the note. The cabbages conveniently taken at that particular moment. Was it possible all three boys had conspired to kidnap Rosie? Perhaps she had walked innocently up to the farm and they had seized their chance. Was it even possible that she was being held at the house right now? But we had shouted for her. She would have heard. Even if she was gagged and tied up she could have thumped around, knocked over furniture . . . unless she was unconscious. I shuddered. It was too horrible to think about.

James fell asleep in my arms and I laid him gently back in his cot. I wondered when Darcy would come home and if he'd found out anything important. If those boys had written the note, then I was sure they were not sophisticated enough to have worried about leaving fingerprints on it. Or on the envelope. How many hours until midnight? Would Darcy be in danger if he hid near the crossroads? Would he be able to track down the kidnappers after they delivered Rosie safely? And the worst question of all . . . was Rosie still safe?

The long gallery was empty and I retreated to the safety of the morning room, which was luckily Fig-free. The morning papers lay on the low table by the fire. Headlines screamed:

MISSING FILM STAR!
NEW SHIRLEY TEMPLE TAKEN!
ALL ENGLAND HUNTS FOR LITTLE ROSIE.

All England was hunting and yet it seemed that she must still be nearby, if that note had not come through the post. Drat Darcy, I thought. If he hadn't taken the motorcar I could have gone into the village and asked questions there. But here I was, stuck alone and worrying, unable to do anything.

Were they still filming outside at our front door? I got up and as I crossed the foyer, there came a resounding knock at the door. I hesitated, wondering if this was part of their film and I'd get shouted at for opening the door and thus spoiling their shot. But when it came again I opened it to see a young policeman standing there. "Beg pardon, your ladyship," he said, "but there's a woman at the gate who's demanding to see you. She claims she's the Duchess of Rannoch. But I told her she couldn't be because the Duchess of Rannoch is already staying here. So then she says . . ."

"Darling!" A clear voice echoed across the forecourt. "This brute of a man was keeping me from seeing my only child!" And my mother glided toward me on her high heels, her blue eyes sparkling from under a large silver fox hat, her arms open.

The policeman looked at me for reaction. "It's all right, Constable," I said. "It's my mother. The dowager duchess."

"Begging your pardon, then, your ladyship," he said. "But I thought, you see . . ."

"It's all right, my good man. You were only doing your duty." She turned that well-known charm on him and he blushed like a schoolboy. She had that effect on all men.

"Let's go inside. It's cold out here," I said.

"Not nearly as cold as Berlin," she replied. "Darling, I haven't taken my mink off for a week."

"What are you doing here?" I asked. "Why didn't you send a telegram to let us know you were coming?"

"What am I doing?" She slipped her arm through mine as we went up the front steps. "Why, come to see my darling daughter and my adorable grandson, of course." She paused, with dramatic timing on the top step, and looked around. "What are those caravans and tents doing on the estate? You can't have turned the place into a holiday camp. Not in the middle of winter. What on earth is going on? Is that a film camera? Don't tell me they are shooting a film at your house."

"Right first time," I said. "We have been invaded by a film company."

She paused again, gloved hand up to her cheek. "But wait. Not the same film that is in all the papers? The child star vanished?"

"I'm afraid it is."

"How absolutely ghastly. What do they think happened to her?"

"We're afraid she has been kidnapped," I said, not wanting to share the details of what we now knew. "Darcy's helping the police."

"But filming is still going on?" She stared at men who were moving cables.

"I suppose they only have a limited time in England," I said, charitably. "They are shooting all the scenes that don't involve Rosie."

Her eyes opened wider. "Good God," she said. "Is that Gloria Bishop? Darling, she must be almost my age and yet she's still getting the leading lady roles?"

"She's playing Catherine of Aragon," I said. "It's a film about Henry and his wives."

"I was in a film like that, don't you remember? We went to Hollywood together. Didn't I play Catherine?"

"It never got finished. The director was murdered."

"Oh yes." She stepped ahead of me into the foyer. "Such a shame. I believe I was rather good as Catherine. I don't think Gloria has what it takes. Not queenly enough. She came from humble origins, you know." She took off the fox fur hat and handed it to me as if I were a lackey.

I looked at my mother and chuckled. "Mummy, you weren't exactly born in a castle yourself."

She drew herself up to all five foot three of her. "If I had humble origins I have chosen to forget them," she said. "All anyone needs to know about me is that I am the dowager duchess of Rannoch, and soon to be Frau von Strohheim."

"How is Max?" I helped her off with her coat. "I'm surprised they let you travel on your own. When you were with that group of ladies in Paris you had a minder."

"That was because Frau Goebbels was with us. She has to be looked after," Mummy said. "Besides, I came with Max. It's only a weekend thing. Some function with the German ambassador and a few of the right sort of Englishmen."

"Fascists, you mean? That Blackshirt lot?"

She shrugged. "I really couldn't say. You know me, if there's a party I go along. And I've never asked my men about their politics or religious beliefs. As long as they keep me amused and in diamonds I really don't care."

She strode ahead of me into the drawing room, where a fire was burning brightly and a pleasant warmth greeted us.

"Mummy, you should care," I said, closing the door behind us. "Germany is becoming really dangerous, Darcy says. Hitler is planning for war."

"Not with England, darling. He adores the English. He told me so. He told me I was the perfect flower of English womanhood. I'm starring in a few little propaganda films, you know. Inspiring German women to be thrifty for the sake of the fatherland. They assure me it's all very harmless."

"I don't think it is harmless, Mummy. You do realize that once you marry Max you'll be a German citizen and therefore not allowed to leave, even if you want to."

She shrugged and gave a little pout, something she always did when anyone crossed her. "I may not actually marry Max. His mother has died, fortunately, so we don't have to be proper and legitimate and I think Max likes the idea of freedom as much as I do. We get along frightfully well, you know. And my German is coming along in leaps and bounds. We actually converse at times. Although I don't see much of him. He's so terribly busy these days with all his factories doing so well."

"Making guns and tanks." I gave her my most severe frown.

"I really don't know what they make." She shrugged again. "And I'm sure English factories are also making the same sort of things to keep up. Besides, I just told you. There won't be a war with England whatever happens. So don't let it worry you. Be glad that your mother is well and happy and adored."

She sank onto the chair nearest the fire. "It's awfully quiet. Are we all alone in the house?"

"Sir Hubert's home."

"Really?" Did I detect a flicker of interest in her eyes? "For long?"

"I couldn't say. He was in Hollywood, advising on a film about mountains, which was where he met this lot. I sense that Gloria Bishop and he . . ."

"Gloria Bishop? Surely not. She's not his type. She must be flinging herself at him, eyeing a title. Some actresses do that, you know."

"Is my father no longer staying?" she asked.

"He escaped when he heard that Fig and Binky were coming. They've been here for a week or so, visiting schools for Podge."

"They're not sending him to school already, are they? The little mite can't be more than four."

"He's going to be seven, Mummy."

"My, how time flies," she said. "It won't be long before I'm forty."

I did have to laugh at this. "My mathematics isn't that bad. You had me when you were twenty-four and I'm now twenty-six."

"Age is just a number. I look forty," she said. "Or rather I look thirty-nine."

This was true. She did. Her face, beneath its skillfully applied makeup, was perfect; not a hair was out of place. Of course a lot of money was spent on that face and hair. "So are the film people staying here too?"

"No. They've been put up at the country club on the way to Haywards Heath. They have started coming into the house to warm up, and then to shoot various scenes, and Sir Hubert has invited them to dinner, which they've jumped at."

"Are they staying for dinner tonight?"

"I haven't heard," I said. "Everyone has been cut up about the child's disappearance."

Mummy looked around. "I hope you can find a place to squeeze in little *moi*," she said. "You know me. I don't need much. Just a tiny corner to sleep in."

I laughed again. "You know very well that you want luxury and adoration. I expect Max is staying at the Ritz. Why aren't you staying there?"

"Max is staying with the German ambassador," she said, then leaned forward to share a confidentiality. "And I gather that a certain person may be joining them for dinner tomorrow. It was thought my presence might make things awkward."

"Certain person?"

She tapped her finger to the side of her nose, then mimed a crown on her head.

"You mean the king?"

She gave a careless wave. "I still can't think of him as that, but yes, David the king."

"Golly" was all I could say.

Chapter 24

November 7
Eynsleigh

I hate to say it but my mother is the last person I wanted to see at this moment. As if we haven't got enough to worry about!

We settled Mummy in a suitable bedroom. She had wanted the one now occupied by Mrs. Simpson's possessions—"But I always stay in that one!"—but I thought it wiser not to mention that the lady had recently stayed with us. Mummy was not good at holding her tongue. She said she was going to freshen up, then came downstairs looking incredibly glamorous in an ivory trouser suit with a red cashmere shawl flung carelessly over her shoulders. That's when it hit me. Either she wanted to make sure that Sir Hubert's eyes did not turn elsewhere or she had known about the film people all along and wanted to remind the film world that she was still as desirable and glamorous as Gloria Bishop or Lana Lovett. Of course she had known, sly minx.

The moment these thoughts passed through my mind I felt that usual weight of disappointment that came with my mother. It wasn't me she wanted to see at all. It was Hubert or film directors or both. As usual I didn't matter. She did come up to pay attention to her grandchild, although insisted on covering herself with towels in case he dribbled or peed on her Chanel.

"So why isn't he up in the nursery, darling?" she asked, holding him at distance, just in case. "I remember Zou Zou and I outfitted that nursery with everything a baby could possibly need."

"It's being occupied by Podge and Addy and their nanny at the moment," I said. "Besides it's so much more convenient to have James here when I'm breastfeeding him."

"Not still doing that! Darling, what about your figure? Your boobs will droop, you know."

"I really don't mind," I said. "This is more important to me." And I took James back from her. He responded with a beaming smile.

"You say your brother's nanny is up in the nursery? Where is yours, then?"

"I don't have one yet. I have a nursemaid, who does all the less pleasant things like changing nappies."

"But my dear girl." She put a firm hand on my arm. "You must have a nanny. Otherwise that child will rule your life. You won't be able to travel, go to dinner parties. . . . It's time you got back into the social swing. Darcy will expect it, you know. He's never exactly been the hermit type."

"We're just fine as we are for the moment, thank you," I said, bouncing James and making him giggle. "And I do intend to get a proper nanny, eventually. But we have to think of the expense. We're not exactly rich, in fact right now we're poor farmers."

She gave that lovely tinkling laugh. "Don't be silly. You know I'll pay for a nanny or Zou Zou would, or I'm sure Sir Hubert would."

"Mummy, I don't like taking other people's money," I said. Unlike you, I thought but did not say. "Shall we bring him downstairs?"

"Isn't it rather bad for them to be spoiled with too much attention?" she asked.

"I'm sure I didn't have too much attention in my early years," I said with a grin. "But no, I don't think it's bad for them. It makes him feel loved and wanted."

I brought James down to the drawing room and rang for tea. And as we were having tea Mummy was rewarded with Sir Hubert bringing in the stars and directors.

"Oh good. I hoped tea was being served," he said. "These poor people are at the end of their tether. Every newspaperman in the country is now lurking and trying to get into the grounds. One even climbed a tree and fell onto one of the caravans. So I brought them in to cheer them up." He stopped, froze, stared at Mummy. "Claire!" His voice cracked. "When did you arrive? I had no idea you were coming."

"Just arrived, darling," Mummy said, extending her hand to him as if she expected it to be kissed. "Last-minute, spur-of-the-moment thing. Max has meetings in London so I thought I'd see my adorable grandchild."

"Good heavens," Gloria said. "You're Claire Daniels. I'm a great admirer."

"How kind." Mummy still had the hand extended.

"I remember you were in Hollywood not too long ago," Gloria said. "We chatted in the cafeteria on the Golden Pictures lot."

"Of course," Mummy said, giving no indication that she remembered ever meeting this woman. "Won't you all sit down. I'm sure the kitchen can come up with enough cakes for all of us, if we're not watching our figures, that is."

I got up and pulled the bell. The film people sat, staring at Mummy in fascination. In contrast to her they were now all dressed in their street clothes and there was nothing glamorous about them. Grant Hathaway came over and perched on the arm of Mummy's chair. "I can't believe you're no longer working, with those looks," he said, gazing at her long and hard.

"She married a duke, remember," Gloria said.

"You're a duchess?" He looked impressed. "We've already met one this week. Two is a bit overwhelming."

"I'm merely the dowager," Mummy said modestly, returning Grant's gaze. "My husband the duke is no longer with us." And she'd been through several husbands since then although she failed to mention it. I felt the electricity in the air. "And of course I'm not averse to accepting the occasional acting assignment if someone makes me the right offer." Her gaze swept the room, then she asked, innocently, "Where is your sister-in-law, the current duchess, by the way, Georgiana?"

"I haven't seen her all afternoon," I said.

"Let's hope she hasn't been kidnapped too," Grant said, getting an embarrassed chuckle from the others.

"Not funny, Grant," Gloria snapped. "Now what is being done about that poor child?"

"Darcy has it under control," I said. "Don't worry. There's nothing we can do except wait and pray."

"Which poor child is this?" Mummy asked.

"The child star who has vanished," Cy Marvin said.

"Probably had enough of acting and gone home to lead a normal life," Mummy said. "I know I felt that way when I was a child star."

I hadn't known she was a child star, or was she just saying that so they all thought she was younger than her true years?

"As I said, Darcy is taking care of it, Mummy," I repeated forcefully.

Sir Hubert's eyes were fixed on Mummy in the chair, Grant sitting rather close to her and the look that was passing between them. "I can't believe you are here, Claire," he said, "and looking marvelous, as usual."

"Thank you, my darling," she said. "And you're not looking so bad yourself. That tan really suits you."

"Yes, I was in Hollywood," he said. "Lots of swimming pools."

"I do love a man with a tan," Mummy said and glanced up at Grant, who was of the ultimate bronzed face. Oh dear, I thought. I hope she's not making a play for yet another man. But then it struck me that perhaps she was finding a way to leave Max before Germany got too awful.

Mrs. Holbrook came in. "You rang, my lady, Sir Hubert?"

"Mrs. H, can you possibly find enough tea and cakes for these starving people?" he asked jovially.

"I'll do my best, sir," she said. "I believe Queenie has been baking again."

She had hardly left when Fig came in, looked around her in horror and then started to creep out again.

"Do come and join us, Duchess," Grant said.

She gave an embarrassed half smile.

"They were worried about you," I couldn't resist saying.

"I was in the library, writing letters. I write to Mummy and Ducky every week, you know. Ducky and Foggy are back at their villa in France for the winter, lucky things."

Ducky was her sister, married to the lecherous Foggy. The villa in question was a miserably small house on a backstreet in Nice but I said nothing. Fig came in and perched awkwardly on one of the upright chairs. "Is Darcy not back?"

"I don't know when he'll be back or if we'll see him before this evening," I said and turned to address the company. "So you're finished filming for the day, I presume."

"We can't do much more without Rosie," Cy Marvin said. "Who knows what will happen now. We may have to scrap the whole damned thing unless she's found soon."

An awkward silence descended. I was conscious of the deep ticktock of the grandfather clock, the crackle of burning logs on the fire and then, mercifully, the rattle of a trolley. To my horror Queenie came in, red-faced from pushing it. When she saw who was in the drawing room her face went even pinker.

"Bloody hell," she muttered. "I brought your tea, missus. Do you want me to pour for you?"

"I think I'll pour, thank you," I said, getting up hurriedly and knowing how disaster-prone Queenie was. If tea went over Mummy's cream pantsuit we'd never hear the last of it.

"Then I'll hand around," she said. "And I baked some lovely little cakes." She pointed to a mound of small rock cakes.

"Oh, interesting." Lana studied them. "I don't think I've eaten these before. What do you call them?"

"Me? I call them drop-deads," she said. "That was our family name because my mum's cakes were so heavy that you could kill someone with one."

"How amusing." Lana gave a nervous chuckle. "Then I must try one." Queenie picked one up and plopped it onto a plate, handing it to Lana. "Here you are then, missus."

Lana took a bite, then nodded. "It's rather good. I'm impressed."

Queenie went bright red again.

"That will be all for now, thank you, Queenie," I said.

"Oh, I don't mind staying to see if they need a second cuppa." She gave me a look of defiance.

"On second thought, you pour and I'll hand around," I said. We managed this without any accidents, although I just stopped Queenie from dropping sugar lumps into each cup without asking.

"I'm afraid my cook is rather starstruck," I said.

"Well, there is quite a lot of star power for one room," Mummy remarked.

Queenie's head jerked around. "Blimey. I didn't notice your mum," Queenie said. "Whatcha, missus."

"Claire Daniels is your mother?" Lana asked.

"How is that even possible?" Grant said, idly sliding a hand over her shoulder. "Unless you had a child at twelve."

"Flatterer." She gave him that dazzling smile. "I may not be in the first flush of youth but I work hard at keeping my looks, as I imagine you do, Gloria darling."

Gloria shot her a look that was not friendly. "I don't profess to be a day over thirty," she said.

We all looked up as wind suddenly buffeted the windows, followed by a great squall of rain.

"Oh no. What next," Lana exclaimed. "Whose idea was it to come to this goddamned country. Rain, fog, sleet, hail. Give me sunny California any day."

"But at least we'll have realism in our shots, Lana honey," Cy said.

I had just realized that once again Dorothy was not with them. Did they have no concerns about her being kidnapped? Or was she not such a valuable commodity as Rosie? And this time quiet little Nora Pines was not included either.

"I've got a splendid idea," Sir Hubert said. "Why don't you all stay for an early supper? I'm sure Chef can rustle up something simple." He looked at me.

"I should go and ask him what he had planned for dinner," I said, not at all relishing this task. I did not think Pierre would take well to yet another meal sprung on him. Did they not realize that a real chef started prepping his meals hours in advance? I excused myself and went down to the kitchen. Chef, as I suspected, was not pleased.

"Who do these people think I am—a magician? I wave my wand and poof, a meal appears."

"What were you planning for our meal tonight?" I asked.

"The boeuf bourguignonne," he said.

"Then wouldn't there be enough of that, if you did some more potatoes and vegetables? It's only five extra people."

He shrugged. "I can try. Then what do we eat? Your staff? Grass, like cows?"

"I'm really sorry, Chef," I said. "I didn't invite them."

"Is okay, my lady," he said. "You are good person. I make omelets for the staff and scalloped potatoes. And Queenie can make one of her puddings."

Queenie! The thought shot through my head. I'd left her alone in a roomful of celebrities. I rushed up again, just in time to hear her say, "Sorry about that. This pot does drip sometimes."

I was relieved to find the person she had dripped on was Fig and not one of the celebrities. I took over. We had a leisurely tea, Sir Hubert gave them a tour of the house, which was not wise as they found several other rooms they would love to utilize, and then we sat down for supper. The boeuf proved to be delicious and Queenie made a good apple crumble and custard. We had just finished and were talking about summoning cars to transport them back to their hotel when we heard a noise. The sound of a large crowd. It seemed to be cheering.

"What is that?" Cy stood up.

"I don't know. A football match, maybe? A local team won?" Sir Hubert stood up, frowning. He headed for the door.

We went outside. The crowd was at the gate. I felt a little like Marie Antoinette except that they sounded happy. A policeman was coming toward us.

"What is it?" I asked.

"It's the little girl. She's been found. She's safe."

Chapter 25

November 7
Eynsleigh

I am so relieved. It seems that everything is going to be all right after all.

We clustered around the policeman. "Where? How? When?" He was peppered with questions.

"Ask her yourself," he said. "She's coming here now, in a car, with her mum."

The gates had opened. The crowd pushed in, accompanying a motorcar. I was surprised to see that the car was ours and the driver was Darcy. Happiness surged through me, and pride. He had found her and brought her home, safe and sound. My husband, the hero.

Flashbulbs went off all around the car. Newsmen shouted

questions as the doors opened. Darcy got out first, then opened the back door. Mrs. Trapp appeared first, followed by Rosie, bundled in a miniature fur coat, looking like a character from *A Little Princess*. Her mother turned to the crowd.

"We'll have a press conference here tomorrow morning, when Rosie will tell you everything about her awful ordeal, but please go away now and let me rejoice in my daughter's safe return," she said. "She needs time to recover. Please leave us alone."

I did notice that Rosie paused and turned back to the crowd on the steps, giving a little royal wave, before going into the house. So she had already recovered somewhat. We all went through into the drawing room, where coffee and liqueurs had already been wheeled in on a trolley. Phipps was standing ready to serve.

"Blimey," he exclaimed, forgetting that servants do not speak in the presence of their masters, especially not using swear words. "They've found the little girl. I've got to go and tell them downstairs."

And he ran off. We took our places, Rosie sitting very close to her mother by the fire. "It's so good to be warm," she said. "I was so cold. I thought I'd freeze to death."

"Where were you? What happened to you?" Gloria asked her. "And did this kind gentleman rescue you?"

"No," she said. "I rescued myself." She glanced up at her mother, who hugged her tighter.

"Such a brave little soul. I'm so proud of her. My daughter. She's a little heroine, that's what she is. I'll never forget this day for as long as I live."

"So what happened, Rosie? Tell us everything," Sir Hubert said.

She glanced up at her mother again. "I snuck off," she said. "I know I shouldn't have. I'm sorry, Mr. Marvin. But when I knew that Addy was going to be rehearsing the scene as my stand-in I thought I'd finally got a chance to see those little pigs. So I went up there to the farm and I was looking at the pigs when someone came up behind me."

"Did you get a chance to see who it was?" Sir Hubert asked.

She shook her head. "I started to turn around but then something was put over my face. It smelled nasty and next thing I knew I was in a dark cold place."

"A man or a woman?" I asked.

She thought about this. "It had to be a man because he was tall."

"Did he say anything? Did you smell anything?"

"Smell? The pigs were smelly, then that stuff over my face and it was awful. I couldn't breathe."

"Chloroform," Sir Hubert said.

"So someone must have been waiting and ready." Gloria looked at us for confirmation. "How could they have known she was going up to the pigs at that time?"

"It must have been someone on-site," I said. "One of your crew, or our farmhands."

"The farmhands? No, surely not." Gloria sounded most emphatic. I looked at her. "They were extras for us. Such nice boys. Reminded me of . . ." She broke off.

"Somebody knew," Darcy agreed. "I've given the list of everybody on this site to Scotland Yard and they are checking into it."

"So let Rosie tell her story," her mother insisted. "Go on, baby."

"I was in a dark cold place and my legs were tied up. I couldn't move. I started yelling but nobody came. Then I saw I was in some kind of shed. There was straw on the floor and someone had put a cup of water and a bit of bread. But I felt sick from that nasty stuff." She snuggled closer to her mother. "I kept shouting but nobody heard me."

"You were all alone in that shed, all this time?" Sir Hubert asked.

She nodded. "I did drink some water in the end but I wasn't hungry. I thought I was going to die."

"And nobody came to check on you?" I asked, making eye contact with Darcy as to whether he wanted to go on with this line of questioning.

"Nobody. I think someone came to the outside a couple of times because I heard footsteps and breathing but nobody answered when I shouted. They probably looked in through one of the little holes in the walls. I think they wanted to check I was still there."

"So who finally rescued you?" Sir Hubert asked.

"I saved myself," she said. "I kept trying to undo the knots around my legs but my hands were too cold, I couldn't do much. But in the end I managed it and I stood up. It was a real old shed. Kinda falling down, you know. And I found there were cracks between the boards and I could see out. I was in the middle of a field with a wood on one side."

"No houses around?"

"Nothing," she said. "A plowed field and a wood. That's all." She stared out at the fire, as if she was still processing this.

"And then?" Lana asked impatiently.

"I thought the walls looked old so I wondered if any of it was rotten, so I started pushing and kicking and then one of the boards got really loose. So I started kicking it some more and it broke. I didn't dare come out before it was dark, in case they were watching. But as soon as it got dark I managed to squeeze out. I didn't know which way to walk but I found a path that went through the woods and kept going and then I saw what I thought was my mom's cottage. And it was. And this nice man was there too." She looked across at Darcy and smiled at him. "He asked me questions. I told him where I'd come from and he went back and looked."

We turned to Darcy. "The shed was locked with a padlock, all right. But it was pretty deserted. I'd say it hadn't been used for years. We'll check whose farm it's on, of course, but I imagine the kidnappers had scouted it out and decided it would be ideal."

"That points to a local person," I said. "Someone who knew the area. We can't overlook one of the crowd outside the gate. One of them could have been waiting for the right moment, seen Rosie go up to the farm and come around from the outside."

"Good point." Sir Hubert nodded. "So what will happen now?"

"We'll have police watching the shed and the crossroads and hopefully we'll scoop up the perpetrator. I suspect he or they are quite naïve and just seized on the opportunity to make a killing." There was a little gasp from Mrs. Trapp. "I meant make more money than they had ever dreamed of," he said hastily. "They probably never meant the little girl any harm. So now you can all go home safely and it's just watching and waiting."

“Thank God for that,” Cy Martin said. “Do you feel up to filming tomorrow, then, Rosie honey? Because I’ve got our passages booked on a liner sailing at the end of the week.”

“Sure do, Mr. Marvin,” she said. And she gave him a bright smile.

“That’s my little trouper,” Rosie’s mom said. “But we have to take time for a press conference for her tomorrow. We owe it to the newspapers and the newsreels.”

“I guess we can do that,” he agreed. “Not a bad idea to get advance publicity for the film. We may rush production through and get it out while all this is fresh.”

I looked across at him and frowned. He seemed so callous and unfeeling. Was it possible he had orchestrated this entire kidnapping to make publicity for his movie? I wouldn’t put it past him!

Chapter 26

Sunday, November 8

So Rosie is safely back and I believe we are getting closer to solving this crime!

I voiced my suspicions to Darcy when we were finally alone in our bedroom. He stared at me long and hard, then he said, "Something similar went through my mind. Let's just see what I find at the crossroads tonight."

"You will be careful, won't you?" I asked.

"I'll have police backup," he said, "and as I mentioned before, these are amateurs. Small fry. I don't think they'll even show up. I suspect they'll check on the shed, see that Rosie is gone and then run for it."

"I do hope so," I replied. "But then we may never catch them."

"We'll do a thorough fingerprinting of everything in the

shed," he said. "Something may turn up, although those rough boards won't give us any clear prints. But on the cup, for example."

He left about eleven. I got into bed but couldn't sleep. It was a wild night and I lay listening to the wind buffeting the windows, worrying about him. What if they were American gangsters? They were known to shoot everything in sight. But if they were local amateurs mightn't they also carry a gun? And panic and shoot wildly? It was just before one that Darcy returned. He closed the door quietly behind him. "Just as we thought," he said. "They never showed up. And not at the shed either. It's a local farmer who owns it. He's been questioned and said that he hasn't used that shed for years. He was quite upset when he heard what had happened. And he hadn't seen any suspicious people on his farm, but then the shed is about as far away from the farmhouse as possible and there isn't much outside activity in those fields in the winter. Only one small interesting fact—he owns Rose Cottage."

"Ah. So he knew who was staying there. That is interesting," I said. "He could have passed that news along to all sorts of people."

"Exactly. We'll just have to keep our ears and eyes open and have the police ask lots of questions locally. Somebody might know something and have spilled the beans. Someone might even have gone to the papers or the police."

"I do hope so," I said. "I've been so worried. First Mrs. Simpson and now this. For a while I started to believe that the two had to be connected and it was a major crime organization of some sort. Thank heavens it's not. Now I just want this to be over, those film people gone and to get back to our normal life."

"Amen to that," he said. He started to undress. "I hope you're nice and warm, because I'm frozen."

"Don't you dare put your cold feet on me," I exclaimed. "Get a hot-water bottle."

THE NEXT MORNING the press conference was a production fit for a Hollywood film. Rosie was dressed in a white fur hat like my mother's, a blue velvet coat with matching fur trim. She looked like a Russian princess as she stood on the steps outside our front door and recounted her story as flashbulbs went off around her. She was remarkably poised and controlled for a tiny tot, but I reminded myself that she probably hadn't realized the extent of the danger. It had been a big adventure to her now that it had ended safely. Children are remarkably resilient. The morning papers had shouted the news: SHE'S SAFE. TINY STAR RESCUES HERSELF. BRAVE LITTLE FILM ACTRESS. Even the sedate *Times* was effusive in praise.

Something was gnawing at the back of my mind as I watched the press conference from an upstairs window, James in my arms. I analyzed my thoughts again. Almost like a Hollywood film. Almost as if it had been staged. And I asked myself whether it was possible that Cy Marvin had orchestrated this whole thing to get publicity for his movie. And yet I'd swear he was as much taken by surprise as we were, really annoyed that his production was being held up, and his actresses were definitely in shock. I needed to find out. I went back to Darcy, who was on the telephone.

"No red flags among the Hollywood lot," he said. "A couple of communists. One indecent exposure, but nothing like a kidnapping. A couple of locals have a record but it's for things like drunk and disorderly and battery. Nothing like this."

"I think I'd like to take a look at that shed for myself," I said. "And to have another word with Jacob. There was something not right yesterday. He's normally so friendly and he wouldn't make eye contact with me. Didn't you notice it too?"

"Yes," he said. "I did notice something. It could be as simple as worrying that he'll get into trouble for staying in the village to talk to his girlfriend. On the other hand . . ." He paused, then nodded. "All right. Let's go, then," Darcy said.

I handed James to Maisie, put on my outdoor clothes and boots and off we went. The press conference had just wrapped up but a lot of people were still loitering, refusing to leave the grounds and hoping to get autographs from the film stars. Darcy had brought the dogs and we kept them on leashes until we were well clear of the excitement. After that they bounded ahead, relishing the frosty day, flushing a pheasant and chasing after a rabbit. This was their idea of a good day. Donnie and Bill were out working but there was no sign of Jacob.

"He's in the house, sir," Bill said. "Not feeling too well today."

"Oh dear," I said. "Let's go and see if there's anything we can do."

They looked wary about this but we went up to the front door and opened it. Jacob was sitting in a battered old armchair by the stove, nursing a big mug of tea. He jumped up guiltily, spilling tea as he did so.

"Something wrong, my lady?" he asked.

"Just concerned about you," I said. "The other boys said you weren't feeling well."

"Just a bit of a head cold, I expect," he said. "I got pretty chilled on that cart taking the veg into the village."

"Well, that was understandable," I said. "I hear you were out a long time. All morning, in fact."

His face flushed bright red. "So they told you," he said. "I didn't mean no harm."

"No harm doing what?" Darcy asked. "Taking a little girl on your cart with the vegetables? Handing her over to somebody?"

An incredulous look shot across his face. "No. Nothing like that. I had nothing to do with the little girl, I swear it. If you really want to know I'm sweet on a girl at the newsagent's, so wanted to talk to her. But nothing bad."

"But something's upsetting you. You've not been yourself for the last few days," I said. "Ever since the film people came. Did anyone ask you to do something that made you uncomfortable? Anyone put you in a difficult position?"

He looked away. "Not exactly."

"Would you like to tell us? We wouldn't judge you for it," Darcy said.

"No. Nothing. Never mind," he said. "I tell you it's nothing. All right?"

We saw that no more was forthcoming. Had one of the Hollywood visitors tried to involve Jacob in the kidnapping or even perhaps propositioned him? Was that why he was staying shut up in the house when he didn't seem too sick to me? Either way it didn't matter now. They'd soon be gone and he could get on with courting the girl at the newsagent's.

We left him with the promise that one of the other boys would go to the big house to bring him hot soup.

"I agree. There's something that's not right there," Darcy commented to me as we walked away.

"I know. But I don't think he'll tell us. Perhaps he was asked to help with the kidnapping but refused. Now he's scared to show his face."

Darcy headed out along the track that led from the farm toward the lane and then the village.

"Are we looking for signs of a vehicle?" I asked because I didn't see any the other day.

"There are the cart tracks here," he said. "I suppose the kidnapper could also have used a cart, but then I think he could just have carried her. The shed isn't too far from here. See, this path goes right to it. But no cart could have come down here."

We started down the path. It was overgrown and clearly not used much. No sign of big boots that we could see. After a few minutes we came out to a plowed field and Darcy pointed. "There's the shed," he said.

"Goodness. It is close."

"So someone could have carried her," he said, "although she is quite a hefty child, isn't she? Perhaps there were two of them."

The padlock had been removed and the door now swung open. It was as Rosie had said. Straw covered the floor. The cup and plate had already been removed. The one board had been broken where she had escaped.

"I wouldn't have thought that she could have squeezed through that narrow a gap," I said to Darcy.

He walked around, examining the floor, which was damp. He kicked aside the straw. "There is no sign of a child's footprint here," he said. "Is it possible this is a movie set we're looking at? Are we being hoodwinked?"

"I've been thinking that for some time," I said. "That note. There was something not right about it."

"Like what?"

I went through the words in my head. "Would our local people use the word 'cops'? Isn't that too American?"

"Unless they were trying to sound gangsterish and tough," he said. "They may have been watching American films."

"That's true. But you know what else. The note said 'You'll not.' We'd say 'You won't.' I think it was written by an American."

I saw his eyes flash as he registered this. "I think you're right," he said. "So do you reckon Cy Marvin staged the whole thing for publicity?"

"He did seem genuinely annoyed more than anything that this was costing him money."

"The mother is clearly relishing this adoration of her child," Darcy said. "It couldn't be possible that she arranged her own daughter's kidnapping, could it?"

"Who would do that to their own child?" I stared at him, then I said, "What if she was never kidnapped? What if she was never in that shed? We only have her word for it. Come to think of it, nobody remembers seeing her that morning. The wardrobe mistress didn't remember seeing Rosie. She said the mother took her costume from the wardrobe saying she was taking it to

Rosie's caravan. But Mrs. Trapp told me that Rosie was in wardrobe. Then she asked Addy to stand in so that Rosie didn't get too cold before the big scene."

Darcy looked at me, a half smile on his lips. "Let's go and take a look at Rose Cottage, shall we? We might find something interesting there."

"All right."

We set off. Rose Cottage was surprisingly close. So Mrs. Trapp could have spotted the shed on one of her walks and planned the whole thing. The front door was locked but Darcy found a key under a flowerpot and let us in. Nothing much to see. It was a simple cottage with a living room, a kitchen and two bedrooms at the back. No incriminating papers. Nothing.

"I don't know what we'd be looking for," I said. "She's hardly likely to have written a confession in her diary."

Darcy looked around, nodding in agreement. Then he said, "Wait a minute. There has to be an attic." He ran out into the hallway and sure enough there was the trapdoor. He tugged on the piece of rope and a ladder descended. He went up with me close behind.

"Aha. Look up here," he said. Amid the boxes and clutter of a normal attic there was a mattress on the floor that looked as if it might have come from a baby's cot. And a tartan travel rug and . . .

"Cake crumbs," Darcy said, squatting down by the mattress. "They must be very recent. The mice wouldn't leave them alone for long."

"And we know she loves her cake," I said, a big smile spreading over my face. "So she hid up here, the whole time. I bet her mother had this planned all along. Talking about kidnapping and bodyguards and how worried she was. She wanted to make sure that Rosie got into the papers and became a household name. So what do we do now?"

"That's a tricky one," Darcy said. "If we report her to the police she'll be charged and probably go to prison. I wouldn't want that for the child," he said. "As it is nobody will be caught. The case will fizzle and the Trapps will go home. But we will certainly let her know that we know exactly what happened. We'll hold it over her. Get her to sign a confession. And if something like this happens again we will tell the police."

"Bloody woman," I said.

"You've sworn twice in the last few days," he said. "Not at all ladylike."

"It's been quite justified," I said. "First Mrs. Simpson and now this. I don't like being tricked, Darcy. Come on. Let's go home."

We left Rose Cottage and headed back onto the estate. The dogs, annoyed at having to wait outside the cottage, now bounded ahead, streaking in all directions. As we turned toward the house they suddenly sped off toward the woods. Darcy called them back but they didn't come.

"Disobedient brutes," Darcy said as they began barking madly. "Come here. Right now."

The barking continued, high-pitched and continual.

"Something's wrong," I said.

We hurried over the grass and followed the sound, plunging into the woodland. We came upon them in a hollow full of dead leaves.

"What's wrong?" I asked.

They stopped, looking up at me and then down at the ground again. Darcy bent to clear away the leaves. The earth had been disturbed. As he cleared more we saw a white hand, poking out of the soil.

"Oh no." Darcy started to scrabble at the earth, moving aside branches that had been laid across the area. I dropped to my knees to join him. We uncovered the arm, then the face, staring up at us.

"Good God," Darcy said. "It's Gloria Bishop."

Chapter 27

November 8
Eynsleigh

Just when I thought we had everything nicely cleared up this awful thing happens.

For a long moment neither of us said anything. I was conscious of the sigh of the wind, rustling dry leaves, the distant mournful call of a wood pigeon, the harsh caw of a jackdaw. The dogs, no longer barking, and sensing something very wrong, sat watching, quite still. It was as if the world was frozen in time. Beautiful, lively Gloria Bishop lying like a marble statue! It seemed too impossible to be real.

It was Darcy who spoke first. "I think she's been strangled."

"Who on earth?" I asked, my voice sounding unnaturally loud in that frigid silence. "Why?"

Darcy cleared more of the earth from her. "This all seems very fresh."

"It must be," I said. "I'm sure I noticed her when they first arrived this morning."

We saw now that she was wearing a fur coat, but underneath she had on her Tudor costume. She wasn't wearing her headdress, however, and her lovely dark hair fanned out among the dead leaves. Her face was blotchy but with a strangely greenish tinge. I realized this was not a product of her strangulation but the makeup she wore for filming. Green made faces appear white on the screen.

"She was made up and ready to start filming," I said, shaking my head as I tried to make sense of what I was seeing.

Darcy stood up abruptly, staring around. "The killer might still be close by," he said. "Don't move. Stay here."

He walked off. I heard him tramping through the woodland. My heart was beating so loudly I was sure it must echo in the stillness of the day. Gloria Bishop had been alive an hour or so ago. I was pretty sure I had seen her when they arrived, early in the morning. She had gone to wardrobe, changed into her costume and then, for some inexplicable reason, had come up here, away from all the activity. Why? She must have come this way on her own feet. The killer couldn't have carried her all the way from where they were shooting the picture this far into the woods without being noticed. So she had to have sneaked away from the press conference and come up here to meet somebody . . . but whom?

I remembered that her demeanor had changed during her time here. When we first met her she had been chatty, friendly, flirty with Sir Hubert, but then she had become more withdrawn, concerned, worried. Something had happened. Someone had upset her.

Darcy returned. "No sign of anybody but then a person could hide out here for days. It's a pity there are so many leaves underfoot. It's hard to make out footprints. Let's see if she came into the woods on her own feet."

The dogs stood up with me, moving close and wanting reassurance. I patted Holly's head and she licked my hand. They stayed beside me as we retraced our steps back to the meadow. When a rabbit darted out they didn't even try to chase it. At the entrance to the meadow Darcy paused, looking around. "Which way did she come?" he asked. "The direct route from the house would bring her into the woods farther down here." He headed in that direction. "But I don't see any signs. The bracken hasn't been trampled."

"You're assuming that she meant to go into the woods," I said. "That she went in on her own two feet."

Darcy looked at me. "If someone had killed her elsewhere and dragged her here don't you think it might have been noticed? It's pretty exposed. Any of the windows at the back of the house look out in this direction. The boys at the farm would have had a good view."

"The killer might assume everyone is busy. If it was someone from the film crew, they were all focused on that stupid press conference. No one would have seen if Gloria had been lured away."

"She was a grown woman. How could she be lured away?" he asked, his voice now sharp with tension. "It's not exactly the time of year for someone to ask her if she fancied a quickie in the woods."

I had to smile at this. "The one thing that will make it hard is that crowd attending the press conference," I said. "We've no idea who might have been here. Someone who bore a grudge against her could easily have taken her aside to talk to her and then killed her while everyone else was listening to Rosie give her Oscar-worthy speech."

"Who on earth might bear a grudge against an American film star?"

I shrugged. "Maybe some kind of religious nut who thinks she's being sinful? Or a crazed fan who sent her letters she didn't answer?"

Darcy nodded. "I agree, but then how did the person persuade her to come up here? Or was he so incredibly strong that he killed her, then carried her all this way without being seen?"

We crossed the meadow, our feet crunching in icy puddles.

"It makes no sense," Darcy said. "We better get back to the house and call the police. Not that poor old chap with his bicycle and not even Haywards Heath. I'll get straight onto a bloke I know at Scotland Yard. This is a high-profile case if ever there was one."

We came around to the front of the house to find the place in an uproar. The crowd had been dispersed and were now being held well away from the film set, where it looked as if filming was ready to begin.

"Where the hell can she have gone now?" Cy Marvin was

shouting. "Really this is too much. First my child star vanishes and now my leading lady."

"One of your leading ladies," Lana said curtly. "She was here not too long ago. Did she go into the house to warm up?"

"We looked," Nora said. "Nobody in the house has seen her."

"Have you asked that Sir Hubert guy?" Cy snapped. "Those two seemed to have a thing going. Have you checked out his bedroom?"

"He's in one of the sitting rooms with the duke and his wife, reading the morning papers," Nora replied. "None of them has seen Gloria this morning."

"What the hell does she think she's playing at?" Cy demanded. "She's normally so reliable, such a professional, and now she's gone all moody on us. I wish we'd never come to this damned place. We could have shot all of this on the lot in Hollywood and be done by now. But no, the big guns thought it would be more realistic if we shot it live in England. I almost lost my child star and now Gloria." He looked around as if he expected her to materialize. "Is this some kind of stunt, do you reckon? More publicity?"

"I'll take the dogs in and telephone the police," Darcy muttered to me, leading them away by the collars.

I went up to the group of people. "If I could have your attention for a minute," I said, raising my voice over the hubbub. Silence fell as they all looked at me expectantly. I beckoned Cy and the actors closer, not wanting the crowd still lingering farther off to hear. "I'm afraid I have some terrible news. Gloria Bishop is dead. We've just come upon her body, buried in our woods."

Lana gave a gasp of horror. "Oh my God. Oh, Cy." She turned to the director and buried her face in his jacket. He put an arm around her, staring at me in shocked disbelief.

"Gloria? No! That can't be true," Grant Hathaway said, sounding more angry than sad. "How can she be buried in the woods? She was here. I saw her."

I realized they were frozen like statues, staring at me, still trying to process this. It would be more sensitive of me to give them time, to invite them into the house, but I knew I had to ask questions while they were still unsettled.

"When did you see her?" I asked. "Before the press conference or after?"

He frowned, thinking. "It must have been before. She was just coming out of the wardrobe tent carrying her costume when I was going in. I said something to her but she didn't seem to notice me. I thought she was getting into character."

"Anyone see her after that?" I asked.

Heads were shaken.

"It was all so chaotic," Lana said, looking at the others for confirmation. "All those pressmen milling around, those people wanting autographs. It took forever to clear them all out so we could start shooting."

"So nobody saw Gloria once the press conference had begun?" I could see them all considering this. They remained silent.

"Did you see her interacting with anybody at all this morning?" I asked. "Or even in the days before? Anybody who shouldn't have been on the set? Any of the crowd who came in? Anybody who might have upset her?"

As I said this I realized that I had seen Gloria Bishop upset once. She had had a confrontation with Grant Hathaway.

"It's those kidnappers again," Mrs. Trapp said, wrapping her arm around Rosie, who was now in full costume. "They tried to get my child then they went for bigger fry, but she fought back so they killed her accidentally."

I stared at her in disgust. She was apparently willing to carry on with this charade, confident that we hadn't found out the truth. I needed to speak to Darcy.

"So what do we do now?" Lana asked. "I presume someone is calling the police?"

"My husband is," I said. "He's going straight to Scotland Yard, so it might take them some time to get here. But I'm sure you realize that nobody is to leave."

"You don't think that one of us had anything to do with Gloria's death?" Lana asked in a shocked voice.

"The police will want to question everybody," I said. "I suggest you all come into the house. Perhaps the actors can wait in that little sitting room and the crew in the servants' hall downstairs."

"I like the way she makes us servants," a voice growled from the background.

I looked around, trying to pinpoint the voice. One of the cameramen, over to my right.

"I'm sorry, I didn't mean it like that," I said. "It's only that the servants' hall is warm and big enough for everyone. The police will want statements from everybody involved. I'll have my staff prepare warm drinks and snacks."

That seemed to cheer them up. There were no more grumbles.

"Okay, everybody. You heard the lady. Get changed into street clothes and let's get into the warm house," Grant Hathaway said.

Cy drew close to his assistant director. "This is going to ruin us, you realize. Now we've shot all this material for nothing and my leading lady is dead."

"We may have shot enough so that we can fudge the last few scenes," the other muttered, "and if so we've already got the publicity. Gloria's last film . . ."

"Who the hell would want to kill her, that's what I want to know," Cy snapped. "She wasn't the type who made enemies, was she? Always treated the crew well. It will probably turn out to be one of those crazy aristocrats. That dippy duke . . ."

I had heard enough. My brother might not be an Albert Einstein but was the most gentle of souls and he had never harmed another human being. I went ahead of them into the house, entering through the scullery to the kitchen. Pierre looked up from something he was stirring on the stove; Queenie was kneading bread on the table.

"Whatcha, missus," she said. Then she saw my face. "What's up now? You look like you've eaten something what don't agree with you."

"I'm afraid one of the actresses has been killed."

"Which one? Not that lovely Lana Lovett?"

"No. Gloria Bishop."

"Gloria's been killed? Oh no. Not Gloria! That can't be true." And she burst out crying.

"That's enough, Queenie," Mrs. Holbrook said sternly,

coming up behind her. "The last thing we need here is hysterics from you. You didn't even know the woman. It's sad but nothing to do with you."

"Nothing to do with me? She was so nice. She actually spoke to me." Queenie gulped between sobs. "She thanked me for my cakes, just like a normal person." She wiped her tears with the back of her hand, then wiped the hand on her apron. "How was she killed? In a motor accident?"

"No, I'm afraid she was murdered."

I saw a wary look cross Queenie's face. "Jealous lover. You mark my words. That's what all these film stars have. They drive men wild."

I thought Queenie had been reading too many magazines. "I don't think Gloria had a jealous lover here, Queenie. But I expect we'll find out soon enough. The police will be coming and they'll want to question everybody. Do you think you could possibly make some kind of big soup, enough to feed everybody, Pierre?"

"A soup? Of course. I can make a soup."

"Oh, and, Queenie, make a big pot of tea and coffee," Mrs. Holbrook said. "They will all be in shock. And it will do you good to keep working. Take your mind off things."

"Bob's yer uncle, missus," she said, wiping her cheek again. "Don't you worry. We'll take care of it."

"*Oui*, milady," Pierre said, not wanting to be outdone by Queenie. "All will be well."

"You two are the best." I gave them a beaming smile. I hadn't realized until I left them how upset I felt. I had seen dead bodies before. I had even had to deal with murder. But it never failed to shake me to the core. Another human being, alive and enjoying life one minute until someone robbed them of the chance of a future. Gloria had been beautiful and talented and was on top of her world. Who could possibly have wanted her dead?

Chapter 28

November 8
Eynsleigh

We just worked out what we thought was a crime. Now we have a real one. I do hope they can solve it. Poor Gloria.

Darcy met me as I came up from the servants' quarters. "Oh, there you are. I've talked to my contact at Scotland Yard and they are sending a team down here right away. He asked that nobody leave the premises."

"I've already told them that," I said. "I've suggested that the actors convene in the small sitting room and the crew down in the servants' hall and I've asked Pierre and Queenie to make coffee and food for everyone. They are all in shock, as I am."

He eyed me critically. "Yes, you do look awfully pale. How

utterly beastly for you to find a dead body like that. Come and sit down in the morning room and I'll fetch you a brandy."

"No, I'm all right," I said. "It's just . . ." And to my embarrassment tears started to trickle down my cheek. I'd noticed that since I'd had a baby I'd become a lot more emotional. Darcy reached up a finger and wiped the tears away. "Come on," he said. "This really isn't our problem. It's sad. It's shocking but from now on it's up to the police."

I nodded and allowed myself to be steered to the morning room. Sir Hubert was no longer there but Binky and Fig were sitting by the fire, morning papers on their laps.

"A five-letter word starting with *B*, meaning a plucky fellow," Binky said. "I've tried Drake because he was darned plucky, wasn't he? But he doesn't start with *B*."

"It's 'brave,' you idiot," Fig said.

"Oh. Gosh. Right. So it is. Well done, old bean."

"Make room for Georgie," Darcy said. "She's had a bit of a shock."

They looked up.

"We've just found one of the film actresses murdered and buried in our woods."

"Good heavens," Fig said. "What is the matter with these people? First kidnapping and now murder. Do you think the two are connected? What was Hubert thinking when he agreed to invite them here in the first place?"

"I don't think he realized there would be all this drama," I replied as Binky moved along the sofa to allow me to sit by the fire.

"Which of them is dead?" Fig asked.

"Gloria Bishop."

"The one who was flinging herself at Sir Hubert," Fig replied. "I suppose she's the sort who sees herself as a femme fatale and leads on too many men. And one of them snapped." She looked around. "Where is Hubert, by the way? I know he went out for a walk early. . . ." She stopped, jaw dropping, as she considered this. Then she shook her head. "No. Not him. Too British."

I felt my heart lurch. Gloria had led him on and then apparently lost interest. But he hadn't been seriously interested, had he? And he'd always been the most even-tempered of chaps. And pretty withdrawn. You never knew what he was thinking. He'd never . . . Suddenly I remembered something. "Where's my mother?"

"Haven't seen her this morning," Fig said. "She likes to sleep in late, doesn't she? Not like us. Up with the sun, aren't we, Binky?"

"What?" he looked up from his crossword. "Oh yes. Rather. I have to do my walk to check the estate at home. Say hello to our cows, you know. God, I miss them. Good company, cows."

"And you're saying we are not good company?" Fig said frostily.

"Oh no. Not at all. But you know cows. They just stand there and listen and seem to understand. And they never interrupt or tell me I'm being stupid."

At that moment Mummy came in, looking stunning as always, makeup perfect, wearing a buttery yellow cashmere twinset that completely matched her hair. And a double strand of large pearls.

"Well, isn't this nice," she said. "A family gathering. I'm too late for breakfast, I suppose. I had a nice lie-in. Georgie darling, do you think you could ask for coffee and maybe some pastries to go with it?"

Then she pulled up another armchair with remarkable ease for one who looked so delicate. "And what is happening with those film people? I looked out through my window and nothing is going on outside. Are they shooting in here?"

"Filming has stopped," Darcy said. "There's been a tragedy. Gloria Bishop is dead."

"Dead?" Mummy blinked as if she hadn't heard correctly. "What was it? Heart? Drugs? A lot of these film types take cocaine, you know. I've never done it myself. My acting skills have always been up to snuff without having to hype myself up."

"She was murdered, Mummy," I said. "Murdered and then buried in the wood." A thought raced through my mind. "Golly. If we hadn't been out with the dogs she might not have been found for days. They might have thought it was another kidnapping. . . ."

My eyes met Darcy's. I could tell he was thinking something.

"I'll just go and have a talk with a friend of mine," he said. "And maybe then meet the Scotland Yard crew at the station." And off he went.

We sat. I couldn't settle to do anything. I glanced through papers, seeing all those headlines about Rosie. Then I got up. I wanted to be upstairs with James, where the world felt safe and normal. As I came out into the hall Darcy was putting on his overcoat and Mrs. Trapp was just going into the sitting room.

"Isn't it just terrible news, your ladyship," she said. "One tragedy after another. I always thought this production was cursed." Her expression didn't match her words. No, she was not mourning Gloria Bishop. She was thinking more publicity. "I'm going to take Rosie back to the cottage. I don't want her going through more distress being questioned by policemen."

"A word before you go in there, if you don't mind," Darcy said, coming over to us.

"Yes?" Her face seemed quite innocent.

"We've got a team coming down from Scotland Yard in a few minutes," he said. "Wonderful things they do these days with forensics. Fingerprints, for example. I gave them the letter from the kidnappers, you know. And guess what? It was clean. No fingerprints at all."

"See. I knew the kidnappers were clever," she said.

"Except someone had to handle the envelope before it was delivered."

"Of course. They'd handle it at the post office, wouldn't they? Probably wiped over any other fingerprints."

"Quite so," Darcy said. "And then we may have touched it after it was delivered. But strangely enough they've managed to match all the prints on it."

"Oh yes?" Did I see a fleeting look of alarm on her face.

"Including yours," Darcy said.

"Well, yes. When I opened the envelope."

"The only thing is, Mrs. Trapp, that you didn't open the

envelope. Sir Hubert did, holding it with his handkerchief and then slitting it open with a knife. You didn't see the envelope. We showed you the note. So the question is . . . when did you touch that envelope?"

"I don't know what you're getting at," she said. Her face was now red.

"Let me say something else, then. Cake crumbs in the attic at your cottage. Fresh cake crumbs."

"I don't know what you're talking about," she blustered.

"Oh, yes you do. You know very well, which is why you've gone bright red."

She opened her mouth, went to say something, then shut it again.

"We know exactly how you planned this and why you did it," Darcy said. "And when Scotland Yard comes, we'll have to share our information with them."

"No!" The word echoed from the high ceiling. "Don't do that. Would I go to jail?"

"Quite possibly," Darcy said. "Police officers don't like their time wasted."

"But what would happen to Rosie?"

"They might decide you're an unfit parent," Darcy said. "Put her into foster care."

"Oh God. Don't let that happen," she gasped. "She's my world. She's everything to me. I'd die if they took her away."

"If we don't share our information with the police, you would have to swear that there would never again be a stupid publicity stunt," Darcy said.

"Oh, I swear. I swear," she said. She grabbed at his sleeve.

"Never again. I just thought it would put Rosie in the spotlight, like the Lindbergh baby, you know. She'd be a household word. Everybody would want her to be in their pictures."

"You understand that if they arrest somebody else for this, I'll have to tell the truth," Darcy said.

"But they won't arrest anybody, will they?" she said. "How can they? There's no evidence. "

"Sometimes they hit on the wrong person. Like in the Lindbergh case," Darcy said. "He always maintained he was innocent. He just happened to get his hands on some of the reward money and that's how they nabbed him. He was German. His English wasn't good. But he was executed, just the same. We wouldn't want something like that to happen, would we?"

"No. Of course not. No." She was now close to tears.

"So you will come into my study with me and then you write out a full confession," Darcy said. "If we need to use it, we will, but let's hope we don't ever need it."

He led her off down the hall. I watched them go, secretly rather glad that he'd put Mrs. Trapp in her place. I continued up the stairs into the bedroom. Maisie was in with James, changing his nappy. He was awake and making happy little baby noises. I paused in the doorway, thinking how lucky I was to have those I loved around me. I waited until Maisie had gone, then I picked up James, pacing around with him, making little humming noises as I rocked him but at the same time letting my thoughts wander. Who had a motive? The only one Gloria Bishop had clashed with was Grant Hathaway, but he had seemed puzzled by her disappearance. But then he was an actor. Lana had displayed an element of catty jealousy. Nora was the quiet, mousy type who could be harboring feelings of deep resentment. Cy or his assistant director could have tried to make a pass and been rejected. My mother could have thought that with Gloria gone she could take over the part.

Then I shook my head. "These are all ridiculous," I said out loud, making James give me a puzzled stare.

"Sorry, darling." I kissed his forehead. "I didn't mean to startle you. I'm just trying to figure something out. Something that makes no sense at all."

Chapter 29

November 8
Eynsleigh

We are not getting anywhere. It's as if Gloria simply vanished without anyone noticing. Someone from the film crew must know something. . . .

Darcy brought in the men from Scotland Yard right after we'd finished luncheon. Apparently they had already been to the crime scene and had left a forensic team at the site. There were two detectives, a DCI Wentworth and a Sergeant Perry. Both youngish men and not the older aggressive type of policeman like Chief Inspector Harlow. Thank goodness. Darcy set them up in his study and they started by questioning us. We told them how we'd been for a walk, the dogs had run into the woods, and then we'd found the body. They asked for my opinion, what I'd observed of the film people. I told them that Gloria seemed to have changed while she was here. She'd been outgoing to start with and suddenly became more withdrawn and moody.

"Do you have any idea who might have upset her?" DCI Wentworth asked me.

"We didn't really have much to do with them," I said. "They dined with us twice. And once they went with us to the Guy Fawkes bonfire. That's about all." I paused. "Gloria did have a confrontation with the male actor Grant Hathaway as they came in from the bonfire. It seemed to be a continuation of something they'd sparred over before. Oh, and you might ask the assistant, Nora Pines, for her views. She's a quiet little observer but I bet she notices a lot."

"Thank you for the tip, Lady Georgiana," he said. "Yes, the quiet ones are often useful."

He glanced across at his sergeant, who was taking notes. "So what do we know about this lady?" he asked. "A Hollywood type? From California?"

"No. She was originally English," I said. "In fact she said she grew up in this part of the world."

"That's worth noting," he said. "Someone around here might know her. Recognize her. Have a bone to pick with her."

"But she's been gone for years," I said. "She said she left England when she was young."

"A jilted boyfriend from long ago, maybe?" he said.

I shook my head. "I don't think you bear a grudge that long, Inspector." I paused. "All the same, there have certainly been plenty of local people hanging around. They've been trying to see the stars and get autographs. Perhaps you could find out whether one of them approached Gloria at all and she had some kind of confrontation."

"The big question, in my mind," Darcy said, "is what was she doing up in the woods? There is no sign of a body being dragged and anyway there would have been a good chance of being seen from the house. All the back windows look out over the grounds."

"And she was in costume," the DCI said, shaking his head as he tried to make sense of this. "So they'd already started filming. Are people allowed to wander away like that when they are shooting the film?"

"There was a break in production this morning," I replied. "Mrs. Trapp held a press conference for her daughter."

"Trapp? Oh, the one who was kidnapped and who escaped?"

"That's right."

"Funny case, that. The kid saves herself," he said. "You'd have thought if she was valuable enough to them the kidnappers would keep a good watch over her."

"Yes, you would have thought that," Darcy said. "They were clearly bungling amateurs hoping to make a few pounds from rich Americans."

"All's well that ended well there, at least," DCI Wentworth said. "More than we can say of this poor woman." He turned to his sergeant. "Perry, why don't you go down and question the crew members? Ask if they saw Gloria being approached by a stranger, or any suspicious interaction with another member of the cast or crew."

"Right you are, sir." The younger man got up and went out of the room.

"Would you like us to send you the directors and actors, one by one?" Darcy asked.

The DCI nodded, then held up a hand. "First I'd like to telephone the local police. I'd like a few more boots on the ground here, have the woodland fully checked. This may turn out to be one of those tramps who wander around, not always right in the head. He saw a beautiful lady in period costume, thought he was hallucinating. . . . You haven't spotted any tramps on your estate, have you?"

"Can't say I have," Darcy said.

"All the same, worth checking out. And the local chaps can look into Gloria Bishop's background. See exactly where she grew up and if there might be any local connection."

Darcy grinned. "The local chap is an old codger on a bicycle. The closest police station with manpower is Haywards Heath. They brought out a team with a bloodhound when we were looking for Rosie. I expect they could come back to help."

"Right." The DCI was about to stand up, but then he said, "Do you think you could get in contact with them while I start my questions?"

"Of course," Darcy said. "Glad to help."

DCI Wentworth gave him a shrewd stare. "I've heard a bit about you. Foreign Office, right? Undercover?"

Darcy smiled. "If I were, I wouldn't tell you, would I?" And he went out.

"Your husband's got a bit of a reputation," DI Wentworth said.

"A good one, I hope," I replied. "Would you like me to send

in the first person? The director first, I suggest. He's not the type who likes to be kept waiting."

The inspector nodded. "Anything going on between him and Miss Bishop?" he asked. "I've heard about these Hollywood casting couches."

"Oh, I don't think so," I said hastily. "The only man she showed any interest in was Sir Hubert, who owns this house, but it was only a mild flirtation, I think."

"Sir Hubert, eh? Perhaps I should have a word with him first."

Oh gosh, I thought. I hoped I hadn't implicated him in any way. "I'll go and find him for you," I said.

"Before you go, who else lives in this house, then? We'll want to question everybody."

"My brother and his wife, the Duke and Duchess of Rannoch, are visiting with their children," I said. "And my mother is here. The former duchess."

"Blimey," he muttered to himself.

"And before you ask, none of us has had much to do with the film people. They've been a bit of a nuisance actually." I saw a flicker of interest in his expression. "Not enough of a nuisance that we'd do away with one of them," I added hastily.

I ran into Phipps and asked him to find Sir Hubert.

"I think he wanted to go into town, milady," Phipps said. "He asked if Mr. Darcy was using the Bentley."

"When was this?" I asked.

"About an hour ago, I think. I asked him if he wanted me to drive him, and he said no, it was fine. He'd drive himself."

I was feeling rather sick as I walked back along the passage.

I couldn't believe my godfather had anything to do with Gloria's death but he had now given himself a convenient alibi for being away from the house. No. Nonsense. I wouldn't believe it.

I made my way to the small sitting room. It was now rather crowded with every chair occupied. I saw that the Trapps were not present. Had they fled back to the cottage? Lana and Grant Hathaway were smoking and a fug hung in the air. They looked up expectantly as I came in.

"The police inspector would like a word with each of you in turn," I said, "starting with Mr. Marvin."

"I don't know what the hell I can tell them," he snapped, rising to his feet. "I never left the set all morning and everyone can vouch for that."

"Not exactly, darling," Lana said smoothly. "When dear little Rosie here was holding her press conference everyone was paying attention to her, weren't they? The press were everywhere, the entire population of the county was milling about, so in fact any of us could have slipped away for a minute or so and not be observed."

"I think I would have noticed," Nora spoke up. As usual she was sitting on an upright chair far from the fire. "Mr. Marvin told me he wasn't pleased about the interruption and could I make sure it was over as quickly as possible, so I was ready to clear the set as soon as we could."

"So did you see Gloria leave, then?" I asked.

"I'm afraid I didn't," she said, "but I can pretty much guarantee she didn't walk away while the press conference was happening. I was standing over by the cameras, making sure none of them got damaged. She would have had to pass me to go around the house."

"Not if she went in the other direction," Grant said. "If she went around past the stables nobody would have noticed her."

"Why would she do that? It's a long way around and you'd have to navigate all the equipment stored there," Nora said.

"But you wouldn't be observed," Grant insisted.

A silence fell. Cy Marvin stood up. "I suppose I'd better go and face the music," he said. "It shouldn't take long. I've nothing to tell."

And off he went, closing the door after him. Lana stretched out her long legs toward the fire. "Pour me another coffee, Nora honey," she said. "This is liable to go on for a while. Do the police have any ideas? Do they think it has anything to do with the kidnapping?"

"I'm not sure," I said, not wanting to reveal more than I had to. I slid into the chair Cy had vacated. "Did Gloria mention anything to you that might have been troubling her?" I asked. "She seemed preoccupied for the last couple of days."

"We weren't exactly best friends," Grant said.

"Not anymore," Lana said, with a malicious smile. "It will come out, you know."

"Only if you tell them," he replied sweetly.

"No, Cy will tell them. He'll say anything to save his own neck," Lana replied.

"Tell them what?" I asked.

"That Grant and Gloria had a bit of a fling."

"Nothing serious," Grant said.

"It never is with you, darling. You can't keep your hands off anything in skirts, can you?" She looked across at Dorothy, who was sitting on a stool by the fire, holding out her hands to the flames.

Dorothy did not look up but continued to stare into the fire, pretending she didn't hear.

"Was Gloria upset when you broke up with her?" I asked.

"She did the breaking up," Grant said. "Our Gloria was not a paragon of virtue, let me tell you. How many husbands has she had? Four, is it?"

"Was she currently married?" I asked.

"In theory, darling," Lana said. "Ron Davies, the property magnate. He kept her in the style she'd become accustomed to. But he was at least twenty years older than her and probably not too hot in the bedroom department."

"And remarkably forgiving," Grant said with a chuckle.

"She said she grew up in this part of the world," I said. "Was Gloria Bishop her real name?"

"I shouldn't think so, any more than he's Grant and I'm Lana," Lana said. "No, I'm sure it wasn't. Cy will know, or you, Zack. You're the one who signs the contracts, aren't you?"

The producer shook his head. "It's Bishop on the contracts, that's all I can tell you. She must have had it legally changed some time ago."

"Did she ever say anything about growing up nearby?" I asked. "Was it possible she still had family around?"

"All I know is she said it was a bad idea coming here," Lana said. "As we drove back through the village she said, 'I don't know what I was thinking. I was stupid.'"

"But she didn't tell you what she meant?"

"I thought she meant insisting we come here when it's so cold and uncomfortable. And maybe that she was stupid to have designs on Sir Hubert. Perhaps she found out he wasn't exactly rich. She liked them rich."

Cy Marvin returned and sent in Zack Dennison. I didn't want to stay with them any longer and retreated to the morning room, where my family was lounging as if they had no worries in the world.

"So do you have more schools you need to visit?" Mummy asked sweetly. "Or are you taking advantage of a warm and comfortable house when we know that Castle Rannoch is hell on earth at this time of year?"

Fig flushed.

"They are welcome to stay here as long as they want, Mummy," I said. "As are you. Anytime."

"I'm sure she's needed back in Germany," Fig said. "Your German beau will be pining."

"Max does appreciate my support when he's working so hard," Mummy said with a smile. "And life is rather fun in Berlin, you know. Very cosmopolitan. Nightclubs and things. I couldn't vegetate in the country like you people." She stood up. "I've just had a brilliant idea. I could stand in for Gloria for those last scenes. I look rather good in a black wig and our faces are not dissimilar. I think I'll go and suggest it."

"Mummy, not now."

"Darling, they need something to cheer them up at the moment," she said, "and what would cheer anyone up more than doing a picture with *moi*?"

And she made a grand exit.

By the end of the day the entire cast and crew had been questioned and we were none the wiser. Nobody had seen Gloria leave the set. Nobody had any idea why she wished she hadn't come or what might have upset her. Sir Hubert had arrived back by lunchtime, telling us he had just popped to the bank to redeposit the ransom money before anything happened to it. When he heard the news about Gloria he was clearly shaken.

"I can't believe it," he kept muttering. "Such a vibrant woman. So full of life. Who could possibly . . . ?" And he couldn't go on.

There was no attempt to invite the cast to dinner that night. They were driven to their accommodation, with instructions they were not to leave the area, and we understood that the police team were putting up at the local pub.

"That should be useful for asking questions," I said to Darcy when we were safely alone in our room.

"Meaning what?"

"If she was a local girl, someone will remember her."

He considered this. "We were told she came from this part of the world. It could mean Sussex, or even the south of England. It would be too much of a coincidence if she really came from this village, or that anyone here actually knew her. She said that she left England when she was young, and that must have been some time ago."

I felt tears sting in my eyes again. Poor Gloria was no longer anything, a waste of talent and beauty. Someone among that crew or cast must have had a good reason for wanting her dead.

I considered Grant Hathaway. They had definitely had words, but he didn't seem like the violent type and whoever strangled Gloria had been violent. Strangling was a crime of impulse, I was sure of that. A moment of uncontrolled rage. And also one that required considerable strength. So it was unlikely to be a woman. That ruled out Lana, Nora and my mother, although I didn't think Mummy would kill to get a part she wanted. Also the wardrobe mistress, although why she would want Gloria out of the way I couldn't imagine. So one of the male crew members, then?

"What do we know about the other people who came over from America?" I asked. "Have we learned anything of interest?"

"Most of the crew and the directors are staples at the studio and had worked with Gloria before," he said. "There was some background checking done when Rosie disappeared. No red flags show up for any of them. Cy Marvin has a temper but it's mainly verbal. And he describes his relationship with Gloria as purely professional. The others agree with that."

"Will they be coming back here in the morning?" I asked.

"They have to pack up everything to ship it back to Hollywood," he said. "They are hoping they can salvage the film as they'd already shot most of it."

"My mother was all for volunteering to take over as Catherine," I said, smiling at him.

"I wish she would," he said. "I'd like to see her safely in Hollywood. Can't you talk her into not returning to Germany?"

"But she loves it there," I said. "She is universally adored and spoiled by a rich man. She is the ideal Aryan beauty. She truly believes that nothing bad can happen to her."

"Let's hope not," he said. "What was Max supposed to be doing over here?"

"Dinner with the ambassador," I said. "Plus a very interesting guest." I gave him a knowing look. He reacted in startled fashion.

"Not your cousin the king?"

"How did you guess?"

"He's made his pro-Nazi sentiments all too clear, I'm afraid. And of course they'll be wooing him and molding him for when the time is right."

"Golly, you don't think he'd actually sell out England, do you?"

"He might make a peace pact, although of course as monarch he has no authority to do so. But he can certainly influence his people."

I rested my head against Darcy's shoulder. "Why is everything so horrible?" I said. "Have we brought James into a bad world?" I sat up, gazing at Darcy. "If there is another war, you'll have to go and fight."

"I think I'll be more useful to them behind the scenes," he said. "We've already talked about it. But yes, I'll be in danger but so will you. So will everybody this time. Let's pray it doesn't happen."

Chapter 30

November 9
Eynsleigh

It seems we have a clue at last, but it's pointing in a direction I hoped we wouldn't see.

The next morning brought the police as well as all the film people back to Eynsleigh. There was activity all over the place as equipment was packed, tents were dismantled, caravans were towed away. The actors helped with the packing up of wardrobe items. I watched Lana walking across our forecourt with an armful of dresses. There was no sign of Mrs. Trapp and Rosie. I found Dorothy sitting by the fire in the sitting room.

"I tried to help but I'm clearly in the way," she said. "Isn't this so awful? First Rosie and then poor Miss Bishop. Why did we have to come? We could have stayed in California and been safe."

"You think whoever killed Gloria Bishop was not one of your people from California, then?"

She looked stunned. "Oh, no. Everyone is really nice. We've all worked together in Hollywood for ages. If Gloria had fallen out with anyone, we'd have known. Film sets are frightful places for gossip, you know."

"So you think it must have been a local English person?"

She nodded. "Unless it was a gangster who followed her here. One does read about horrible American gangsters. It must have been some kind of criminal who kidnapped Rosie, mustn't it? Perhaps Gloria spotted him, or them, and would have given them away."

I realized I couldn't tell her the truth about the kidnapping.

"At least you're going home now," I said.

"That's right." She gave a little sigh of relief. "I really miss my mum. I can't wait to be back with my family and live a normal life again. I'm glad my acting is making us a lot of money but I really would like to be an ordinary girl and go to school and dances and things."

"You should tell your parents that," I said. "You're not supposed to be the family breadwinner."

She gave an embarrassed smile. "It's just that . . . we were ordinary before. Not poor, you understand, but we didn't have a lovely house with a swimming pool like we do now. I do have to make the most of this, I think, but then maybe I can take a break and go to college."

"Yes. Good idea," I said. "And remember what I said about men like Grant Hathaway."

"I will," she said. "That's what Gloria told me, you know. She said there would be men like him but I should always make it clear that I had high standards and I wasn't interested. She said she made a mistake when she was not much older than me by not knowing how to say no and always regretted it."

"Interesting," I said.

I left her by the fire and met Darcy coming out of the study.

"Well, at least we know one thing," he said. "Her name on her immigration form was Mary Ellis. And there is no Ellis in this village. But we think we've found her birth certificate and she was born only about ten miles away."

"Does she have family there now?" I asked.

"No. No more Ellises that we can trace. That's probably why she went abroad. No more family."

"They might have died in the Spanish flu epidemic," I said. "Lots of people did."

He nodded. "But we're no closer to finding who killed her."

"Shouldn't we go into the village and ask questions?"

"The police are doing that," he said. He put a hand on my shoulder. "It's not up to us, Georgie, or at least it's not up to you. If I can make use of my contacts here and in America I will do so. But I don't want this to upset you. You've a baby to take care of and the fact that some woman was killed on our property is not our fault."

I nodded. "I know. But I feel . . . I mean when you've seen someone who was lively and beautiful like Gloria was and you know that life can be snuffed out in one second . . ." I turned away, worried that I would cry again.

He bent to kiss my forehead. "It makes you treasure what you have even more." He looked up as Fig came down the stairs, followed by Nanny and the children.

"A good long walk, Nanny, that's what they need," she said, waved imperiously, then went ahead down the hallway in the direction of the morning room.

"Even if everything and everyone in our lives are not what we might have chosen," he added with a grin, gave me a wink and went off to the study.

The children were dressed in their outdoor clothes. Nanny paused to wrap scarves around their necks.

"Are you going up to the farm?" I asked. "Do you want to send the children down to the kitchen and get some scraps to feed the animals?"

"Their mother said a good healthy walk," Nanny said. "And a good healthy walk it will be. I've had to clean animal dirt off their boots enough times already."

"Just be a bit careful where you go," I said. "There will be policemen around and maybe dogs."

A warning glance told me that Nanny knew what had happened but certainly didn't want the children to know.

"We'll stay on the path," she said firmly.

"Why are there policemen?" Podge asked. "I saw them yesterday too. Are they still looking for the men who kidnapped the girl?"

"I think they are just making sure everything is quite safe," I replied and got an affirming nod from Nanny.

Something just struck me. The nursery faced the back of the house and the grounds. There would be a perfect view of the meadow, the farm and the woods if anyone looked out of the window.

"Nanny, did you happen to see anybody going toward the woods yesterday morning? Any of the film people? You'd have the best view from your windows."

She thought about this. "I can't say that I did. Not that I have much time for gazing out of windows when I have to make sure these two imps are washed and dressed and have their breakfasts and then do their schoolwork. We can't have his young lordship falling behind if he's to go to a good school next year. And this one is as smart as a whip." She patted Addie affectionately on the head. "Too smart for her own good at times."

"So you didn't notice any strangers at all?"

She shook her head. "The only person I saw was one of your farmhands with a wheelbarrow."

"Coming from where and going where?"

"Coming from around the house and going back up toward the farm, I expect. He came around from the stables side."

"And did you see what was in the barrow?" I felt my pulse quickening.

"I don't know. Potatoes? I think they were potato sacks."

"Thank you, Nanny," I said.

"Come on, Nanny. Can we go now?" Addy asked, tugging at Nanny's sleeve.

"Miss Impatient, aren't you?" Nanny frowned. "What did I tell you about being impatient?"

"Good things come to those who wait," Podge said, looking smug.

"Quite right, young man," she said. "I can see you'll be a credit to me and your parents when you're off to one of these schools in the heathen south." (Nanny was a die-hard Scot and proud of it.)

I watched them go, my heart still beating rather fast. One of the farmhands pushing a wheelbarrow with potato sacks in it. Of course that would be a natural thing to see, but why would potatoes be pushed toward the farm and not from it? And why from the stables side, which was a farther way around to the farm? There was a good explanation for that, of course. The press conference might have still been going on, with all those people making it hard to get past.

You are reading too much into this, I told myself. They might well have been empty potato sacks ready to be filled again, or even sacks full of chicken feed. But the nagging doubt wouldn't go away. My farmhands: Jacob, Bill and Donnie. What did we really know about them? Sir Hubert had hired them as strong young men, used to working on a farm. Had he checked carefully into their backgrounds? Wild thoughts floated around my brain: Gloria morose and uneasy, Jacob suddenly withdrawn. Then I froze, staring blindly out of the front door. Jacob Parsons. If you wanted to choose a stage name, wouldn't you want to elevate yourself a little? Choose something a little grander? Gloria is a lot fancier than Mary, and Gloria Bishop? A step up from a parson.

Chapter 31

November 9
Eynsleigh

Golly, I think we might be getting somewhere at last. It all starts to make sense.

I couldn't wait to tell Darcy what I was thinking. I ran down the hallway, my feet clattering and the sound echoing from the oak-timbered walls. I pushed open the door to the study where Darcy was working, and burst in. Darcy looked up in surprise.

"I think I've found a connection," I said, gasping as I was out of breath, and explained exactly what I was thinking to him. He stared at me, digesting this.

"So you think she's related to Jacob Parsons? His older sister perhaps?"

"And one of the farmhands was seen pushing a wheelbarrow

away from the house, from the side of the stable block. One of the farmhands, Darcy. It had to be Jacob."

"You think Jacob killed her and then wheeled her body away to be buried? Why?"

"Maybe he was angry that she had done so well in life and ignored the family at home."

He frowned. "But we were told her name was Mary Ellis."

"Perhaps she gave a false name when she went to America," I said. "She's been gone a long time. They weren't so strict about passports and things in those days. You came in through Ellis Island and . . ." I paused, giving a whoop of excitement. "Ellis Island. She did take a false name. She didn't want anybody to trace her."

Darcy looked at me long and hard, as if weighing what I had just said. Then he nodded. "We should mention it to the police."

"Can we talk to Jacob first?" I said. "I really like him, Darcy. I'd like to hear his side of the story."

He hesitated. "And if we tip him off and he makes a run for it?"

"Where can he go? In case you've forgotten we are on an island and I'm sure he doesn't have a passport. They'd find him soon enough. Besides . . ." I paused. "He's our employee. We should stand up for him."

"Very well," he said. "But if we find out anything incriminating we have to tell the police immediately."

I nodded.

"Another thing you haven't considered," he said. "If by any reason he did murder Gloria Bishop, he's strong and dangerous. He's worked on a farm all his life."

"Jacob would never harm us," I said. "He's told me how grateful he is that we took him in and gave him a chance."

"Desperate men do desperate things," Darcy said.

"I want to go and talk to him, Darcy. I want to hear his side before we tell the police anything."

He looked at me long and hard, then he stood up. "Very well," he said. "But remember to tread very carefully."

"You are going to come with me?" I heard the alarm in my voice.

"You don't think I'd let you go and confront a murderer alone, do you?" he said, then he gave a little chuckle, shaking his head. "Of course you've confronted murderers alone, and found yourself in some very tricky situations from which you needed to be extricated."

"Not by choice," I said. "I don't exactly enjoy finding bodies or meeting murderers. Things just seem to happen to me."

"Precisely. That's why I'm coming with you now."

We put on jackets and set off. A lorry had arrived and film equipment was being loaded into the back of it. I noticed that all this activity had made a mess of our pristine front lawns. I hoped the film company had paid Sir Hubert enough to re-turf it.

"If this wheelbarrow came from the side of the stable block, perhaps we should check that out first," Darcy said. "Although I expect the police already went through it carefully."

"Good idea," I said. We skirted around men carrying boxes and crates and came to the stables. The first one now served as a garage for our motorcar and Phipps had the former groom's flat above it, since he was officially our chauffeur. The doors were open, the motorcar sitting there. Everything in it was utterly pristine, the floor swept, tins of motor oil and polishing rags on the one shelf. We moved on. There were four more former stables, one now housing odd bits and bobs that were either broken or no longer needed. Another housed gardening tools, a lawn mower, a trellis that looked as if it came from the summer house. I gazed around, not sure what I would be looking for. If someone had come in here and strangled a woman how would we ever know? There wouldn't be blood on the floor or anything else to give away what had happened. The last of the stables was almost empty apart from some sacks of potatoes stacked against the back wall. The floor was swept clean although the faint smell of horse still lingered. On the far wall a high window let in a shaft of sunlight making a light stripe on the floor. As I looked down something sparkled. I bent to pick it up. It was a sequin.

"Darcy, look." I held it up carefully by the edges in case there might be part of a fingerprint on it. "This could have come from her costume."

"A red sequin," he said. "Her costume did have a lot of red on it."

"The high collar was red," I said.

He opened his handkerchief and took the sequin from me, wrapping it up and putting it into his pocket. "We'll tell the police and have them dust for fingerprints. Someone would have had to open the stable door."

Thus encouraged that we might be getting somewhere we came out again and continued to the back lawns. It was a fine bright morning with just a light breeze, the sort of day the dogs would have loved to go on a walk with us. As we came around the house we heard screams, only to find it was Addy and Podge, playing chase while Nanny stood, arms folded, staring in displeasure.

"Adelaide, ladies do not scream," she scolded.

"But Podge wants to put a worm down my neck," Addy shouted.

"She wanted to put a worm down my neck first," Podge complained.

"Children, put the worms down and we're going for a good healthy walk," Nanny said. "You may count how many types of birds you can identify."

She grabbed them both by the hand and they set off, heading away from the farm.

"You see what we need for James," Darcy said, giving me an amused glance. "Someone who will keep him in order."

"But children are supposed to find worms and get muddy," I said. "Didn't you?"

"Ah, but I grew up in Ireland, where everyone is wild and crazy. I learned to ride when I was four and you wouldn't believe what I made that pony do." He grinned at the memory.

That made me look across wistfully at the stables. "I wish we could have a horse or two," I said. "I'd like James to ride."

"And you miss it too."

"I do, actually." I gave a little sigh. "But I realize that horses cost money. And are an extravagance. And we'd need a groom. . . ."

He put an arm around my shoulder. "All in good time, my darling. You've a husband, a house and a son."

"You're right. That should be more than enough." I snuggled up against him.

As we approached the farm we encountered Bill and Donnie, working the plow behind the patient horse. They looked up as we came near.

"Is Jacob still sick?" Darcy called.

"I don't know what's the matter with him," Donnie said, coming toward us. "He don't seem too bad. He don't have no fever but he just says he aches all over. It's not like him, sir. Do you think we should get the doctor to him?"

"We'll take a look ourselves and then see if we should call the doctor," Darcy said.

They went back to their plowing. We made our way through the farmyard, past clucking chickens and piglets that rushed over, noses twitching in anticipation of being fed. Darcy tapped lightly on the door of the farm cottage and we entered. The downstairs room was empty. There were two mugs on the table and half a loaf on the breadboard, together with a slab of butter and a pot of jam . . . the remains of breakfast.

"Jacob?" he called. "Where are you?"

We waited awhile, then heard scurrying movements upstairs.

"Would you come down here, please," Darcy said. "I've Lady Georgiana with me. We are concerned that you are still not well and we need to decide whether to call the doctor."

"I'm all right. Leave me alone," came the voice from upstairs.

"We want to take a look at you. Please come down now," Darcy said firmly. "I don't want Lady Georgiana to have to come up to your bedroom. That would not be right."

Finally Jacob appeared, wrapped in an old blanket. He did look very pale and his eyes seemed hollow. If he was really as sick as he now appeared to be, could he have had the strength to kill Gloria and then transport her body all that way?

"Sit down, Jacob," I said. "Let me feel your forehead."

"I don't have no fever," he said, almost aggressively. "I told you, I'll be all right."

"Is it your stomach?" Darcy asked him.

He gave an embarrassed shrug. "Maybe. I just don't feel right."

"I think we should get the doctor," I said, meeting Darcy's gaze. "This could be serious. Maybe he needs to be in hospital for observation. It could be his appendix and he'd need an operation."

"No. I don't need no hospital," Jacob snapped, looking suddenly alarmed. "Just leave me be. I'll be right as rain in a few days. And I'm sorry I'm not working now, my lady. I'll make it up, I promise."

"We're just concerned about you, Jacob. Not the work," I said. "We want to make sure you're all right, because you haven't been yourself recently."

For a second he looked up, his eyes met mine, then he looked away again. "I told you, I'll be just fine," he muttered.

I pulled an upright chair closer to him so we were on the same level. "Jacob, we want to get to the bottom of what's troubling you," I said. "Something upset you a few days ago. We think it was something to do with the film people. Can you tell us what that was?"

"Nothing," he said. "I told you, it were nothing. I had nothing to do with those folks."

"But you did, Jacob. You were an extra, in tights. I saw you,"

Darcy said. "And they came up to your bonfire on Guy Fawkes night."

"You don't think they paid notice to a nobody like me?" He still sounded aggressive. "They needed extra men for their film so they got me and Bill and Donnie. We had to just stand there and follow the king. That was all."

"You've heard about Gloria Bishop, I take it." I moved a little closer.

"What about her?"

"That she is dead?"

"Dead? I didn't hear nothing," he said. "How did she die?"

"Brutally murdered. Her body buried in the woods. It's on our property, Jacob. We feel responsible."

"I don't know nothing about that," he said. "Why are you telling me this?" He stood up, the blanket falling to the floor and revealing faded striped flannel pajamas. "Why are you going on at me? Just leave me alone."

He started to walk back to the stairs. I noted that he hadn't seemed very surprised about Gloria's death nor did he say that he was sorry.

"Jacob, we don't want you to hang," I said.

He spun around, a look of shock on his face. "Hang? Why would I hang? I ain't done nothing. I've been here all the time. Ask the others. They'll tell you. And anyway, why would I want to murder some American woman?"

"Because she's a family member? She was once close to you?"

There was a moment of silence as if we were all frozen. Outside I heard the clucking of those chickens, the shouts of the boys with the plow.

"I don't know what you're talking about," he said at last. "I've never seen her before in my life."

"The police will find out, Jacob, if they haven't already," Darcy said. "You'll be their most likely suspect. They'll be coming for you. It would be good to confess now. We can help."

"I tell you, I ain't done nothing!" His voice rose alarmingly, filling the tiny room.

"Did you recognize her or did she recognize you?" I asked gently. "Were you both surprised or was she actually looking for you?"

He sank back onto a chair. "Why don't you go away and leave me alone," he said.

"Who was she, Jacob?" Darcy stepped forward, towering over Jacob. "Was she your sister? Your long-lost sister and she'd done so well in life and you were here, barely surviving. That must have made you so angry. . . ."

"My sister?" Jacob looked up now. "My sister, you think?" He actually laughed. "I didn't have no sister. She was my mother. Least, that's what she told me. And of course I didn't recognize her because she went off and abandoned me when I was three years old. So she didn't recognize me either. It was only when she saw my name on the pay slips that she knew."

"Your mother?" I stammered out the word. Gloria Bishop had looked so young and beautiful, she certainly didn't look like somebody's mother. I remembered then that she had told Dorothy she had made a mistake when she was very young.

"That's right," he said. "She said she wanted to talk to me and I thought maybe I'd done something wrong when I was supposed to be acting the part of a man at the court of Henry the Eighth. But then she said she knew who I was. And she could see that I had her eyes. I thought she was, you know, chatting me up the way these film stars do. But then she told me. You could have knocked me down with a feather. And the first thing that came out of my mouth was 'Why the hell did you go and leave me, then?'"

He looked up now, wanting us to understand.

"And what did she say?" I asked gently.

"She said she couldn't take it no more." He sighed. "She said she was only a girl, not even seventeen, when my dad took advantage of her. Forced himself on her. When she found she was pregnant her folks chucked her out and she had no choice but to marry him. And she said he was a bully from day one. He hit her, knocked her about, he belittled her, he made her life hell. And she knew she had to escape before he killed her. And all the time he acted holier than thou, spouting Bible verses at her like she was the sinner. So she got up the courage to run away."

"But she didn't take you," I said. I saw the pain on his face.

"She said there was no way she could take me with her. She had no money, nothing and no way to support a child. She said she thought my grandma would take care of me and she was going to come back for me as soon as she could, she said, but she didn't."

"She became famous and forgot about you."

He was looking down again, staring at his hands. "She said she heard my dad had married again and she thought I'd be all right where I was."

"But I thought we were told that you grew up in an orphanage," Darcy said.

"That's right. I did," he said. "My dad couldn't take care of me, him being a farmer and out in the fields from dawn till dusk, and my grandma died around the same time, so he had to put me in the orphanage."

"But then he married again?"

"He did. Sarah Carter. A right cow she is. She didn't want me. She came with a daughter of her own. So they left me there in that place until I was old enough to work in the fields. Then I was brought back to the farm and worked like a beast of burden. I worked there until I made the decision to go off on my own. I got a job at another farm and I told my dad I wanted nothing more to do with him. I thought he was going to kill me there and then."

"Jacob, I'm so sorry," I said, reaching out to touch his hand. "So naturally you were really upset when you met your mother again. The court will take into consideration that you lost your temper and . . ."

"Hang on. I never saw her again after we had that little talk," he said. "That's why I said I was ill and stayed in the house. I didn't want to see her no more. I didn't want anything to do with her."

He stood up suddenly. "You think I killed her, don't you? Well, I didn't. And I don't know who did."

Chapter 32

November 9
Eynsleigh

It's so strange to have this horrible crime hanging over us while the family is having fun and enjoying life. I do hope they solve it soon.

"We must find the detective inspector and tell him this," Darcy said as we came out of the cottage.

"Must we? They'll arrest him. He'll be their most likely suspect."

"We don't know he's telling the truth," Darcy said. "He comes from a background of violence, doesn't he? A father who regularly beat up his mother. Maybe he thinks this is how men behave."

"He's always seemed such a sweet and gentle lad," I said. "I wish he'd come to one of us and told us how meeting Gloria had upset him. We could have had a word with her and maybe she'd have wanted to make everything right again. She certainly had the funds to do so."

Voices from the direction of the woods made us turn to look. Detective Inspector Wentworth and his sergeant were coming our way. Darcy touched my arm. "Why don't you go back to the house and I'll tell them what we've found out?"

I opened my mouth to say that I'd want to share my opinion too, but he was giving me that firm look and I realized this would be better man to man.

"All right," I said. "But make sure you tell them that he's always been sweet and willing and no signs of bad temper."

Darcy had to smile at this. "I can hardly see myself saying that my farmhand was always sweet," he said, "but I will say that he swears he never left the house and he thinks the other boys could verify this."

"Yes. That's right. Thank you," I said.

Sir Hubert had now joined the children on the back lawn and was demonstrating a kite he had made. They watched in awe as it flew into the breeze and hung there. Sir Hubert handed the string to Podge, who held it with a look of delight on his face. How easily children are pleased, I thought. And it is their nanny witnessing this, not their parent. I wanted to make sure I was there for every milestone of James's life. I really didn't want a nanny.

Addy spotted me. "Look, Aunt Georgie," she shouted. "Uncle Hubert has made us a kite. I get a turn next."

"Well done," I said. "He used to make me kites and things when I was your age."

"You knew him when you were a little girl?" she asked.

"Yes. I used to live here when I was small," I said. "My mother was married to him. It was a lovely time. I had a pony."

"He was your daddy?"

"No. My daddy and my mother didn't get along," I said. "So she married someone else."

I didn't want to tell her that Sir Hubert was the second husband after my father. The first, an Argentinian polo player, hadn't lasted long. And after him she had been lured away by the motor-racing driver who was killed in Monte Carlo. Such a colorful life. So many adventures. But had she ever really been happy? Perhaps she had always wanted the wrong thing—money, adoration, excitement instead of simplicity, security and love. I just hoped she had made the right choice with Max.

Even as I was thinking these thoughts my mother came out of the French doors at the back of the house, stood on the terrace and, seeing Sir Hubert, picked her way over to us.

"Oh, there you are, Hubie darling," she said. "I've been looking for you everywhere."

"Oh yes?" He had that eager, almost boyish look on his face as he approached her.

"You said you might be going up to town and I wondered if I could cadge a lift?"

"You're leaving us so soon?" he asked.

"I only popped down here because Max came over for the weekend and had business to attend to," she said. "He doesn't like me to be away too long. And now that I've seen my daughter and my adorable grandson I can go back to Germany quite content."

"Oh. All right, then," he said. I saw his face fall. He still loves her, I thought. If only . . . I was very tempted to give her a good slap, tell her to wake up and be with Hubert instead of Max. But it wasn't up to me to tell her how to live her life. Not that she'd listen anyway.

"You're an angel." She blew him a kiss. "I'll go and get my things packed. Do you think those nasty policemen will let me leave? It's not as if I ever knew Gloria Bishop and I'm certainly not tall enough to have strangled her."

This was true. She would have had to reach up for Gloria's neck.

"It's time those children were back in the nursery, Sir Hubert," Nanny said sternly.

"Oh, come on, Nanny. They're having a lovely time," Sir Hubert said.

"And I didn't get my turn yet," Addy said, frowning at Nanny.

"His young lordship has his studies to attend to," she said. "If he's to go away to school next September he may be hopelessly behind. I fear his schoolwork has been neglected. I told his parents he needs a tutor but her grace was against spending the money. And I don't have the schooling myself to teach him mathematics."

"I'll be happy to give him a lesson or two myself while he's here," Sir Hubert said. "But I wouldn't worry if I were you. Children catch up very quickly, especially bright children like young Podge."

"Very well. Ten minutes more, then," Nanny said. "As long as you promise to work hard for Sir Hubert."

"Oh yes." Podge looked at him adoringly. "I'll work awfully hard. I like doing sums."

He would have made a perfect father, I thought. He was the father I loved having once, if only for two short years. It was sad that he and my mother had no children. They might have been the tie that kept her at Eynsleigh. But then I remembered that he had gone off on his expeditions, climbing mountains. My mother couldn't compete with that. She had never liked being left alone.

I left them and walked back to the house with my mother.

"I imagine you are glad those people are finally leaving," she said. "Not top-grade film people, I suspect. I shouldn't speak ill of the dead but Gloria Bishop wasn't much of an actress. It was only her looks that got her parts . . . oh, and she has married some very rich men."

This made me think of something else. Who inherited Gloria's money? If Jacob knew he was in her will, might it have been a good motive for murder? Something else to mention to the police. As I came around to the front of the house the first lorry was driving off, piled high with boxes. Nora Pines was standing there with a clipboard, checking it off.

"Is that going to the docks now?" I asked.

"That's right. I've booked us all passage on the *Queen Mary* again in three days' time," she said. "But it's provisional. Maybe just the crew will go back. We're waiting to hear from Gloria's husband whether he wants to hold her funeral over here or to have her body shipped back to California or just her ashes." Her voice broke a little at the end of this. "And of course we don't know when the police will give us permission to leave England."

"This must be hard for you," I said.

"Really hard," she said. "I blame myself."

"Blame yourself?" I stared at her incredulously.

She looked at me, her eyes pleading with me to understand. "I keep wondering if there was anything we could have done to prevent it. To stop it from happening."

"What do you mean? You saw this coming? You suspected it?"

"Oh no," she said. "But usually it's my job to be there in the background and notice everything, and I was so caught up in hearing what Rosie was telling us that I was staring at the podium. I didn't see Gloria leaving. And it must have been during the speech that she walked away."

"You can't blame yourself for that, Nora," I said. "It's not your job to watch every person when you are not actually shooting a scene."

She nodded. "I know. It's just that I'm usually a good observer. Nobody notices I'm there."

"Do you have any suspicions yourself?" I asked. "As you say, you're the observer. You must have seen if Gloria clashed with anybody."

"Only Grant," she said. "She and Grant certainly didn't get along. But if he wanted to kill her he'd have had plenty of other opportunities back in Hollywood. Besides, Grant isn't the strangling type. I happen to know he's squeamish about things. Rumor is he fainted when he had to have blood drawn."

"So he might have shot her from a distance," I suggested.

She had to smile at this. "Exactly. But it takes a particular type of person to strangle somebody, doesn't it? Someone who can't control rage. I haven't seen that kind of behavior from anyone on this set. We've worked together before and seem to get along well enough." She looked down at her checklist. "My suggestion would be the same people who kidnapped Rosie. Maybe they are still hiding out nearby and Gloria stumbled upon them and they had to silence her."

I wanted to tell her what we knew but I couldn't. Let these people think that was what happened. It was good to believe it was some nameless criminal or gangster, because it was too horrible to believe it was an ordinary person, someone who knew Gloria.

It was only as I was going into the house that I realized my mother had stated she didn't know Gloria. But earlier hadn't she said they had worked together once, long ago?

Chapter 33

November 9
Eynsleigh

I think we're getting closer to the truth, but I'm still not sure about Jacob.

I could hear the sound of conversation coming from the morning room but I didn't feel like facing my family and being bright and cheerful when I was so worried. The problem was that I didn't quite believe Jacob. He was normally so open and honest, with a face that looked so willing to please. And all the time he had spoken with us he had averted his gaze. What's more he was the only person with a perfect motive for killing Gloria. She had abandoned him to a most miserable life. Had she promised to make it up to him? Or did he think that she'd go away and forget all about him again? I could understand why she ran away in the first place: trapped into a marriage she didn't want at a time when other girls were having fun, and then finding her husband was a violent bully. But to leave her child behind? I tried to picture any situation in which I'd leave James.

I hung up my coat and went upstairs. It was time for James's ten o'clock feed. The doctor had stressed how important it was to get the baby onto a schedule and keep to it. Six o'clock, ten o'clock, two, six and ten. Luckily he now slept through the night. But it was now ten fifteen and James's indignant cries let me know I had failed him. I scooped him up, sat in the low nursing chair, and the moment I put him to the breast he ate as if he hadn't had a meal in the past three months.

"I can't wait to get you on solid food, young man," I said, tenderly stroking the dark curls that were coming in so like Darcy's. It felt good to be up here, away from the nonsense, to feel safe and secure. But the question nagging at me was, If Jacob didn't kill Gloria Bishop, then who did? One of our farmhands pushing a wheelbarrow. What did we know about Bill and Donnie? Was it possible one of them had a connection to Gloria? Was it possible that one of them had a violent past or, worse still, had lusted after Gloria, caught her and dragged her up to the woods? We hadn't found out if she had also been sexually assaulted. I shuddered. It seemed all too horrible and too improbable.

I heard footsteps coming along the hallway and Darcy came in.

"Oh, there you are," he said. "I was looking for you."

"It's after ten o'clock and the lord and master could not be denied," I said.

"I wish you were so subservient to me," he said. He sat down on the bed. "I saw the police and I'm rather afraid they are going to arrest Jacob. His fingerprints did show up in that stable. . . ."

"Understandable, since the potatoes are stored there. I imagine he'd have come in and out numerous times."

Darcy's gaze held mine. "I know you're fond of him, but there was something off, Georgie. All the time we questioned him I kept feeling he was holding back. There was something he didn't want to tell us."

"I felt the same way," I said. "One thing we hadn't considered, Darcy, and that's his father. The one who drove Gloria away. Might he have wanted to punish her for running off?"

"How would he have known she'd come back?"

"Perhaps Jacob couldn't resist telling him that Gloria had come back," I said. "That is a tremendous load of knowledge for a young chap to carry alone."

"I don't think he'd have wanted his father to know, do you? A man whom he knew to be violent and vindictive? Didn't Jacob say he wanted nothing more to do with his father?"

"Then the father found out somehow," I said. "Perhaps he spotted her going past on her way here. Is his farm close to the country club, I wonder? He could have seen her there."

"I'll check on that," Darcy said. "But I'm wondering, how would he know who she was?" She'd been gone twenty years or so. I bet she didn't look exactly the way she did when she left home. If he'd happened to spot her going past in a car he wouldn't have recognized her. And Jacob hated his father. He'd not have shared the information with him."

"I still think we should follow up on where his farm is. You never know. If it's next to the country club and Gloria confided in one of the servers there that she'd lived in this area, he could have put two and two together . . . spotted the likeness."

"Possible." Darcy didn't sound convinced. "But we do need to get to the bottom of what Jacob doesn't want us to know. The police are checking into the background of the other farm boys. Did they have any connection to Gloria or any past record of violence?"

"You and I could drive into the village and talk to people there," I said. "What if Gloria stopped off in the village on her way here, went into the shop for cigarettes, perhaps, and was seen and recognized?"

"I suppose we could," Darcy said, "but I don't like interfering with a police investigation. I'm sure they are doing good work."

"Then I'll drive in," I said. "I need some things from the shop anyway. And I might just chat while I'm there."

Darcy shot me a disbelieving look. "I suppose there's no harm in it," he said, "but don't you dare go driving out to farms to question people."

"I wouldn't dream of it," I said. I almost ran down the stairs, grabbed my overcoat and went around to the garage. It wasn't easy driving out as there were cables and vehicles everywhere and I had to wait as people grudgingly moved things aside for me. There were still people lurking outside the gate. Not as many as before but enough that I had to crawl past as they stepped aside.

"I bet you're sorry to see them go, your ladyship," one of the women called to me. "Adds a bit of spark to life, don't it?"

I realized then that they had no idea that Gloria had been killed. Perhaps the police had not questioned the local inhabitants yet and the news had not spread around the village. Although with policemen staying at the local pub the villagers must have suspected something was not right. Perhaps they still thought it was the investigation into Rosie's kidnapping. I pulled up and parked outside the newsagent's where Jacob's sweetheart worked. She'd be logically the first person to talk to. I went in and picked up a *Woman's Weekly* magazine and some boiled sweets. "Winter mixture, please," I said. "Two ounces."

"Good idea, my lady," Mrs. Allingham, the older woman who owned the shop, said. "I find the cloves especially are good for sore throats this time of year."

"Is Joanie not working today?" I asked.

She frowned. "I had to let her go," she said. "She was sneaking off too many times to be with that boy during working hours. That girl needs teaching a lesson."

"That boy? Do you mean Jacob from our farm?"

"Oh no. Not him. She was sweet on him for a while but now it's Peter Thompson from over in Ditchling. He works as a waiter at that fancy country club up the road. And he has a little motorcar. I think that's what quite turned her head, but then she always was flighty."

"So where has she gone, do you think?"

"Got herself a job as a maid at the country club, that's what.

Well, she'll find the work there a lot harder, that's for sure. Making beds and scrubbing out toilets!"

"So have you seen Jacob recently?"

"He came in here, asking after her a few days ago," she said. "Oh, he were right put out when I told him. I imagine he's still sweet on her, poor boy. He's not had the best life, has he?"

"Tell me, does his father still live around here?"

"Parsons's farm? It's about five miles going that way, toward Wivelsfield Green." And she pointed away from the road going to Haywards Heath, and away from the country club. So Gloria would not have driven past.

"Does he come in here much?"

"He used to come into the pub here but I think he got thrown out on account of his behavior when he's drunk. Now I expect he drinks at the Bull Inn at Wivelsfield."

"So you haven't seen him recently?"

"I have not," she said. "Not exactly the friendly type. If he comes in for a newspaper he'll not give you the time of day. His wife comes into the shop from time to time. Sarah Parsons. And she's the opposite. Loves to gossip. Proper busybody she is. And she were right starstruck, wanting to know all about the film people, and whether I'd seen them. I told her the likes of them don't stop here for their two ounces of jelly babies." And she laughed at her own joke.

I handed across the money and couldn't think of any more questions to ask. As I was leaving she called after me. "I believe she was with those women who went to your house to watch the filming. Anyway, I heard her husband was right put out that she wasn't there to get his dinner. I gather he said his wife was going to get what was coming to her."

"Thank you, Mrs. Allingham," I said. As I came out an awful thought struck me. Mummy! She had told Sir Hubert that she wanted to leave and be driven to London and I had taken the motorcar. She'd be furious at being kept waiting and Mummy furious was not a thing to relish. I leaped into the car and drove home as fast as I dared along those narrow little lanes. So Sarah Parsons had been one of the women hanging around and hoping to get autographs. And had not been home when her husband came in for his dinner. I knew the working classes called the midday meal "dinner" so that only meant she had been gone for a couple of hours.

As I approached Eynsleigh the gate was open and a lorry was driving out, fully laden with equipment. I had to back up and let it squeeze past. The remaining spectators had to flatten themselves against the hedgerows. Some of them were rather round women and this was not easy. I wondered if Sarah Parsons was still one of them or if she'd learned a painful lesson about not being there to make her husband his lunch. Then, as I finally drove up toward the house, I remembered conversations I had overheard and paid no attention to at the time. A woman called Sarah had been there asking about getting autographs. Could she have told her husband about Gloria Bishop? But then she wouldn't have recognized her either. And who would want to tell a husband about his ex-wife? Then I remembered something else. One of the men who joined the search party had been aggressive and spouting the Bible, matching the description of

Jacob's father. What if he had come to look for his wayward wife to fetch her home to prepare his lunch, and he had seen Gloria? He might not have recognized her but she would certainly have recognized him. Her look of horror would have given her away. And when he said his wife was going to get what was coming to her, perhaps he meant Gloria, not Sarah.

Chapter 34

November 9
Eynsleigh

Now we just have to find a way to prove what I suspect. Oh golly, I do hate this. How I long for my peaceful life again.

I had no idea how I would prove any of this. There were other men that Mr. Parsons was talking to who could attest he had been on the grounds the day that Rosie went missing, but who would have seen him the next morning if he came back to kill Gloria? I still suspected Jacob knew more than he was telling. I left the Bentley outside and rushed into the house. I could hear Mummy's voice coming from the morning room.

"I'm frightfully sorry," I said as they looked up.

"What have you done now?" Fig asked, giving me that usual disapproving stare.

I was about to apologize to Mummy, when I noticed she wasn't wearing her mink or dressed for a journey.

"You didn't want to leave?" I asked.

She shrugged. "I telephoned the embassy and Max had been invited to lunch with one of those lovely Mitford girls and her husband. So I thought Hubert and I could travel up later. He said he'd drive me all the way so that I can avoid those horrid dirty trains." And she gave him her most adoring smile.

"Mitford girls?" Fig said. "Not the one who's married to Mosley? Ghastly person. As if he can ever convince the British to become Fascists. We are far too sensible."

"Hear, hear," Binky said. "You might enjoy watching those goose-stepping idiots, Claire, but they will never catch on over here."

Mummy turned rather pink. "Well, of course Max has to pretend to go along with them," she said. "And there are a lot of good things to be said. Streets are clean. Trains run on time. All of Max's friends are optimistic about Germany's future again. I'm not exactly a fan of all this hiking and singing folk songs that they are encouraging these days but I do look rather good in a dirndl."

Fig caught my eye. For once we were in agreement.

"Take off your coat, Georgiana, unless you are going out again," Fig said.

"I need to find Darcy," I said.

"Those policemen were here a few minutes ago and I think he went with them." Sir Hubert looked around.

"Went where?"

"Up toward the farm, I think."

I didn't wait a second longer. I hurried out again and headed for the farm. There was no sign of anybody in the fields so I went straight into the farmhouse. The small room was crowded and there was a fug of smoke. The three farmhands were there as well as three policemen, the detectives and a bobby in uniform, plus Darcy, standing over by the Welsh dresser.

"I tell you, none of us knows anything," Jacob was saying angrily. "Ask these two. I never left the house yesterday or the day before. I've been ill, all right."

"Jacob Parsons, I'm arresting you for the death of Gloria Bishop," DCI Wentworth said. "You are not obliged to say anything but anything you do say may be used in evidence against you."

"It's not true!" Jacob stood up. The policeman in uniform took a step toward him.

"He's right. Listen to him," Donnie said. "He was here all day. He didn't leave."

"And where were you?" the inspector asked.

"We were out working in the fields, like usual," Donnie said. "We were both rather annoyed that Jacob wasn't doing his share. It's plowing season."

"So you were working in the fields, eh?" The detective gave a smirk. "Not exactly watching the house every second, I'd imagine."

"I was in my pajamas," Jacob said. "It would have been noticed soon enough if I went for a walk. And I'd have frozen to death in this weather."

They looked up as an icy draft came in from the front door and they noticed me.

"You want something, my lady?" DCI Wentworth asked.

"I have some information I'd like to share with you," I said. "It may have a bearing on this case."

"All right. Spill the beans."

"Outside, if you please," I said to him, nodding also to Darcy. "I don't want everyone to hear."

"Stand guard over the prisoner, Blake," he said and followed me outside. Darcy came too. "All right. What is it?"

I told him what I'd overheard, what I knew and what we'd found out about Gloria and the Parsonses. "I suspect that Mr. Parsons came to Eynsleigh, looking for his wife because he was angry she hadn't come home. And while he was here he saw Gloria. And she recognized him. It was reported to me that he told someone his wife was going to get what was coming to her. They thought he meant Sarah, but what if he meant Gloria? And he came back the next morning and that's when he killed her."

"Interesting," DCI Wentworth said, "but I have to go on evidence. And I have Jacob Parsons with the best motive and with fingerprints in that stable where we think she was killed."

"And on the wheelbarrow?" I asked.

"What wheelbarrow?"

"The one used to transport her into the woods to be buried."

"Transported? You know about this?"

"I know that Nanny looked out of the window and saw one of our farmhands coming from the stable block with a wheelbarrow. She thought it was full of potatoes because she saw sacks. But why would you take potatoes away from where they are stored?"

DCI Wentworth looked at me shrewdly. "One of your farmhands. That's only more incriminating to Jacob Parsons."

"But what if it was his father? Nanny doesn't know exactly who works on our farm. She looked down from high above and saw someone dressed as a farmworker pushing a wheelbarrow. The sort of thing you see all the time. Nobody thinks twice about it."

"We didn't see a wheelbarrow, did we?" DCI Wentworth looked around. "Not one in the woods or in any of the sheds."

"There's one over in that field, but presumably it belongs to the farm and is kept up here," his sergeant said, indicating a barrow standing among the cabbages.

"So naturally it would have the prints of whoever used it last," Darcy said. "One of the boys here. But you could just possibly extract a print from someone else who has used it recently?"

DCI Wentworth stared first at the wheelbarrow and then back at us. Then he gave a little nod and went back into the cottage. We followed him.

"All right, men," he said. "That's it for now. We'll be taking you with us for further questioning, Parsons, but I don't want anyone discussing this at the moment. No gossip down at the pub, you understand?"

The boys nodded. Jacob looked so white I thought he might throw up.

"Oh, just a minute," Darcy said. "I see you have a wheelbarrow up here. Do you mind if we borrow it? Those film people were looking for a wheelbarrow to transport things and we couldn't find the one that normally lives in the stables."

"Right you are, sir," Donnie said. "Shall I go and get it for you?"

"No!" Jacob snapped the word. "That's our barrow. It belongs up here. We need it. Let them buy their own barrow. They've got plenty of money."

I moved closer to him. The policeman still had his hand on Jacob's arm, holding him firmly.

"Did you get the barrow for your father, Jacob?" I asked in a soft, gentle voice. "Did you help him wheel away the body?"

"Being charged as an accessory to a crime is better than swinging for murder, Jacob," Darcy said. "You can say you didn't know why he wanted the barrow. Unless, of course, you did help him kill your mother and transport her body up to the woods. Then it's a very different story."

"No!" he shouted again. "No. I wanted nothing to do with it. He came and told me what he had done. He said he hadn't meant to kill her but she was rude to him. She laughed at him and told him she wasn't going to give him any money. He should be paying her for what she went through. Then she was about to walk away. He grabbed her. She fought back."

"Were you there? Did you witness this?" DI Wentworth asked.

Jacob shook his head. "He came to me and told me to find a wheelbarrow. He didn't say what for. I brought it and saw her lying there, covered with sacks. Then he told me to wheel it up to the woods and he'd dig a grave. I didn't want to. He told me he'd kill me too if I didn't help him. Just as easy to be hung for a sheep as a lamb, he said." Jacob looked up, his eyes begging us to believe him. "He was a powerful man, my dad. He'd beaten me up enough times to know he could kill me if he wanted."

"So you wheeled the body to the woods?"

Jacob nodded. "And he made me help him bury her. It was horrible. I mean, I was angry at her for deserting me but she didn't deserve to die, did she? And then my dad grabbed me and he looked right in my face and he said if I breathed one word to anybody he'd come for me and those would be the last words I'd ever say." He took a gulping sob. "I was so scared. I didn't know what to do. I thought maybe they wouldn't find her for ages and then they wouldn't recognize her anymore."

"You've told us now, Jacob, and I believe you're telling the truth," DCI Wentworth said. "These people, Lady Georgiana and Mr. O'Mara, speak highly of you. We're going to take you with us now, for your own safety. You can make your official statement at the police station. And I can guarantee you that no harm will come to you. Your father will be arrested and behind bars."

"Will I also be arrested for helping him? I really didn't want to."

"I think a judge would understand your predicament. It's not a crime to carry out something under fear for your life."

"Really?" He looked hopeful.

Chapter 35

THURSDAY, NOVEMBER 12
EYNSLEIGH

Finally our life is returning to normal, just in time for the country to be in complete upheaval. Oh dear. I am dreading what will happen next.

The news made the national headlines. Famous film star murdered by local farmer. Now instead of autograph seekers we had the same pressmen milling around trying to get shots of the crime scene and quotes from the inhabitants. We forbade our servants to speak to the press. We had a policeman watch over our farmworkers. Jacob had returned after his father was safely behind bars. He was still very shaken and we told him we didn't expect him to work until he felt better.

"Oh no, milady," he said. "Working's good for me. If I work

hard enough I don't have time to think. And right now I don't want to think. I've thought of myself as an orphan for most of my life and then I found both of my parents and now I've lost them both again and I really am an orphan."

"It must be very hard for you, Jacob," I said. "But since neither of them were ever the sort of parents you deserved I'd put the past behind you, if I were you. Find yourself a nice girl, settle down and then be the sort of dad you'd wished you had."

He gave me a sad little smile. "I thought I had found a nice girl," he said. "But it turned out she liked another bloke better."

"She was too flighty, Jacob. You deserve better," I said. "The right one will come along, I promise you."

He nodded. "And thank you for sticking up for me, my lady," he said. "You and Mr. Darcy and Sir Hubert, you've been right true blue. Real decent folks. Lots of people like you don't worry about your workers as long as the work's done, but you really do care. I reckon it was the luckiest day of my life when you offered me this job. I'll work hard and I'll make you proud."

"We're delighted to have you here, Jacob," I said. I wanted to put a hand on his arm but that wouldn't have been proper. Instead I walked away with tears in my own eyes. I too had grown up without the love and support of parents. My mother had bolted when I was really too young to remember her. My father spent most of his time at the casinos in the South of France, where it turned out he had another family. But the difference had been that I had been taken care of. I had lived in a castle in Scotland and my nanny had been warm and loving.

My mother had bolted again, this time back to Max. When I had tried to talk to her to make her reconsider whether this was a wise move she had patted my cheek and laughed at me. "Don't be so silly, darling. Max adores me. Everyone adores me, even Herr Hitler."

Her picture had appeared in the same newspaper where the headlines proclaimed the arrest of Jacob's father. *Local Farmer Confesses to Killing Famous Film Star.* And beside it *German Ambassador Hosts Glittering Reception. Spotted Among the Guests Former Star of Stage Claire Daniels Along with Her German Beau, Millionaire Industrialist Max von Stroheim.*

She looked lovely, as always, with a white mink stole over a slinky black evening gown. And again I had that touch of sadness that she hadn't come here to see me, or my baby. I was always an afterthought.

The film crew had departed, leaving nothing more than some ruts and gouged patches in our lawns. The amount they paid Sir Hubert was not what he was expecting since it wasn't clear that the film could ever be finished. They were going to try to splice in some shots of Catherine from earlier scenes. Luckily the film ended with the execution of Anne Boleyn so Catherine was not needed in the final scenes. Mummy had been rather miffed, I suspect, that Cy Marvin didn't think she could take over as Catherine and immediately invite her back to Hollywood. I don't think she would have gone but she would have liked to be asked.

I walked with my godfather as we inspected the lawns after the final lorry had departed.

"They made a bloody mess, didn't they?" he said. "I wonder now if it was worth it."

"This must be hard for you," I said.

"To get my house back and be able to use my morning room again? Not hard at all." He gave a little smile.

"I meant Gloria Bishop. I thought I detected a spark between the two of you."

"Nothing more than a harmless flirtation, my dear. I suspect Gloria was the type of woman who enjoyed the chase. Once she had snared the man, she lost interest. Besides, she had a very rich husband at home."

"Do you think she was interested until she saw Eynsleigh and that we weren't extremely rich?"

He chuckled. "I don't think her motive had anything to do with us, Georgie. When she found out I lived at Eynsleigh and realized where it was I think the idea struck her that she could go back to her old haunts and maybe see her son. She thought that nobody would recognize her, which was probably true. But all the same by doing so she signed her own death warrant."

"Poor woman," I said. "But you are not too heartbroken?"

His smile now was a winsome one. "Oh, my dear, there has only ever been one woman for me. You should know that."

"My mother, you mean?"

He nodded. "Your mother. I was foolish enough to think she was in love with me, which she was, in a way. She was attracted to me because I was a dashing explorer. We met at a reception when I'd just climbed the north face of the Eiger and I was the hero of the hour. She was vulnerable at the time, having just left that dreadful Argentinian who had a slew of mistresses. So she fell for what I was, but once married to me she didn't like me going off on expeditions and leaving her alone. So it was doomed to failure really. But if I'd stayed home and become a farmer she would have soon been bored with me. I didn't have the sort of money to whisk her off to the South of France or wherever the mood took her."

I slipped my hand into his. "I'm so sorry. But I wish you'd tell her how you feel now."

"My dear, I can't compete with a millionaire who gives her everything she wants in a society where she is queen for the day."

"For the day is right. That's what I worry about. I don't think Germany is a safe place to be, do you?"

"Maybe for her," he said.

"For now," I replied.

We turned and headed back to the house.

AND SO SANITY and normality returned to Eynsleigh. I wrote to my grandfather begging him to come back in time for Christmas. Fig and Binky lingered on for another week but when it was clear they had visited every school within fifty miles they decided they had better go home. Binky was kind enough to invite us up there for Christmas but Darcy tactfully declined, saying the journey would be too long and cold for the baby. Thank heavens.

"Maybe we should have taken a look at some of those schools with them," Darcy said. "We'll have to put James's name down somewhere."

"James is not going to boarding school at seven," I said. "It's far too young. I won't allow it."

He looked at me with amusement. "The protective mother

hen," he said. "What are you going to do, hire a tutor and keep him home here?"

"No. I agree that children should go to school and mix with others but I'm sure there are good day schools close enough until he's thirteen. Then I don't mind at all if he goes to your old school."

Darcy nodded. "That seems a good enough plan. And by that time he'll have younger siblings to look after their mother while he's away."

"Golly, don't let's think about that yet," I said. "One baby seems like quite enough work."

Darcy laughed and ruffled my hair. "Well, if you will keep getting involved in solving crimes . . ."

"I promise to stay home and be the model housewife and mother," I said. "I'll give dinner parties and run the Girl Guides."

This made him laugh. "I hope you can hold the fort," he said, "because I have to go up to London again. I may be late. Don't wait up for me."

"Another of your secret trysts?" I teased.

"Oh definitely," he said.

It was after midnight when he finally returned.

"Your ladylove kept you late," I said as he undressed.

"Not my ladylove. Your bloody cousin, if you'll pardon my language. I've just spent six hours with him while he worked his way through the Scotch and got more and more morose."

"He's still anguishing over what to do?"

"No, worse than that. He's made up his mind to walk away."

"Walk away?" The words came out so loudly that I was afraid I might have woken James. "You mean abdicate?"

"That's what he intends to do. His attitude is to tell Parliament if he can't have the woman he loves then he can't do the job of being king properly."

"Darcy, that's awful. He can't mean it. It's just a threat to make Parliament agree to letting him marry her."

"No. He really does mean it, Georgie. There were several of his closest friends assembled today around him. All trying to make him see sense. And he has shut his ears to all of us. He is going to spill the beans to the newspapers all about Mrs. Simpson. He'll play for their sympathy, how he's being kept from marrying the love of his life. He hopes to get them on his side in one last vain attempt to sway Parliament."

"That's awful. I still can't believe it. I always thought that in the end he'd buckle down and do his duty. I suppose she's to blame. She's not content to be a mistress. She really believed that he could issue some sort of proclamation and change British law."

"If you want my opinion," Darcy said, "I think it's more on his side than hers. He's absolutely besotted with her, whereas she . . ." He hesitated. "I think she enjoyed the fantasy of becoming queen but if he does walk away and she finds herself an ordinary person, out of the limelight, she might start to find your cousin rather dull."

"I never understood what he saw in her in the first place," I said. "It's not as if she's warm and sexy."

"Maybe David is a bit of a sadomasochist," Darcy said. "Look at how she treats him. She bosses him around and he comes running like her lapdog. It's just not healthy. But it's not as if he's a lovesick boy. He's a grown man in his forties. We have done what we can to advise him. We can't stop him if he wants to make an awful mistake."

"What would happen to the monarchy if he walked away?" I heard my voice tremble. This was, after all, my family, my traditions.

"His brother will have to take over."

"Bertie?" I asked. "You mean Bertie will be king? Elizabeth will be queen and the princesses . . ." I stopped and looked at him in horror. "But he'd hate it. He'd hate it more than David does. You know he stutters and he doesn't want to make public appearances. It would be an utter disaster. The anti-monarchists will use it to suggest that Britain no longer needs a monarch."

"I'm afraid there's not much more we can do, unless you'd like to volunteer to be queen," he said.

"You know I renounced my claims to the throne when I married you," I said, giving him a stern look because he was smiling. "Poor Queen Mary. All of her worst fears are coming true."

THIS PROVED TO be the case. Later in the month the first newspaper articles appeared with Wallis Simpson and David together and mentions of their great love story. Kept apart from the woman he loves, said the headlines. Dilemma for our king. Everyone took sides. Many people thought he ought to marry the woman he loves as ordinary people can do. But equally many thought that he was head of the Church of England and as such cannot condone divorce.

Shortly after the newspapers had broken the news to the shocked population I received a letter with a crest on the envelope. Not only a crest but a royal crest. Oh golly. I tore it open with trembling hands.

My dear Georgiana,

I am sure you have been made aware of the dreadful happenings at Buckingham Palace. I wonder if I can entreat you to call upon me at your earliest convenience. I have always found you both wise and comforting and I know you have been part of this distressing saga since the beginning.

It was signed Mary R.

When the queen summons it is not at your earliest convenience. It means now. So the next morning I left James in Maisie's care, giving instructions to feed him a bottle at the correct times, and I caught the train up to London. A taxicab whisked me to Marlborough House, where Queen Mary now lived since David had taken over Buckingham Palace.

She was sitting on a pale blue brocade sofa in a room with all of her beloved antiques around her. She still looked severe and upright but somehow frailer than before. She held out her hands to me. "My dear Georgiana. What a lovely treat to see you. Let me ring for some coffee. Do take a seat."

I managed to kiss her and curtsy at the same time, proving that I was getting less clumsy with time. She patted the sofa beside her and I sat.

"You have no doubt read the newspapers," she said. "I still can't believe that he will go through with it. I know your husband was among those trying to talk sense into him. But he won't listen to anyone. He is determined to marry her."

"I'm afraid so, ma'am," I said.

"You remember all those years ago when I first caught wind of this new woman who had attracted his attention, I asked you to go to the house party and spy on them."

"I do remember, ma'am," I said. "In those days I couldn't think what he saw in her. Oh, she's elegant and can be witty. . . ."

"And very cruel," Queen Mary said. "You know how she makes fun of poor Bertie's stutter, and of Elizabeth's dress sense. She calls her Cookie because she looks like somebody's cook."

"Yes, I know," I said. "And she calls Princess Elizabeth Shirley Temple because she's a goody-goody."

"And this is the woman David thought could be queen of England." Queen Mary shook her head, dislodging a hairpin from the perfectly arranged gray curls. She looked up as a footman appeared at the door.

"You may serve coffee, Emerson."

"Very good, Your Majesty," he said, backing out again.

"Does he really think he can convince the British public to be on his side and force the government's hand?" she went on. "He must be mad. That woman has bewitched him. I am very much afraid, Georgiana, that he will carry out his threat and abdicate. Renounce the throne."

"I'm afraid he will, ma'am."

She reached across and grabbed my hand. "And what will that mean? Poor Bertie as king? You know how awkward he is in public situations. He'll be a disaster. And those poor little girls. They've had such a happy life until now."

"Maybe Bertie will have the grit his brother lacks," I said. "After all he married a good woman and they have a really happy family."

"Elizabeth is definitely made of the right stuff," Queen Mary said. "She'll be his backbone, his champion."

"Yes." That was all I could think to say.

Coffee was wheeled in and cups were poured for us. We waited until the door was closed again.

"Do you really think that David and the Simpson woman are desperately in love?" she said. "I thought that kind of love only happened in novels, or in ancient history. Héloïse and Abelard. Romeo and Juliet."

"Romeo and Juliet were still children," I said. "I'm sure that kind of intense feeling is possible when you are sixteen but not two people in their forties. But Darcy said he thinks David is besotted with her."

"But she's not quite so enthusiastic about him?"

"That would be my feeling," I said. "She liked the idea of being royal. Not being Mrs. David Windsor."

"So there may be no happy ever after, whatever he chooses," she said. "Why could he not have been sensible like my husband's father, King Edward? He had his mistresses. Alexandra turned a blind eye and they were really quite happy. They both knew their duty, you see. Just as I married George when his brother died. I did my duty. And it turned out well. We were happy too."

I took a sip of coffee, making sure I didn't slurp or spill in the saucer.

"And so we sit here, waiting for doom to fall," she said with a sigh. "He'll have the final answer from Parliament any day now, and then he'll have to make his decision public."

I nodded.

Our talk turned to gentler things. How my baby son was progressing. What we were doing with the estate.

"You would be most welcome to come for a visit, ma'am," I said. "Although I should wait until the weather is warmer. Country houses can be rather cold."

"Most kind of you, my dear." She patted my hand. "I intend to go to Sandringham for Christmas as usual. It was my dear husband's favorite house. To think that this time last year . . ." She broke off, looking away so that I couldn't see a tear on her cheek.

I stood up. "I should return home before the baby needs his next feed. He's still very small."

"You don't have a wet nurse?" Then she shook her head. "Of course, this modern generation, they want to be involved in their children's lives. Look at Bertie and Elizabeth. They do everything as a family. It's good in a way because he's going to need all the support he can get. Take care, my dear. I'm glad you have found yourself a decent man and have a happy life ahead of you."

"Thank you, ma'am."

I was about to curtsy and leave her presence, when she looked up suddenly and said, "I don't think he had the makings of a very good king, do you? He was Peter Pan. He never grew up."

She rang the bell to signify that audience was over. I curtsied again and backed successfully from the room. On the train home I couldn't wait to get back to my house and my family.

Epilogue

On December 11 the king made a broadcast to his people, announcing his intention to give up the throne for the woman he loved. We sat in the drawing room, listening to his clipped voice coming from the radio. It seemed almost impossible to believe it was happening. From the servants' quarters came the sound of sobbing. There was not a dry eye in the country. That night David went abroad to join Mrs. Simpson, who had been staying on in France and one of the first things they did as a couple was to visit Hitler in Germany. So his mother's prediction was probably right.

And we? Our life has returned to one of comfortable domesticity, that is if Darcy doesn't have to go abroad on undercover missions. We still have two trunks of Mrs. Simpson's clothes. I'd think of wearing them if she wasn't so horribly skinny.